I0846781

Against the Tide

Against the Tide

Book 1 of the Caines Island Stories

Sherry Comstock

Sherry Comstock

To My husband, Keith
and
to my children, James, David, Kenneth and Sarah.

No author publishes a book in a vacuum. They always have a large supporting cast. Many thanks go to my husband, Keith , for all his words of encouragement along the way. My children listened patiently and proved feedback as I spoke of Callie as if she were a breathing person. My daughter, Sarah, served as an early reader and provided wonderful insight. My sister, Terry, was ready with support and was unstinting in her efforts as a follower on my budding social media platform. Finally, thanks go to my critique groups; our discussions helped me become a better writer.

1

Late Spring 1970

The ocean glittered with shimmering shades of pink, gold, and blue, reflecting the sun's rays as it worked its way above the horizon. The only sound is the squawking of seagulls as they soar and dip along in the wake of small fishing boats heading out to sea. Callie eased her baskets to the ground. *Not too much further.* She sat down and leaned against a live oak tree dripping with Spanish moss. Resting her baby in the V made by her legs and belly eased the strain on her back. She looked down, lifted the sling's flap, and smiled at her sleeping daughter. After a few minutes, she got up slowly to avoid jostling Kimberly, gathered her things and continues down the crushed oyster shell path. Before long, she was at the pier.

Callie set out her wares: shrimp, crab and a few seagrass baskets woven by her neighbor, Alma. The baskets are in demand and always sold out. Callie tried to keep things simple by bringing just enough to sell each day. *Kimberly will be a year old in a few months, and she's getting heavier by the minute. I'm going to have to find a cart or something soon. But first, I've got to figure out a way to stay on the island.*

Her mother wanted her to sell the house and move in with them. When Kimberly went to school, she could go to work in the mill. At least, those were her mom's thoughts on the matter. Her dad stood on the sidelines of this debate, knowing Callie would make up her own mind. Every visit or phone call from her mom involved some idea of rearranging their home to accommodate the two of them. Just last night, her mother was making the pitch again. Callie replayed the conversation in her head.

"Well, honey, you know we've left your room set up. The den could be Kimberly's nursery and playroom." Her mother's voice had the extra sweetness she added when trying to convince Callie to do something she didn't want to do.

"Momma, that's sweet, but where would Dad watch sports? You know he's got the Braves in the summer and then there's the Gamecocks during basketball season. And don't forget football."

"We can put the TV in the living room." Her mother countered.

"You don't care about any sport but baseball. What are you going to do when it's football season?" Callie laughed at her mental picture of her mother's impatience as her dad became excited and coached his favorite players from the comfort of his recliner.

"We'll get through that easy enough. We want to help you while you get on your feet. I didn't have to work while you and your brother were little. I don't want you to have to, either."

"Thanks Momma. But I really want to hold on to the house where Kimberly was born. Joe and I fixed it up together. Besides, it was Aunt Sally's. It needs to stay in the family. I've already made enough to pay the property taxes next week."

"But what about other expenses? And Kimberly's getting older. She's going to need even more of your attention. How are you going to do both?"

"I know it'll be hard. Raising Kimberly without Joe will be hard, no matter what I do. At least this way she will be with me. The social security check will start up soon and that will help. I'll figure out a way to make more money." Callie closed her eyes, hoping her mother wouldn't pick up on her frustration through the telephone.

"Your Dad and I are just trying to make things easier for you."

"I know, Momma, and I don't mean to seem ungrateful. I've got to try my idea first."

People strolling in from the boardwalk onto the pier broke into Callie's thoughts. Most chatted with vendors as they considered the wares for sale. Seemingly, many people enjoyed seeing what was available almost as much as they interested in finding a bargain. Others were there with a little more intent.

"Hi, Callie. Glad you've still got some shrimp. The kids are coming, and I was wanting some shrimp to go along with our oyster bake this evening."

"Good to see you, Ethel. All the family well?"

"You know Jack's back troubles him from time to time, but he's okay. Jill and her family are doing good. I hate they moved up to Fort Mill, but I guess you got to go where the work is. It'll be good to see them."

That was the last of her seafood. *Another good day.* Callie thought to herself. Kimberly woke up as Ethel headed down the pier. Callie adjusted the sling and put Kimberly to her breast as she sat crossed legged on the pier in the shade of her umbrella. Her long, dark brown hair and a lightweight muslin blanket screened the baby from the sun.

Alma's baskets always took a while longer to sell. She wove beautiful baskets but didn't use patterns favored by the Gullah artisans. "I learned basket weaving from them, but I won't cash in on their heritage. My people made baskets, too, but I paid little attention when I was younger," she once told her. A descendent of the Kiawah tribe, Alma was proud of her heritage. Her ancestors were farming and fishing here when the first white settlers arrived on the island. *Okay. With what I saved; I've made enough today to pay the light bill. Next in line is the phone bill.* Callie thought with relief.

Further down the pier, Callie noticed Max had set up a stand instead of spreading things out on the pier like most other vendors. He was selling straw hats and shirts. Callie thought to herself, *It would be more convenient to work from a stand. I wouldn't have to carry everything back and forth each day. I would make so much more money if I brought vegetables from my garden to the market, too.* After the last basket sold, she gathered her things and made her way over to Max.

"Hey, Max. How's business?" Callie sifted Kim's weight to ease the pull on her back.

"Was going pretty fast there for a bit. How 'bout you?" Max was a tall, ebony skinned man with flecks of gray in his hair. A fisherman in his younger days, Max had been selling shirts and hats since the rigors of fishing became too much for his aging body. Besides, his son didn't want to follow in the family fishing business. Steve was going to be a lawyer.

"My seafood sold out early. Had to wait a bit longer to sell all Alma's baskets. How did you wind up getting this stand?"

"Well, Steve told me the town supervisors wanted to encourage more sellers and tourists here at the pier. I set this up after getting a license for it. It's been good so far. If you're going to keep selling here, look into it."

"I just might do that. See you later. Gotta get Kimberly home now."

On her way home, Callie's mind reeled as she thought about building a stand of her own. *I could offer more things, like produce from her garden and loose sundresses for the tourists. Except for the license, I wouldn't need to put out more money. Lord knows I don't have any extra money. Not sure how Momma will take this. I know she didn't go back to work until Bobby and I were in school, but I don't see that I have much choice. Besides, it's 1970 and things are changing.*

Even with these thoughts swirling through her mind, Callie felt a surge of pride as she walked past her house to Alma's and looked at her home from the roadside. A modest white Cape Cod, with screened porches wrapping around three sides. Domer windows added character, although they only gave light to the attic. A neat, fenced yard surrounded the house. Small peach trees grew to the right of the driveway and should bear fruit this year. Late azaleas bloomed under the magnolia and live oak trees. Flower beds filled with zinnias, yarrow and rose campion followed the porches. Spanish moss streamed from most trees. Callie smiled to herself, thinking, *Joe and I did well.*

Alma waved from her front porch as Callie turned into the walk. "How'd we do today?" Alma was several years older than Callie. Even now, after years of working in vegetable fields, Alma stood tall and was fiercely independent. Her coppery skin and straight black hair belied her age. It had taken Callie a while to talk Alma into letting her take the baskets to the pier. Eventually, Alma understood it was Callie's way of repaying her for all the eggs and other things Alma saw as "just being neighborly" that she did for Callie.

"Sold out again. Here's your money from the baskets." Callie reached into her pocket with a smile.

"Come on in and have some iced tea. Let Kimberly loose on the floor." Alma turned to the front door. "Have a seat while I get the tea."

Immediately, as she stepped inside, Callie felt the cool air from the whirling ceiling fan and felt relieved. "That sounds great," Callie said as put her daughter on the living room floor and sat in one of Alma's comfortable armchairs. She loved the combination of the white shiplap walls and the bright oranges, reds and browns of the large rugs Alma had placed around the room. Their colors often seemed to reflect upward, reducing the starkness of the white walls covered with paintings and photographs. A large stone fireplace held center stage. Alma had filled it's mantel with more framed photographs.

"I'll be right out," Alma called from the kitchen.

Over the cool drinks, Callie told Alma about Max's stand and how she wanted to set up a stand herself.

"Sugar, that might be good. You'd need more stuff to sell, though."

"You're right. But I can sew the dresses myself. I've got a fairly good fabric stash to start with. I'd have to save more to buy the license and building materials." Callie bubbled with enthusiasm.

"Who's going to build it?" Alma sat her glass on a coaster out of Kimberly's reach.

Callie thought for a minute. "Me. Joe taught me some stuff when we were working on the house. I've still got his tools in the shed. I'm sure Dad will help me work out the plans."

Alma's dark eyes looked nearly black in the house's cool shadows as she frowned in thought. "See how much it costs. We might be partners. I got a little put back from the baskets you've been selling for me."

"I'll see about it and let you know. Let me take this glass to the kitchen. I'd better get Kimberly home and cook something for supper."

It took several weeks for Callie to work out a plan for the stand's simple construction in between selling on the pier and her other work. Her dad drove down from Columbia to go over her plan and help her figure out how much lumber she would need. He agreed she could get most of her supplies from the salvage yard and save some money. Josie gave her a ride to Mt. Pleasant to buy supplies.

She and Alma worked out a partnership deal. When she wasn't on the pier, Callie sewed sundresses. Alma worked hard to build up a stock of baskets and fans. Callie's mom stopped promoting the move to Columbia and was going through her stuff to find things to use in displays.

Callie was relieved her mother was diverted from talking about her and Kimberly moving to Columbia, at least for a while. On her way from the pier Callie thought, *I love living on Caine's island. Not so many cars. No one is in a big hurry. No worry about neighborhoods. We've got the basics of electricity, running water, phone service and indoor plumbing. And the people here act more like family, everybody lending a hand to their neighbor without taking advantage.* Even in the seventies, Caines Island was a rural oasis overlooked by the burgeoning city of Charleston, South Carolina. Although Callie's parents lived on the island when she was a small child, they had followed the textile mills inland before she started school.

Today, some people worked in Charleston. Others worked on farms or in shops on the island. Many, like Callie, sold seafood or other products on the pier. Few women worked outside the home unless they were teachers, nurses, waitresses or store clerks. Callie didn't know any women who owned a business, even a small one.

At last, building day arrived. Mike, Brenda's husband, gave her a ride to the pier and helped her unload her tools and building supplies. Today, Alma kept Kimberly at her house. Even though the morning was still cool, Callie was sweating in her jeans and loose top while giving herself a mental pep talk. *I know I can do this. Don't have any choice. I've bought and paid for this stuff. I've got to finish this today. Can't have many days where I'm not selling, my budget will fall apart if a do. Maybe I shouldn't have been so stubborn and waited until Dad could come help.*

With a farewell wave to Mike, Callie looked at her rough drawing and sorted out her materials. There was an electrical outlet at the end of the boardwalk. Callie planned to cut her lumber there so she could use a power saw. Taking a deep breath to steady her nerves, she started making cuts for the frame. Getting ready to take things to her site on the pier, she saw two of her neighbors, Brenda and Josie, walking down the path toward her.

"Hey, I heard you had a building project today. We can lend a hand until the kids are back from school," Brenda said as she and Josie got closer.

"I'd appreciate the help, but I can't pay anything." *These two had already done a lot since Joe died.* Callie thought. *When the news of Joe's death made its way through the community, Brenda and Josie organized the neighbors. For nearly a month, neighbors had delivered meals to the house. Brenda or Josie sat with me on the porch talking or just letting me cry on their shoulder. I just never want to take advantage of my friends.*

"Who's talking about money?" Josie answered with a frown. "Would you sell some stuff for us like you do for Alma? I'm glad to help either way."

"Alright, I can do that. Look at this sketch." Callie said, holding her plan so the others could look at it. "See how the top half of the wall folds up to make a small shade? See the hinges for it? Getting it to close up tight is where I think I might have some trouble. It's got to keep the weather out."

"Okay, I see. We did something like this for the window awnings on the house. I remember how to do that." Brenda said, tracing the awning's section of the plan with her finger.

With their help, the stand was together within a few hours. Drenched in sweat, the three women trudged back down the pier to the shade of nearby palmetto trees next to the pavilion. Callie smiled as she took iced tea, cut up watermelon and a couple of pimento cheese sandwiches, cut in half, from a small cooler and passed it around.

"It's not much, but I didn't know I'd have a crew today," Callie said apologetically.

"It's enough to take the edge off," Brenda said after taking a long drink of iced tea.

"What are you doing tomorrow?" Josie asked in between bites of her sandwich.

"After supper, I'll bring Alma's baskets and my sundresses to the stall for tomorrow. I've got to get the shelf and stuff for the displays down here, too. Probably take a few trips. Then I'll get the shrimp and crab as usual tomorrow morning."

"I've got the truck for shopping tomorrow. I'll be glad to pick you up on my way out," Josie offered.

"Thanks, that would help a lot. I really appreciate your help today. Let me know what you want to sell."

After eating, all three women gathered up the tools and began the walk home, their steps crunching on the oyster shells. Everyone was excited about the stand's prospects. Josie and Brenda turned off as their street came up, leaving Callie alone to walk to her front porch and drop off her tools before crossing over to Alma's and picking up Kimberly. Her excitement over finishing the stand overcame her tiredness. *I'd be a lot more tired if I didn't have their help. Not sure I'd have finished without them. I know I wouldn't have finished this early.* As she set her tool bags down, Alma and Kimberly surprised her by opening the screen door.

"Hey there, my precious girl." Callie smiled as she took her daughter from Alma's arms.

"I figured you'd be tired after today, so we came over here to start some supper. It's not too early, is it?"

"Oh, Alma, thank you. That sounds great. I'm famished since I shared my lunch. Man, it's hot out in that sun. I'll freshen up a bit and tell you about today while I help finish supper."

"Just clean up a bit. Supper's waiting on the back of the stove. Greens, rice, chicken, and gravy. I'll get the table ready." Alma turned to go to the kitchen.

Over supper, Callie recounted the day and expressed her surprise at Josie's and Brenda's unrequested but much needed help.

"I couldn't believe it when I saw them walking toward me. They're good friends and all, but I didn't expect this." Callie smiled as she thought of her friend's timely help.

"People respect you. They know how hard it is to raise a child on your own. You're fighting to stay, and we want good people here."

"Still, it was awful nice of them to help. We talked about them bringing some things to sell at the stand." Callie said pausing a moment before giving the food her undivided attention.

"Consignment could be a good way to have more merchandise." Alma agreed.

After they ate, Callie began clearing the table. "I'll get the kitchen cleaned up. Then Kimberly and I'll get the baskets and dresses down to the pier. Josie's picking me up tomorrow before I check the pots. I could probably wait until then. Silly, but I'd like to see something at the stand now. Tomorrow is Saturday. Should be a good day."

"I imagine putting something in the stand will make it seem even more real. I'll get the kitchen while you do that. My baskets and fans are by the front door. Kimberly can just crawl around until you get back."

"Thanks. It'll go faster without Kimberly," Callie said.

Glad for the early start, Callie gathered the bags with her dresses and went next door to pick up Alma's things. This would also give her a few minutes to think. Tomorrow, hopefully, will be too busy for much thought.

On her walk back to the pier, breezes, redolent with the smells of life by the ocean, drifted her way; fresh earth turned by farmers and salty air with a just a hint of decaying vegetation. Cattails with their velvet brown seed pods and slender leaves waved in the breeze as gulls flew overhead. Closer to the pier, sandpipers kept up their ceaseless dance with the waves as they looked for food along the ocean's edge. Seeing the sandpipers made her remember how she and Joe often watched birds together.

Tears filled her eyes as she allowed herself to think about how much she missed him. Since his death in a construction accident nearly six months ago, times had been harder. Callie had put the small life insurance benefit check in a savings account for Kimberly. She had made enough money selling seafood to pay the property taxes and utilities, and had a little to spare. *With the stand, I'll make more money. Maybe I can save and buy a truck in a few years. Lord, I hope I'm right about this. There's absolutely no wiggle room in my budget,* Callie thought has she reached the stand. With a sigh and a couple of blinks, she squared her shoulders, opened the stand, and stored the items for tomorrow's sale.

Back home after Alma left, Callie harvested watermelon and cantaloupe from the garden while Kimberly played peek-a-boo between the plants. She moved the board, crates, and other display pieces from the shed to the porch with the melons. Her mother had found a few old fruit crates in her shed, so she added those to the growing pile. It was almost dark now. Callie picked Kimberly up and went into the house. Her daughter nuzzled close into her shoulder, eyelids fluttering, nearly asleep.

"Hey, my precious. You've been crawling around in the dirt. No sleeping yet. Let's get you a quick bath. Then you can sleep."

Before Callie finished the first lullaby, Kimberly was asleep. *Now I can get a nice, long, hot bath. Man, I'm sore from all the work today. I'll sleep well tonight.* She barely managed not to fall asleep in the tub. Throwing her nightgown over her head, Callie crawled into bed. She paused just long enough to pull Joe's old shirt out from her nightstand drawer and put it on her pillow. As his lingering scent eased her worries about tomorrow, she drifted off to sleep.

Callie was up well before sunrise. She quickly pulled on a loose blouse and skirt. Slipping on her Keds, she then braided her dark brown hair before coiling it around her head. Her deep tan set off her brown eyes and belied her German and Irish heritage. Callie had coloring like her dad; Kimberly had the Irish deep auburn hair, blue eyes, and fair skin like her grandmother.

"Good morning, baby girl. Did you have a good sleep? Come snuggle with momma and have a bit to eat."

Josie pulled into the driveway as Callie was adjusting Kimberly in her sling a short while later. "Morning. Hope you got some rest. I was sure tired last night." Josie said, pulling down the truck's tailgate.

"Oh lordy, me too. I almost fell asleep in the tub. It won't take long to load. Everything is on the side porch," Callie said as they started loading things into the truck.

"Got nothing but time today, at least until three thirty this afternoon," Josie laughed at her own joke. She was always the joker in their group.

They pulled the crab and shrimp pots in record time. Back at the pier, Josie and Callie carried everything down to the stand. Josie promised to stop by again on her way home.

With Kimberly in her playpen, Callie set up the stand. Alma's fans sprouted from crocks. Fruit boxes supported the board, and she lined it with chow-chow and jam. Watermelon and cantaloupe sat on the pier between the boxes. Sun dresses danced in the breeze as they hung from hooks along the awning. Seafood, on ice, sat on the upper counter.

"Callie, you've done yourself proud." Max stopped at Callie's stand on his way down the pier. As usual, a huge smile spread across his face and up around his eyes.

"Well, thanks Max. I borrowed some of your ideas after I saw how you set up your stand. You made everything so attractive. And I made it eight feet by eight feet like yours. Then Kimberly's playpen can sit in there." Callie smiled back at her friend.

"Ah, now that was thinking. I see you've added a few things. It's good to have a variety. Like the way you bunched the fans like flowers in the old crocks, too." Max stood back to take in the display.

"Thanks. Now that I don't have to carry things back and forth every day, thought I would bring some of the extra produce from the garden. Brenda and Josie made the jam and chow-chow."

"And you were smart. Looks like you'll be able to break down the stand and get it off the pier if we get a storm warning. We built mine that way, too." Max put his hand on his chin as he looked over the stand's construction.

"You never know what might happen." Callie shrugged to emphasize their lack of control over the unpredictable coastal weather.

"Well, let me get myself opened up. Folks will be heading down to the pier soon." Max picked up his bags before walking down the pier.

Business was brisk. Callie made notes about the day's sales. During the lulls in customers, Callie sat with Kimberly on a blanket for a while, as they played with blocks. After lunch, Kimberly napped in her playpen, strategically placed within the stand. Callie sat on a stool next to the playpen. *I can hardly keep my eyes open. Hope someone stops by soon. Is that Momma and Dad? I sure didn't expect to see them. This will perk me up.*

"Momma, Dad, it's great to see you." Her mother's auburn hair glistened in the sun. Her dad's short, dark hair was showing a bit of gray at his temple. *Funny, I never noticed before.* Callie thought as she stepped out from the stand.

"Honey, I couldn't let your opening day go by without seeing how things were going." Her mother gave Callie a hug. "You've got a beautiful display set up. The labels on the fruit boxes really catch your eye as you walk down the pier, and the gingham oil cloth will be easy to wipe down. Where's Kimberly?" Her mother's head swiveled as she took in the surrounding area, looking for her granddaughter.

"She's back here with me. Sleeping," Callie said, pointing beside herself.

"Well, there's plenty of shade. Doesn't the noise bother her?" Her mother frowned slightly.

"No, most people aren't that loud. Besides, she's used to it. We've been coming down here much of her life."

Callie's dad had been quietly looking over the stand since he said hello.

"You girls did a good job following the plans. Looks like it will hold up well." He nodded to emphasize his approval.

"Thanks Dad. I appreciate your help in working things out. How long are you staying?" Callie said, thinking it was a long way for her parents to come and then go back home in the same day.

"We thought we might stay 'til after breakfast in the morning. Don't know what you were planning, but I brought some chicken and thought I'd see what else you've got to go with it."

"Thanks Momma. The house is open. Kimberly'll be fine here." Callie hoped to reassure her mother.

Not long after Callie's parents left, Josie, Brenda, and Alma stopped by. "How's it going? Everything looks so good." Alma stood back to look at the stand.

"Thanks, it's been good. Everyone's probably at lunch now. Your stuff has been selling well, too."

"Think we'll take a walk and check out the competition before heading home. Alma, you want to walk with us?" Josie looked down the pier at the other stands.

"No, I think I'll sit for a while. I wore out these knees of mine. They'll really bark at me tonight if I don't rest a bit." Alma sat beside Callie on an empty crate.

"We'll stop back to take you home, Alma." Brenda waved as they started down the pier.

By five o'clock, Callie and the last of the vendors began closing. Her dad drove back to the pier to help close the stand and give Callie and Kimberly a ride home. They talked about the day's sales and how much an older truck would cost. Callie avoided talking about what worried her the most. *What will Momma think? True, she found the crates and things to help create the displays, but is she really okay with my decision? This seems a little too easy.*

At the house, Callie's mom met them on the porch. "Come on in here. Supper's on the table."

"We're coming. Let me get Kimberly from the backseat." Callie leaned into the backseat of her mother's car, where the infant lay in a long oval basket, which sat across the seat. Alma had woven it for her from the softest seagrass and then lined it with lavender and white gingham fabric. A cushion on the bottom made sure Kimberly was comfortable.

Walking into the kitchen, Callie set Kimberly on the floor in her basket, her eyes grew wide as she saw the table. "Momma, this is a feast. Chicken, potato salad, squash, and the melons too. Let me get Kimberly settled in the high chair." *This will last me a week.*

"Well, you're going to be busy. I thought I'd make enough so you could have a cold supper tomorrow. Your favorite lemon meringue pie's in the Frigidaire, too." Her mother brought tea glasses to the table.

Kimberly played with the watermelon on the tray of her highchair while the adults dug in. "Momma, this chicken is so good, nice, and moist on the inside and crispy outside. I better watch out or I'll be so full; I'll be miserable."

"Thank you. I thought you might be hungry after today." Her mother played with Kimberly in the highchair. "It's good to see this high chair get some use. A lot of people nowadays don't seem to like the wooden ones."

"I like having some things from my childhood. And I always liked the fluffy lamb on the back of the seat and the way the tray flips over the back is handy. You're never looking for a place to set the tray down."

"I'm really glad you like it," her mother said.

Sitting around the table after supper, Callie and her parents went over her notes and talked about her experience selling on the pier. They all agreed working the weekend would be so profitable, Callie could probably take off Tuesdays and Wednesdays, since those days were slow. Then she'd have time to sew, play with Kimberly and do whatever else needed doing around the house.

"Oh my, it's gotten so late. I've got the bed in the sewing room made up, if you're ready for bed Dad." Callie stood up from the table. "I'm surprised Kimberly's still awake."

"Think I'm going to find that bed," her dad said and headed toward the sewing room.

After Callie got Kimberly down for the night, she and her mother finished washing the dishes

"Momma, I hope you're not horribly upset because I didn't move in with you." Callie looked at her mother from the corner of her eye as they stood side by side at the old porcelain double sink. The sink with its attached drainboard was there when Callie and Joe moved in and she fell in love with.

"Upset? No child. I only want what's best for you and Kimberly. Try this selling thing. You might still need to move." Her mother smiled at Callie.

Forgetting her hands were wet from rinsing dishes, Callie embraced her mom. "Oh Momma, will you ever give up?" *I know she won't give up. I'll just have to show her I can take care of Kimberly and myself.*

Laughing, she moved away from Callie while ignoring the questions. "Look, now my back's wet. Let's go sit on the porch for a spell so I can dry off."

"Alright, I'm still too excited to sleep," Callie said as they walked to the front porch.

The next morning, after a quick breakfast, Callie and her dad emptied the crab and shrimp pots, leaving her mother with Kimberly. Doubling back to the house, they picked up Callie's mom and Kimberly before going to the pier. After they unloaded the seafood, said good-bye, and hugged each other at least a dozen times, Callie's parents headed home.

Things went well over the summer. Callie made a wooden cart with a padded seat for Kimberly and a large area for merchandise. Its substantial wheels rolled smoothly over the crushed oyster shells. The addition of vegetables from the garden had been popular with locals and tourists.

During the busy summer, Callie harvested peaches from the two trees in the side yard. She canned several quarts and made peach jam. *If I can or freeze what we don't eat from the garden, then I won't have to buy much more than staples at the store. Trading seafood and produce for Alma's eggs and an occasional chicken will balance things out when Kimberly starts eating table food. If I do it right, I can put back enough to cover the winter months when not much is happening on the pier.*

One evening, Callie's dad surprised her with a phone call. "Hey, Callie-girl. I've been thinking, talking with your momma. Anyway, we took out an insurance policy for your business. It's not much, just a few thousand."

"Dad, isn't that expensive? I mean, I'm right down on the pier." Callie leaned against the kitchen cabinet.

"Don't worry. I've paid the premium for six months. You can pay me back at the end of the year. Who knows? It may come to nothing, but hurricane season is coming. It's been worrying us. You and Alma got everything tied up in this."

"Thanks, Dad. I hope we don't need it," Callie said before hanging up the phone.

2

Early Fall 1970

Kimberly had her first birthday in September. It was a quiet day with her parents, Alma, Max, and Louise joining the small celebration. Callie made a shrimp boil with fresh vegetables. Alma, Max, and Callie began planning for a bigger celebration in October. Callie wanted to share the stand's success with her neighbors, since most of them had a hand in getting it set up.

Near the end of the month, the storms arrived. Callie became adept at breaking down the stand and packing the merchandise for storage. Several times, Josie helped get everything to the house and back down to the pier once the storm passed. This time, the forecast was for a full-fledged hurricane. Islanders shook their heads at people who wanted to "ride out a hurricane". Of course, most of these people lived in towns or cities along the coast, not an island that the storm might totally engulf.

With the stand dismantled and everything stored, Callie began boarding up the house's windows and porches. Her parents were on the way back from Columbia. They had already made a trip yesterday to get Callie's canned and frozen foods to safety. A friend took Alma's chickens to keep them on their farm in Conway.

Callie had just finished boarding up her house as her parents pulled into the driveway. Alma and her mother swiftly loaded a few suitcases into the trunk while Kimberly, delighting in the brisk wind, ran in circles, laughing as she tried to catch leaves floating in the wind. Callie and her dad made quick work of boarding up Alma's house.

That finished, everyone piled into the car for the trip to Columbia. The neighborhood looked like a ghost town, but a few people were staying to help those who couldn't board up their homes alone. By dark, there would be no one on the island except a few weathermen and other storm watchers staying until the last minute for a big story.

Callie and her daughter would stay with her parents while Alma stayed with her sister. Exhausted, Callie fell asleep once the car got on the highway. Kimberly curled up on the seat between Alma and her. *The ocean surged over the island, swallowing it in a series of waves. Towering waves crashed into her house. Powerful tides pried away boards, sweeping them out to sea. Winds howled over the island, whipping trees back and forth like seedlings. Nothing living visible, just the pounding waves.* She woke up abruptly as her dad closed the trunk at Alma's sister's, her heart still pounding. *It was just a dream. Everything is going to be alright. The island's survived hurricanes before.*

The next few weeks crawled by as Callie waited to be allowed back on the island. Struggling to stay positive, she tried to make plans for repairs to the house. Of course, she couldn't really plan until she knew how much damage the hurricane caused. In the meantime, she helped her mother can the last of the produce from the garden and played with Kimberly.

The evenings were long. Frustrated, knowing the setbacks caused by the hurricane would wreak havoc with her budget, Callie renewed her resolve not to use the insurance money she had set aside for Kimberly. Even though Callie was busy with Kimberly and helping around the house, she found it strange not to be so tired that she just fell asleep at night. Thoughts of Joe were always on her mind now. *I wish you were here with me. You've always helped me find my way. I can't even have a good cry. If I cry, it upsets Kimberly. And if Momma caught wind of it, well, she'd never shut up about Columbia. I'll be strong because I have to*

—for Kimberly. Hopefully, the house won't need too many repairs. Long after midnight, she fell asleep with Joe's old shirt bunched near her face.

Callie was up with the sun, and excited officials were finally allowing them on the island. Thinking she'd have a few minutes to herself before Kimberly woke up, she was surprised to see her mother had already started the coffee. Grabbing a cup, Callie headed to the back porch.

"Morning, Momma."

"Hey, Callie. What are you up to today?"

"Dad and I are going to the island to check on the house. Want to come with us?"

"No, think I'll stay here." Her mother frowned and wrinkled her nose. "Don't really want to go climbing around in all that mess. No telling what's got into the houses. You can leave Kimberly with me, though. She and I will have a fun day."

"Well, if, you're sure. Now that she's walking, she gets into stuff pretty quick. Don't know what we're going to see today, so it might be best if she stays with you. Thanks, Momma. I'll get dressed. Then I'll be ready when Dad is."

"Dad drove over to the mill; he's not scheduled today, but there's a meeting or something going on. Said he'd be back soon."

Finishing her coffee, Callie went inside to get ready. *Momma's being awfully sweet. I just hope I can get back to the island soon. Maybe we can avoid a fuss about where I'm choosing to raise my daughter.*

When her dad returned, he and Callie set off for the island. Even in mid-October, the weather was still warm, 75 degrees according to the radio. Although the truck's windows were down, it was hot. *Why did I wear jeans? It's so hot and now my clothes are stuck everywhere.* If she wasn't fidgeting, Callie was looking mournfully out the window.

"This trip is taking so long." Callie pulled her hair up into a ponytail after having just let it down a few minutes ago.

"Only seems that way, since you're nervous about the house."

"I simply want to get back home. You and mom are great. I appreciate what you are doing, but I have a life on the island." She turned in the seat to look at her dad.

"Callie-girl, you know you have options now. I know you've been able to save some of the social security checks this summer. And you might have money from the insurance Momma and I took out on the business."

"I know I sound like a whiny teenager, and I'm sorry. I just feel I need to get back out on my own or else Momma's snare will catch me and I'll be in your house forever." Callie shook her hair loose from its ponytail, shifting her gaze from her father to back out the window.

"It's not that bad, is it? Momma is trying to help and protect you." Her dad took a moment to throw her a beseeching look.

Callie shrugged, shaking her head. "I know she means well but, I'm grown now, with a daughter. I wish she would support my ideas instead of trying to think of ways to make me stay with you. You can't take care of me forever."

"Do what you think is best, but try to take it easy on your momma."

"Okay, Dad. I'll try." Callie rolled her eyes as she turned back to the window.

Nearing the island, they could see evidence of flooding from coastal rivers where their banks had not been able to contain the rising waters of the hurricane. Flooding carried its own brand of destruction; it uprooted trees and tangled debris in their branches and stained walls with mud. Abandoned chairs on rooftops stood witness to the inhabitants' anxious wait for rescue from the rising water. The devastation grew worse as they got closer to the coast. Boats broken from their moorings looked strangely adrift, as they sat beached so far inland.

Finally, we're actually on the island. Lord, this looks bad. Piles of debris along the side of the road. At least the crews got the fallen trees from the roads, but now they're just dirt tracks. The storm washed away the oyster shells.

The power company's big trucks made huge ruts in the soggy road as their crews worked to restore electricity to the island. Her dad stopped to talk with a crew working near the turn for Callie's road and found most of her neighborhood had power. Making their way slowly along the potholed dirt road, Callie saw a few houses damaged beyond repair, walls or roofs completely gone. Some houses sat partially off their foundation, tilted as if a giant's hand had tried to push them over.

"Stop, Dad, that's Mike's truck, and it's all loaded up." Anxiously, Callie leaned forward to see around her dad. "Mike, is everyone okay?"

"Yeah, we are. The house took some damage but its fixable. This is Brenda's parents' stuff. Their house took a harder hit than ours. We salvaged what we could. Right now, they're with family in Columbia. How about you, Callie?" Mike leaned out the truck window. Dirt streaks ran across his face; his shoulders sagged.

"Good to know you're okay. Haven't seen the house yet. We're on our way there now. Call me if you need anything. I'm with Momma and Dad. Brenda knows their number."

"I'll get her to call you. Well, I better get going. I've got to unload this tonight and come back for another load early tomorrow. See you later." Mike's truck lumbered on down the road.

Callie was quiet as they continued dodging potholes. Her body slumped against the seat again. *Please let the house be okay. I can get by if the house is okay.*

"Your place sits up off the ground on some pylons so your flooding shouldn't be too bad. You probably have some damage. Hopefully, we can repair it."

As they turned into the driveway, Callie's heart sank. The winter garden and shed were gone. Her peach trees were still standing but bedraggled and tilted from the strong winds. The white Cape Cod had lost most of its shingles and a good bit of its siding and all of its black shutters, but otherwise, the house still looked intact. As her dad grabbed a crowbar from the trunk, Callie pulled her pony tall through the loop in her ball cap and walked up to the house.

Pulling down a sheet of plywood, they stepped onto the porch, sand crunching under their feet. Runnels crept across the porch where some water had gotten in and water stains on its haint blue ceiling, but no evidence of flooding. Inside, sand covered everything, but again, no serious water damage.

"We'll have to get it checked out, but I think the house will stand a few more years. The floors seem solid. That brick work under the porches and around the house is just decorative. I can help you repair it and show you how to do it while I'm at it."

"That's good, Dad. I think I can do a lot of stuff: cleaning, painting, and small repairs. I think we'll be with Momma and you a while longer. It'll take time to get the house ready for us to move back in."

"Going to break your momma's heart," her dad laughed, dodging the ball cap Callie threw at him.

"Let's see if Max is home before we go to the pier. I have a house to live in. Now I just need a place to work. He'll know what's happening at the pier," Callie said when she finally stopped laughing and caught the cap her dad tossed back to her. Putting on her ball cap, she threaded her ponytail through the back loop before following her dad to the truck.

On the short drive to Max's, they saw people were returning to the island. Most clearings held huge burning piles of uprooted trees placed there by the power company's crews as they cleared the lines. Even from the road, Callie could see neighbors working on their homes, repairing a roof, or putting up new siding. They, too, had smaller burn piles for debris.

Max's truck wasn't in the driveway when they stopped. Someone had covered the roof with a tarp, but they had repaired the siding. Her dad waited in the truck as Callie knocked on the door to see if Max's wife, Louise, was home.

"Hey, Louise. How are you and Max making out?"

"We're in good shape. Been back for about a week now. Max'll be sorry he missed you. He's working with his brother. Bill's got a contract clearing out rubble from public areas. Come on in and have some iced tea and a bite to eat."

"No, thanks. We just drove down to check on the house but, I wanted to be sure you two were okay before checking out the pier and heading back to Columbia. It's kind of hard to do the round trip in a day, but there wasn't much choice for this trip."

"We'll all have to get together once everyone is back." Louise hugged Callie tightly.

"That sounds like a good idea, a community party. We'll all be ready for a celebration by the time we clean this mess up. I'll stop by when I'm down from Columbia again. Give Max my love." Callie hugged Louise before returning to the truck.

Officials still had much of the beach area around the pier cordoned off. Even from a block away, Callie couldn't believe the devastation. The pier's planks were gone. Some lay askew on the beach in a haphazard pile, as if the storm had grown tired of carrying them and simply dropped them before moving on. The pier's pylons, with its planking supports hanging loose and trailing in the ocean, stood like lonely sentries in parallel lines. But there was nothing to guard, just a few boarded-up buildings along the boardwalk. It didn't appear that anyone had investigated the buildings yet.

Callie blinked tears from her eyes and struggled to keep her voice steady. "Things were looking up. Dad, I don't know what I'm going to do. This is too much, losing Joe, the hurricane, now the pier's gone."

"Well, at least you and Kimberly are safe. You've got the insurance on the house and the business. You'll do what all island people do, rebuild, or move." Her dad gave her a hug, trying to take the harshness from the situation.

Callie looked around her dad's shoulder, away from the ocean, in the general direction of her home. Despite the devastation, she could envision the area once everyone came back to restore their homes and businesses. It would be a thriving community again.

"It's going to take a while, but I'm coming back to the island. This hurricane doesn't change anything."

3

Late September 1970

Callie and Alma sat sipping ice tea on the front porch enjoying the warm fall day. Kimberly crawled around the chairs, tables, and potted plants clustered on the porch. For the moment, Kimberly ignored the few small toys Callie brought for her as she explored the hidden world under the porch's furnishings. Begonias, with waxy, shiny leaves and blossoms of red, white, and pink, were everywhere in the porch's shade. Bright red geraniums lined both sides of the wide steps leading up to the porch. Alma's sister, Carol, loved gardening and could usually keep everything on the porch blooming well beyond summer. But even these pots would soon have to come inside for winter.

"So, Callie. What are your plans for going back to the island? Don't see you staying in Columbia." Alma leaned back in her rocking chair. There was a sadness about her nearly black eyes even as she smiled.

"We've got someone doing an inspection. Just want to be sure the house passes before committing to repairs. Guess I'm just waiting; can't really make any plans until I hear what the inspector says. What are you going to do?" Callie sighed in exasperation.

"I'm in the same boat as you, waiting. The best years of my life were spent in that house. I'd like to spend the rest of them there."

"You've been on the island for years. I've known you most of my life, but you've never told me about when you first came to the island and being friends with my Aunt Sally and my momma. I wish I understood

Momma better. You never know if she's going to blow hot or cold. Sorry I never got to know your Nate. From the way you talk, he was a fine man. How did you guys meet?" Callie leaned closer to Alma.

"I worked on the Mount Pleasant truck farm owned by Max's parents since I was about ten. I'd pick the crops early in the morning. Then I'd get them crated up for delivery to the Piggly Wiggly or the stand we ran up by the road. Nate would come pick up produce for his father's store. He started hanging around the stand while I was working." Alma smiled and stopped talking as she remembered the first time he asked her out.

"Come on Alma. Just go to the supper club with me on Friday. They've got jazz and good food. It'll be fun."

"No, you know my parents don't hold with listening to that kind of music. You can come for a late supper, though." I was so nervous. I couldn't look at him.

"Is it alright if I come as soon as I get cleaned up after work?"

"Sure, we can sit on the porch a while before I have to help with supper."

Alma ran her hand through her long, jet black hair, pushed the shining curtain over her shoulder and deftly tied it into a loose bun as she started talking again. "At first, my parents weren't so sure about Nate. Being a Native American wasn't considered cool back then, and Nate was pale white with blonde hair and blue eyes. How did Momma put it? 'Your daddy and I aren't sure about his intentions'. Occasionally, we went for drives in his truck, but most of our courting took place at church, or at our parents' home. At first, his parents didn't approve of our dating either. That part wasn't easy, going against our families. Since we spent all our time with either his family or mine, eventually, both families came to accept it.

Like most young men back then, he got caught up in the war effort and joined the Navy. We married just weeks before the ship deployed. Back then, a couple often lived with the man's parents until they could set up housekeeping on their own. Then the young wife would learn to cook and do things just the way her husband liked them. But since he would go to war soon, we stayed in my old room at my parents' house until the ship left."

"Gosh, how long was he gone and how did you stand it? Worrying about him." Callie leaned closer to catch Alma's soft-spoken words. Kimberly played with wooden blocks at Callie's feet.

"Sugar, you know how it is. You do what you have to. I knew he was the one. We dated five years before we got married. So, I just kept going to work. We wrote letters, but they didn't get delivered regularly. Especially once he got into a war zone." Alma sat quietly, lost in thought for another few minutes.

"Momma, was there any mail today?"

"No, baby. Jonesy didn't stop today." Momma stopped stirring the pot and looked at me close like. "Come on, let's have some tea on the porch before supper."

I wait on the porch swing, rocking it back and forth with my feet. The jerky, uneven motion went along with my jangled nerves. The tall magnolia's fragrant blossoms look like small bowls. Spanish moss envelopes the oak trees like a lover. I usually love the trees, but today they are just making everything worse. Momma came out to the porch and sat beside me on the swing, steadying my jerky, rocking to a gentle, even pace.

"What's got you so uneasy today? Has your 'friend' come to visit?"

"Yeah, when my monthly was so late, I started hoping I'd have a baby to help me get through this, to have a part of him if something terrible happens."

"Oh, sugar. You'll have lots of time for babies. Now, you can just save toward that house y'all want."

Alma's eyes refocused as she came back to the present. "Since I didn't get pregnant before he left, I just kept working. I helped Momma and Daddy, but saved most of my money. The government rationed everything then. Momma tried to teach me basket weaving, but then, I just didn't seem to care about it, even if it was a tribal thing. I was so foolish. With no baby, I sewed a lot, decorated towels, made quilts and volunteered at the colored hospital. Like most girls of my time, I already had a hope chest when we married. By the time we set up housekeeping, I had everything ready, even baby clothes. It was four years before he got home."

"Was he okay when he got back? I've talked with some men who were in the war. They were different when they got back. Like my Uncle Johnny, he couldn't abide loud noises and went off to live by himself." Callie reached over to help Kimberly get out from a maze of chairs and table legs.

"My Nate came back okay. For a while he couldn't bathe often enough and said when we had a house, it would have a shower. Seems they rationed water for showers on the ship. He went back to his old job making deliveries for his father's store. At first, we had a hard time finding a house. Some people think I'm a light-skinned Black woman. You know how it was and can be now. And especially back then, many white folks thought Black folks should live in their own neighborhoods and were more obvious about it. We'd look at a house, make an offer and then suddenly they'd tell us they had sold the house already. Nate would be furious, even more than me, and I was pretty fired up about it. Still, I knew we couldn't win fighting them head on.

I developed a plan. We'd drive around the neighborhoods. If we saw a house we liked, Nate would go back to see it without me. He told me 'I don't like this, Alma. They shouldn't get away with treating you this way. It's bad enough they treat Black people like this.' I argued being mad wouldn't change anything and just give us indigestion. Anyway, that's how we found the house.

It was beautiful. Painted light green, like it is now. There were three large oak trees, delightful shade. Large front and back porches. We bought furniture and a wringer washing machine. We put the swing on the porch, added the glider and a few chairs. Put in the flower gardens. Man, we were living high on the hog. There were a few neighbors, but they didn't seem to care about anything except our being decent people. Your Aunt Sally wasn't there yet. My parents and siblings weren't that far away. We visited them on the weekend, or they would come out here.

I lost my first two babies at seven and eight months along. We buried them in the christening gowns I'd made for each of them. I stopped working at the truck farm. Doctors couldn't tell me why I lost my babies. I was beside myself with grief. That's when the Sullivan sisters taught me how to weave baskets in the Gullah fashion. Somehow, their patience and the slow, careful nature of basket weaving kept me from drowning. They were such dear friends.

We were as loving as ever. Over the years, it became obvious there would be no babies. After the first two, I couldn't carry one for over three, four months along. I'd go through the excitement, the hope that this time it would be different and then the despair of losing yet another precious child. Still, doctors wouldn't help me not to have babies. We didn't have the pill then. There was one doctor who wanted to do surgery, but I was afraid of going through the change so young. Besides, from the stories I heard, I didn't trust them to do right by me. Eventually, we repainted the nursery, and that became my sewing room. In time, I learned to enjoy other people's children. We got together with neighbors. Seafood, jazz music. I had finally come to understand and love its soulfulness.

Sally and Claude built the house next door just after I lost my second baby. We didn't get on right away; both of us wrapped up in grief, as we were. You know she lost her middle child due to sickness. She and the family would come for the weekend. Often Sally and the children would stay longer. Anyway, things kept throwing us together. The chickens fascinated the children, and they were always trying to find the eggs. We each took long walks and joined in community things. We found we had similar interests and understood each other's grief without needing to explain things."

Kimberly stopped playing and climbed into Callie's lap, mesmerized by Alma's soft voice. As she sensed Alma's sadness, Kimberly held her arms out to Alma with a smile. Alma took her into her lap and held her close. Kimberly reached up to stroke Alma's arm, much like Callie soothed her.

Alma shuddered as she threw off memories of the past. "Enough of that. Got to live in the now. Save Sally and your momma for another day. When are you going back to the island to do some cleaning up?"

"I'm going down tomorrow. Dad said I could use his truck. Do you want to come with me? I'll be taking Kimberly, but I can still help you get something done at your place. I'm planning to stay overnight." Callie began gathering Kimberly's toys, tossing them in a loose bag.

"Sounds good to me. Call me just before you're ready to leave. You know I'm up early." Alma stood to hand Kimberly to Callie.

"I'll do that." Callie called over her shoulder as she started down the porch steps.

The next day was cool, but with no hint of rain in the air. Callie's mother wanted her to leave Kimberly in Columbia. "There'll be times when I can't take her, but we're just cleaning up some stuff. I've got some of her toys and her playpen. It'll be great for her to get back to the house. She's not completely weaned yet, anyway." Callie turned to look at her daughter playing in the living room.

"She doesn't need to be crawling around in that mess." Her mother stood back from the kitchen sink.

"What she needs is to be with her mother and in her own home. I'll make sure she's okay." *Now she thinks I can't take care of my daughter.* Callie fumed silently as she went into the living room and picked up Kimberly. *Now I sound defensive. I am a great mother.*

"Do what you will. You're always so stubborn." Her mother stormed off toward her bedroom.

Callie huffed on her way out the door. *I can't breathe when I'm in Columbia. The air is just clogged up. The mills. Yeah, the river falls are beautiful, but those mills surround them and just block out everything. And then there's Momma —*

Kimberly started fussing in Callie's arms. "Sorry, baby. Momma's fine. Just stewing some. We're going home today. Let's get you settled in the car and then we'll get Aunt Alma."

Following the river led to a beautiful sunrise. Water droplets from the falls acted as prisms, creating multiple rainbows dancing in the sun-rays. Beyond the falls, the river snaked its way alongside the road. *It's a beautiful sunrise, but it needs an ocean under it. Be good to hear the waves again.*

A few hours after collecting Alma, Callie pulled into her driveway on the island. The house looked sad with its missing siding and shingles. Still, the porch running along three sides of the house was sturdy, and it's screening pretty intact. Screened porches and ceiling fans made island life bearable since one kept out mosquitos and the other kept you cool.

The larger magnolias were leafing out again. Soon the live oaks would too. *It's going to be hard work, but I can get this house livable again.* Callie thought to herself. The inspector's truck was already there, to her surprise. She hadn't expected him for at least another week. Grabbing her daughter, Callie climbed out of the truck. Alma was close on her heels. It didn't take long to find him around in the backyard, coming from under the house.

"Hello? I'm Callie. This is my house. How's it going?"

"Afternoon ma'am. I didn't think anyone would be here today."

"No, I'm still staying in Columbia until we can move back in. We can move back, can't we?"

"Yes, you need a new roof and a few other things. Your electrical wiring looks intact from what I can see. Just be sure the stove is off when you turn on your breakers. I'll send you a written report." Callie took a deep breath and let it out slowly.

Alma spoke up, worry creasing her brow. "Have you been next door?"

"Yes, ma'am. You're in good shape too. The reports should get to both of you in a couple of weeks. We're a little backed up right now, as you can imagine. It's safe for you to clean up. Glad I was here. Y'all shouldn't have been in the house before I gave the okay. Bye now."

The inspector tossed his clipboard in the truck, climbed in, and backed down the driveway.

Kimberly began fussing. "Hungy, Momma." Callie fluffed the red curls plastered to Kimberly's head. *Joe was dark-haired like me. Funny, she has red hair like Momma. But he always said his grandma had red hair. She does have his blue eyes, though.*

"Okay, baby. We'll eat soon. Let's make a place on the porch for a picnic."

Once they unloaded the car and cleared some sand from the porch, Alma and Callie set out pimento cheese sandwiches and opened some peaches. After Kimberly expressed her pleasure with the offerings, the two women set out a plan for the day.

"Since we have electricity here, what do you think about cleaning up the kitchens first? Then we can leave the refrigerators running," Callie said.

"Seems good to me. If we each have a kitchen and a bedroom, we can get back here sooner. Hope we don't have trouble with the septic." Alma frowned thoughtfully before taking a bite of her sandwich.

"Oh Lordy, I didn't even think about that. Guess we'll know soon enough if there's a problem. Let's start at your place. Then when Kimberly's tired, I can just lay her down here and keep working. I think she'll rest better at our house."

Even though the women worked steadily, it took a few hours to get Alma's kitchen and bedroom clean. Sand was everywhere. In cabinets, windowsills, if there was a crack in something, sand got in it. By the time they were through, they knew Alma's stove and refrigerator worked. Her bedroom was clean. The bathroom needed more scrubbing, but it was functional. They piled old bedding and mattresses on the porch. Maybe later, Max and his brother could haul them off. Either that or they'd have to start a burn pile like everyone else.

"Kimberly's about ready for a nap. I'm going home to get a place ready for her to sleep. For now, I'm just going to put the playpen in her room. She can sleep in my room for a while, if necessary, so we don't have to worry about getting two bedrooms ready right away." Callie watched the baby rub her eyes.

"Leave her here until the playpen's ready. Then we can all go over together." Alma offered, straightening up from the cabinet she was scrubbing. "I can block the door going to the living room and she can play here with me."

"Alright. I'll be back shortly."

It wasn't long before Callie returned and they transferred everything over to her house. "It'll take me a little bit to get Kimberly settled if you want to take a break," Callie said as they stood in her living room.

"If I stop, it'll just make it harder to get going again. I'll start in the kitchen. You take your bedroom once Kimberly's down. It'll get something done in each of the rooms. First, let's drag out that old bedding before you lay the little one down."

Kimberly drifted off to sleep easily, and Callie joined in the cleaning efforts. Using a flat shovel, Callie pushed sand from her bedroom through the living room, onto the porch, and finally out in the yard. With the bulk of the sand out of the room, she vacuumed and wiped everything down with a mild bleach solution. Mildew had gotten to most of the clothes left in her closet. She hung what she thought she could save on the back porch clothesline and added those beyond salvage to the pile on the porch.

That done, she joined Alma in the kitchen. "Wow, you've made quick work of this.""Well, this in the drainer is ready to use. I've stacked up everything here to the left that still needs washing. I bleached the upper cabinets but still need to get the lower ones done. You didn't have a lot of breakage in here."

"Oh, that's good. I'll start in the lower cabinet then. When Kimberly wakes up, we can go to Piggly Wiggly to get something for dinner and breakfast tomorrow."

"Probably a good idea. Glad we'll have the refrigerators and freezers cleaned and plugged in. Next time, we can bring some stuff with us since we know everything works." Alma stood up from the table. "I'm going to put my feet up for a bit. Come get me when you're ready to go."

"Sure. On our way out to Piggly Wiggly, I want to go by Brenda's and Josie's and see if they've been able to move back. This place wouldn't be the same without those two around." Callie sat on the floor to start work on the lower cabinets.

When Kimberly woke up, they drove over to check on Josie and Brenda. Mike and his brothers were working on the roof. Brenda was boiling shrimp in the sparse shade of a magnolia. "Hey there, Alma, Callie. Good to see you guys," Brenda called as Callie and Alma walked across the yard.

"Hello, I was hoping to catch you here," Callie said, shifting Kimberly to her other hip. "How's it going?"

"We're doing okay. You know Momma's place took a major hit. Funny how that works. Her place isn't that far from us. Anyway, she and Dad aren't coming back. Momma said this was just one time too many. They're going to stay with Aunt Bess in Columbia for a while." Brenda brushed a tear from her eye.

"Sorry to hear that. I know you and your momma are close," Alma said.

"Well, they're getting up there in age. I can't really blame her. Even though we kids said we would do the repairs and cleaning, she just couldn't face setting up the house again. Dad didn't even argue this time. How about staying for supper?"

"No, thanks. We just stopped to see how you're doing. Got to get to Piggly Wiggly before they close. And we're going back tomorrow. How's Josie doing?" Callie asked, shifting her daughter again. There was still too much debris on the ground for Kimberly to roam, as she usually did.

"They were here until about an hour ago. They'll be back for good in a few weeks. How are your places?"

"We both need a new roof." Callie tilted her head to include Alma. Glad Joe and I didn't decide to use Sheetrock when we were redoing the house. The shiplap is a lot easier to clean and doesn't mildew so quick."

"You got that right Callie," Alma said. "At least we can wash down the shiplap with bleach. Our appliances are all working. So that's good."

"When we get back to Columbia, I need to check on the phones and then see if I can buy a truck. Dad's been sweet letting me use his, but I need to have something of my own. I hate missing this good haul of seafood. Lord knows the money would be handy with repairs and all. But then there's no place to sell it right now, anyway." Callie tightened her lips into a straight line, thinking about the money she'd lose.

"Yeah, they're working on the phone lines now that everyone has electricity. I've heard talk they may not replace the pier. Something about 'structural integrity' and how much money it would cost. I don't know that they've made a final decision yet," Brenda said.

"We'll have to see. Hopefully, they'll have an open meeting, and give us a chance to voice our opinions. I see the guys are finishing up. Let us get to the store. Glad I got to see you today and that you're doing okay," Callie said as she hugged Brenda before going back to the truck.

Brenda called out as Callie and Alma were walking back to the truck, "Hey what are y'all doing for beds?"

"I brought a lot of blankets. Figured I'd make a palette on the floor like we did when we were kids," Callie said as she turned back to look at her friend.

"We've got some old army cots. We don't need them now." Brenda turned toward the house, looking for her oldest son. "Matt, get two of the army cots and put them in the back of her truck."

"Yes, ma'am." Matt hurried to the large shed behind the house.

Callie retraced her steps to give Brenda another hug. "Thanks. That will be much better."

"They're a little narrow but, at least it'll be softer than the floor." Brenda gave her friend another tight squeeze before going back to put supper on the table.

Callie got Kimberly settled in the car seat. When Matt returned with the cots, she and Alma were already in the truck. He pounded the back of the truck as he stepped away to let Callie know the cots were loaded. "Thanks, Matt," Alma yelled, waving from the window as Callie backed out of the driveway.

Unable to resist, Callie drove down by the pier. The roads were open, but nothing else. The boarded up building looked shabby. Clean-up crews had stacked the pier's planks neatly along the beach and pulled down the boards hanging from the pier's pylons. She shook her head and sighed. "I don't know what I thought would have changed down here. Let me turn around and we'll get on into town."

Back on the island, Callie dropped Alma at her house. "I'll put the soup on as soon as I get home. Come over whenever you're ready." Callie leaned out of the truck window. "Oh, yeah. Want me to bring the cot in for you?"

"No. Just set it by the driveway. I'll get it after I get the bags in."

Callie turned off the truck and put the extra cot by her friend's driveway. Reversing down Alma's driveway, Callie backed into her own. Putting the keys in her pocket, Callie left Kimberly in the cab with a teething biscuit as she unloaded the groceries and cot onto the front porch. Going back to the truck, she rolled up the windows and picked up Kimberly.

"Come on, my sweet girl. Let's see if Momma can get dinner started and then do some more cleaning."

Kimberly smiled up at her mother, grabbing Callie's hair to hide behind. "Where's Kimberly?" Callie cooed. The toddler moved Callie's hair away. "There you are. Okay sweetie, it's going to be the playpen for a while longer until Momma gets this mess cleaned up. But from here you can see me while I keep working in the kitchen. Okay?" As Callie sat her in the playpen, Kimberly began playing with her toys.

Sometimes I think she knows what I'm saying. Callie thought. *She's not fussing at all about being in her playpen. But then it's not like she spends much time in it. She usually roams through the house. Hopefully, I'll have it clean enough for her to crawl around before too much longer.* With the soup on, Callie continued cleaning, stopping only to make a pan of cornbread.

By the time Alma came over, Callie had scrubbed the kitchen floor and washed the remaining dishes. To keep things simple, the women served themselves from the pot. Callie placed the cut up cornbread on another plate and put some vegetables in a bowl so they could cool for Kimberly.

"Dang. I didn't think about Kimberly's highchair." Callie pursed her lips as she thought. "Oh, I've got that old, tall kitchen stool. Be right back Alma." After wiping it off, Callie dragged the old aluminum kitchen stool in from the porch. It was one that functioned as a step stool too if you pulled out the lowest section. Once she had Kimberly secured in the chair with a towel, Callie joined Alma at the table.

"Oh, Alma. Living next door to you has been like having Aunt Sally back."

"Having you and Kimberly here has been good for me, too. I was getting a little lonely. You two have surely livened things up."

Callie and Alma had planned to be back in Columbia before supper the next day, but with one thing or another, they got a later start than planned. Callie stopped at a payphone so she could call her parents and Alma could call Carol. It was full dark by the time she got to her parents after dropping Alma at Carol's. Callie knew her dad was already in bed. He had become a supervisor before Callie married and was happy working days instead of rotating shifts, even if it meant going to bed early. She sat in the car for a few moments.

Her parents lived in a mill house. Once he became a supervisor, the family moved to a slightly better house and her dad had made improvements over the years, but still a mill house. It was much like any other house in the community, white asbestos siding with a carport. The builders had clumped all the houses together. A few years ago, the mill added a heating and air conditioning system. There were a few trees and her mother planted flowers and kept a small vegetable garden out back. But everything about Columbia felt unnatural to Callie, artificial and constraining. *Oh, let me get this child inside.*

After wiping her off with a damp washcloth to remove sand stuck in the little rolls in her legs, Callie tucked Kimberly into the crib. She was asleep before Callie turned off the light. *I hope Momma's gone to bed. Didn't see her when I came in. I'm just too tired for an argument tonight, but I need something to drink.*

"Oh, I see you made it home, finally." Callie's mother was now waiting in the living room, her arms planted firmly on her hips. "How are things on the island?"

"We got some of the sand out at home and at Alma's. We both have a working kitchen, bedroom, and bathroom. Josie and Brenda are working on their places. I didn't see Max, but they are back in their house. The inspector was at the house today and said the house is structurally sound. We should have his report in a couple of weeks. Had to go to Piggly Wiggly since nothing is open on the island yet."

"So, you're still planning to go back there? Why?" Her mother's eyes narrowed, and her face flushed with anger. "There's a really cute three-bedroom bungalow three blocks over from here, in the neighborhood Sally lived in. Just fix up the island house and sell it."

"Momma, I love you, but I don't want to live in Columbia." Callie closed her eyes, willing herself to stay calm.

"Why do you insist on making things hard on yourself? Just stay here. Close. If you go back to the island, this will just keep happening." Her mother shook her head.

"It's where I want to live. It's where Joe and I started out. Maybe one day the house will get ruined, but until then, I want to live in it." Callie felt tears spring into her eyes and Squeezed them shut. *I'm not going to cry, and I don't want to argue with her.*

"You're just so pigheaded. Listen to reason." Her mother crossed her arms over her chest.

"Look, I'm tired. I'm going to get a quick bath and go to bed. Even though I'm not going to the house tomorrow, I've got things to do besides help you and look after Kimberly. I need to find a truck and a roofing company."

Callie knew the argument wasn't over, but went into the bathroom to forestall saying things she would regret. She kept thinking about this argument with her mother. *It will come to a head eventually, but I hope our relationship won't change too much. Why does she think I can't handle things on my own? I'm a grown woman with a child.*

The next day, Callie's mother was out for the morning, running errands. Before she left, they hardly spoke, and even then, it was with excessive politeness. Making a few phone calls improved Callie's sour mood. Although the roofing company couldn't get to her for another month, they would cover her roof with tarps right away to avoid any further water damage. She left a few messages for owners of trucks she had seen advertised in the paper and had phone service restored at the island house. Callie felt she was making progress. *Now let's get these floors cleaned while Kimberly's sleeping.*

She was hanging the mop out to dry when she heard a car in the driveway.

Going to the front of the house and looking out the living room window, it surprised her to see Alma and Carol getting out of the car.

"What are you up to today?" she asked as she opened the front door.

"Nothing much, just visiting folks." Alma paused long enough to give her friend a hug and peer around for Kimberly as she stepped into the living room.

"Come on in. Coffee or iced tea? I made some peanut butter cookies this morning."

"I'd like coffee and a few of those cookies," Carol said.

"Come on to the kitchen, then." Callie smiled as she led the way.

"Me too. Where's Kimberly? I'd hate to miss seeing her." Alma looked around the living room as they followed Callie to the kitchen. Her voice dropped off to a whisper.

"She's napping, but should wake up soon, Alma. Not to worry, she sleeps through everything."

"Any luck finding someone to do the roof? I can't get anyone until next month," Alma asked as she sat down.

"Same here. They'll go out and cover it with tarps now, though. I've left messages for some people with trucks for sale. With the phone on, I'm tempted to just go back to the island now. Momma was really pushing for me to stay in Columbia last night. This morning she was extra nice, like people do when they're mad at you."

Carol laughed. "Maybe *now* would be just a little too soon?"

"Yeah, how grown up would it be to say I'm leaving and then ask for Dad's truck? He would loan it to me, but it would make things awkward for him with Momma. That wouldn't be right." Callie grinned.

Both older women laughed, agreeing with her. "Carol and I are going down tomorrow. You and Kimberly want to go with us?" Alma asked.

"That sounds good. I'll be able to get my laundry and a few other things done today. I try not to make extra work for Momma," Callie said, excited to get back to the island without having to ask her dad to borrow the truck again.

The women talked a while longer. Alma admired the lemon motif in the kitchen and the deep purple African violets on the shelves next to the sink.

"I'll be sure to let Momma know. She made the curtains and place-mats herself. When I was a child, she sewed all my clothes. She taught me to sew. I'm working on curtains for Kimberly's room now." Callie looked around the room, smiling, as she thought about the work her mother put in to keep the house warm and welcoming.

"If we're going to go see Brenda's mother, we'd better get moving, Carol. You know they bought a place just down the road, Callie.

We wanted to check with you about tomorrow first. Give that baby a hug for me," Alma said as Callie walked them to the door.

After the trip with Carol, Alma and Callie fell into a routine over the next several weeks. At least once a week, they went back to their island homes, staying overnight to continue the work of cleaning, painting, and making small repairs. Sometimes Callie borrowed her dad's truck. Other times, Carol took them down. Once her Dad went down with her and helped her repair the brickwork that skirted the house. Callie still hadn't found a truck. She felt buying a truck and getting Kimberly's room ready was all she needed to do before moving back home. There was still a lot of work to be done, but she could do that while she was in the house.

4

Early October 1970

Callie finally found a used Ford pickup truck after her trip to Caines Island with Carol and Alma. Its red paint was a little faded, and it had a stick shift on the column, but the mileage was low. When her dad checked it over, he reassured her she'd learn to drive it easily. Today, she was on the road in front of her parents' house, trying hard to remember to engage the clutch so she could shift without grinding the gears and to avoid releasing the clutch too soon, which would stall out the engine.

She had been practicing for at least a half hour when her dad pulled up beside her and laughed. "Is that a burned clutch I smell?"

"Well, I had some trouble earlier." Leaning out the window, she grinned at him. "Think I got it now. I'll go down to the end of the road and turn around. See you inside in a few minutes." She waved to her dad and as he pulled into the driveway.

Callie joined her parents in the kitchen for coffee after peeking in on the still napping Kimberly. "How was work today?" Her mother had recently crocheted lemon shaped coasters since they always used mugs for coffee, rather than a cup and saucer.

"Alright. This crew is pretty good, and usually there's no problem. Think you've figured out that truck?" Her dad asked.

"Yeah, it's not too bad, and once you get going, it's like any other truck. For once, I don't mind being tall. If I were any shorter, I'd never get the clutch engaged," Callie laughed, stepping away from the table before shaking her hair out of her ball cap.

"So now that you've got the truck, are you planning to go back soon?" Her mother asked, turning to stare at her daughter as Callie sat down with her coffee, careful to put her mug on a coaster.

"I was planning to go tomorrow and probably move back for good this weekend." Callie ignored her mother's stare.

"You know, the house I told you about is still available." Her mother separated each word distinctly to underline her desire for Callie to remain in Columbia.

"Momma, let's not get into it again. I love being near you, but I don't like living in Columbia. With the truck, Kimberly and I can come visit. You won't have to drive all the time. I'm not sure Alma's ready, so I'll be back soon since I promised to help get her stuff to the island."

"Bob, can't you talk some sense into this girl? She's just asking for trouble going back to that island." Her mother pushed her chair back abruptly and went to the kitchen sink and stared out the window.

"Lydia, you know as well as I do, our daughter is headstrong." Callie's dad got up from the table to stand beside his wife and slipped an arm around her waist. "Like all of us, she's got to make her own way. Who knows, she may want to marry again someday. How's she going to do that stuck here with us?"

"Okay, let's don't go planning my entire future for me right now," Callie laughed. "I've got to fix the house, find a job, and raise a daughter. Any man out there has got a long wait. Momma, how can I help start supper?" Callie asked, hoping to divert her mother's tirade.

"It's pretty much done. I've got a pot of soup on, and I'll just make some biscuits," her mother said. Callie knew the discussion wasn't over, but still felt relieved.

"Alright, it smells so good. I always love your vegetable soup. I'll set the table. Kimberly should be awake by then."

Over supper, Callie outlined her plans for working on the island house. Mostly she would focus on finishing Kimberly's room, since she had painted it on her last trip to the island, "Joe and I had planned to paint her furniture but didn't get around to it. I hope I can get it painted before we move in."

"Why don't you let her stay here? Since you plan on staying overnight. Painting will be easier without her underfoot. I don't have anything but laundry for the next couple of days. It'd be great to spend time with her," her mother asked, looking fondly at Kimberly.

"Okay, thanks Momma. I will." Callie smiled at her mother and thought. *I'll never understand why she can be so sweet while insisting I should sell the house when she knows I'm dead set against it. Sometimes it's like she's two people. She really loves Kimberly, though, and is good with her.*

Early the next morning, Callie loaded the truck with her remaining foodstuffs, most of their clothes, and other things for the house. Her parents had a small portable crib Kimberly would use while visiting. Back inside, she sat with Kimberly in her lap. *I know she'll be fine with Momma, but I hate leaving her.*

"Alright baby girl, Momma's going to the island house and won't be back for a couple of days. I want you to be a good girl and listen to Grandma, okay?" Callie whispered in her daughter's ear.

Kimberly smiled, nodded yes as she squirmed out of Callie's lap and crawled into the living room. Callie and her mother watched Kimberly root around in the toy box. Squeals of delight erupted when she found her doll.

"Momma, I'll get back as early as I can on Thursday. She still likes a lullaby or one of the short books I have in the bedroom before she goes to sleep," Callie said as she hugged her mom. "And the phone is on, same number I've always had."

"Don't worry. We'll be fine. Just be safe traveling," her mother said, engrossed in Kimberly's play as she looked over Callie's shoulder.

"Okay, I will. Love you and thanks, Momma," Callie replied, forcing herself out the door. *I've never been away from Kimberly, except for a few hours. This is going to be so hard.*

The crew was already hard at work replacing the roof when Callie pulled into her driveway. They had gotten to her sooner than expected and should finish today. Quickly, she unloaded the frozen food and put it into the freezer. Continuing on, she took the boxes of canned food into the kitchen. They could wait until later to go into the pantry.

Turning her attention to Kimberly's room, Callie hung the hardware for the curtains she had sewn while in Columbia. She set up the crib since it was already white. Having roughed up their finish with sandpaper earlier, she painted the dresser, rocking chair, toy box, and bookshelf white. *When everything dries, I'll put a coat of polyurethane on it to keep it from chipping. Then I can empty the boxes of clothes and toys. I just want everything in her room ready when we're back home.*

During her last trip to Caines, the furniture store in Mt. Pleasant delivered the new mattresses for her bedroom and the sewing room. Thankfully, they also put them on the beds. After making her bed, she put her clothes away. She hadn't gotten around to making curtains for her room, so she draped fabric over the windows. *I need to remember to set up my sewing room once I finish in the kitchen.* A knock at the door brought her into the living room.

"Hey, Josie. Come on in," Callie said, hugging her friend tightly.

"Was on my way back from town and saw an unfamiliar truck in the driveway. I've gotten used to the roofers trucks. Is it yours? Are you back for good?" Josie grinned.

"Yes, that's my truck. I'll be back for good this weekend. Momma's got Kimberly today. Wanted to have her room ready before we moved back in. Come on in the kitchen and have some iced tea."

"Sure, is that paint I smell?" Josie asked, wrinkling her nose.

"Yeah, I painted Kimberly's furniture. Here, come take a look," Callie said with pride.

"Oh, Callie, this is gorgeous. Love that you painted all her furniture white."

"Thanks, everything was so mismatched before. I thought painting the furniture would help everything go together better, even though the furniture has different styles."

"It sure does, and when she's ready to get out of the crib, it all will still work." The women turned to leave the room. "Are these her curtains here on the couch? Those little daisies are so cute."

"Thanks. Sorry, the kitchen is a mess, but it's we won't get food poisoning, I promise," Callie said, walking toward the kitchen.

"It's me, not the ladies' garden club. Don't worry about it. Everybody has at least one room in a mess, especially right now." Josie waved her hands in a dismissive gesture.

After shifting boxes to the counter, Callie and Josie sat around the kitchen table. They caught up on each other's lives since the hurricane. "So, tell me, what have they decided about the pier?" Callie asked with a slight frown.

"Last I heard, they aren't going to rebuild it. The supervisors say it would cost too much to rebuild it safely. It seems Folly Beach had a more substantial pier. That's where most tourists go, anyway. Max still has a petition going around asking them to reconsider." Josie shook her head and shrugged.

"I'll have to catch up with him and sign it. Selling on the pier was easy for me. I've got the truck now, but I still want to do something that will let me keep Kimberly with me. Already, Momma's not excited about me coming back to the island and now they're not rebuilding the pier. I can hear her say 'I told you so.' Oh well, I'll figure it out." Callie rested her chin on her hand.

"The supervisors said they would rebuild the pavilion and boardwalk. It looks like a couple more store owners are cleaning up, but they've still got the diner boarded up. Pete says he's not sure he will stay open." Josie looked down at her watch. "Oh, look at the time. My boys will be home from school soon. I'd better run." Josie jumped up, putting her glass on the counter.

"Thanks for stopping by. I'll see you Saturday. Let me walk you to the door," Callie said.

After Josie left, Callie put away the canned food. The roofing crew was finishing, making sure they didn't leave any trash or nails anywhere. She started painting the living room before going to see Max and Louise.

Although people were getting back into their homes, it still surprised Callie that there were still so many fallen trees alongside the road. The county had scraped the roads, so there weren't as many potholes as before. Eventually they'd get around to spreading oyster shells again.

Max and Louise were on the front porch when she pulled into the driveway. Once they settled on the porch with some ice tea, Callie asked about the petition. "Are you still collecting signatures about rebuilding the pier? I'm ready to sign."

"Yeah, we're still collecting. I've got it right here." Max reached over to a nearby table.

"Do you think this will make a difference? I'm not sure what I'll do if we don't have a place to sell from." Callie leaned over the clipboard to add her name to the list, signing with a flourish.

"We're all hoping it will, but I was going over the numbers for repairs with Steve. It doesn't look good for us. Rebuilding while meeting today's codes is pretty expensive. Glad I've got work with my brother while they figure this out." Max shrugged a shoulder.

"I heard the diner is still closed and the general store might close." Callie gave Max the clipboard.

"Yeah, the Jenkins are moving for sure. They weren't prepared for this part of island life. Think they're going to Charleston or maybe further inland. I heard they'll eventually sell the diner but haven't seen any signs," Louise said.

"Pete opened up again pretty quickly, but his kids have moved away, and there's no one to help him but Lyla. Her health's not too good. So, who knows?" Max turned the palms of his hands up as he shrugged again. "Several of us helped him get the store cleaned up, but he still seems worn out by it all."

"If they don't redo the pier, maybe we could find a space to do an open-air market. I really don't want to go off the island for work." Callie crossed her fingers.

"I don't know any space on the island that would be big enough and would have any traffic. They approved replacing the pavilion, but a large part of that will be an amphitheater for concerts by local music artists and a few picnic tables. From what Steve has told me about the plans he's seen, it doesn't seem like there's a good place for an open-air market there, either." Max rubbed a hand over his head.

Discouraged, Callie frowned. "Well, I'll find work in a shop if I have to. I surely don't want to sell the house and live in Columbia," she said with a sigh. "But I have to go back tomorrow afternoon and I still have a boatload of stuff to do at the house. I'll be back this weekend for good. I'll see you then."

Determined to finish most of the painting before moving back on the weekend, Callie worked until late in the evening, painting the living room and hanging curtains in Kimberly's room. Before she left tomorrow, she would finish unpacking Kimberly's clothes.

Thursday morning, back in Columbia, Callie bought one of the car seats she had read about. Made of molded plastic with a thin vinyl cushion, it had two large rectangular holes just large enough to slip the truck's seatbelt through. It took a while to get it tightened down in the truck's seat. Looking at the lightly vinyl where Kimberly would sit, Callie was glad she bought a cover that fit over the molded plastic car seat so Kimberly would be more comfortable. She wasn't sure how she felt about the whole setup. But since she'd be driving alone most of the time, she thought it would at least keep Kimberly in one place.

Friday, after her dad came home from work, he and Callie loaded the truck and covered everything with a tarp. Callie's mother played with Kimberly and avoided talking about the move. *I'm not sure why*

Momma's so quiet. Well, I'm not going to poke the bear. I know this is just a ceasefire before the next assault.

When Saturday arrived, Callie spent the early morning stripping her bed and putting away the toys Callie's mom kept at her house for Kimberly. Her mother was still eerily quiet, and her dad was helpful, as always. He checked the tie downs on her furniture at least six times before she was even ready to leave.

Finally, Callie had done everything she could think of to avoid leaving her mother with extra work. She would miss them, but she was eager to get back home. Picking up Kimberly, Callie went out to the truck. Her parents followed. Pausing by the passenger side of the truck, they began the long process of saying goodbye. After each grandparent hugged Kimberly at least three times, and her dad rechecked the tie downs on the truck bed yet again, Callie put Kimberly in her car seat and hugged each of her parents.

"Call us when you get home," her mom said as worry lines settled on her forehead.

"I will, Momma," Callie said, smiling softly.

"Now when is Alma going back?" her dad asked as he tugged on a tie down one more time.

"Probably two weeks. I'll be back to help her," Callie said as she got in the truck.

With a wave to her parents, Callie backed out of the driveway. A small cooler on the floorboard held snacks and drinks for Kimberly. There was also a cookie, and a drink tucked beside her in the car seat. For now, Kimberly seemed content to play quietly. *I hope she stays happy. She's generally good in the car, but I haven't been the driver and only other person in the car before. I'll stop if I have to, but I'm hoping we can drive straight through.*

Soon, the truck's motion lulled Kimberly to sleep. About halfway, Kimberly started fussing. They made a quick stop for a diaper change and for Callie to go to the bathroom. Kimberly drifted off to sleep again once they got back on the road. By the time they made it to the island, the stops and turns woke Kimberly up again.

"Hey, baby girl. Was that a good rest?" Callie smiled as she quickly glanced at her daughter. "We're almost home. Here's that cookie Grandma put in the truck for you. Oh, and there's a drink beside you."

"Tank you, Momma." Kimberly smiled around her cup.

As they pulled into the driveway, Kimberly started bouncing in the seat. "Home. Home," she giggled.

"Yes, baby girl, we're home." Callie went around the truck and picked up her daughter. "Oh, you're soaked again. Let's get you inside and changed."

After changing Kimberly and getting her settled with a snack on the porch, Callie began unloading everything she could move herself. Mike and Brenda said they would come by after supper to help get the couch inside. For now, she busied herself putting away other things brought back from Columbia and starting a load of diapers. Last night she had been too tired to do them at her parents. Especially now that Kimberly was into everything; keeping up with her laundry seemed like a never-ending chore.

It was hard for Callie to admit, but it seemed almost too quiet after being in Columbia. *It'll be different when everyone's back. Besides, it was always quiet on the weekends.* Callie turned on the radio and found a station playing the Temptations. *I remember dancing to this with Dad when I was little.* She danced around, putting things away and singing to Kimberly. "I can't help myself. I love you and nobody else, sugar pie honey bun." Kimberly toddled around, trying to copy her mother's dance moves.

With laundry in the dryer, Callie fixed a quick supper. *It's good to be back home. Back in my kitchen.* Shortly after she had cleaned up the kitchen, Mike and Brenda arrived.

"Hey, there. Come on in," she called, stepping out onto the front porch. "I've missed you," Callie said as she hugged her friend tightly and moved to the front door so she could see Kimberly.

Mike made it to the porch, too, and stood with his hands in his jeans pockets. "My brother's right behind us. Show me where you want the couch. After we get it inside, he'll take me home so you and Brenda can visit," Mike said.

"Sorry, Mike, I know you must be tired coming over right after work. I sure appreciate this. Come on into the living room. How about here against this wall? Then I can see the driveway and porch through the window," Callie said. She had always loved the windows in this room. Three nearly floor to ceiling windows, right next to each other. Opening them a little at both the top and bottom and turning on the ceiling fan, kept the house comfortable during the heat of summer.

"Okay. I hear my brother now. Here's the keys, Brenda. See you later, Callie," Mike said, standing in the doorway.

"Thanks again for moving the couch for me," Callie said as Mike turned to go back to the truck. She and Brenda went inside.

Callie scooped Kimberly up from the living room on her way into the kitchen with Brenda. "Come on, let's get a cup of coffee. I've got more stuff to put away and then ironing to do once Kimberly's clothes are dry. But that can wait until later. Kimberly, let's get you some milk."

"So, what have you got to do in the next few days?" Brenda asked. After pouring two cups of coffee, Callie settled Kimberly in her highchair with a cup of milk and a few small toys.

"Well, Alma had some materials delivered to build a new chicken coop. I'll be working on that. Here friends in Conway would like us to get her chickens as soon as possible. When that's done, I need to get to work building a shed. Besides all that, I have to find some kind of job." Callie grinned and shrugged.

"You didn't tell your parents about the pier, did you? Come on, Callie." Brenda shook her head. "They're going to be so mad. Your mom especially will blow a gasket."

"What are they going to do to me? Momma's already mad I that moved back. I think Dad will understand. Maybe?" Callie shrugged again, thinking, *I'm not really that sure he'll understand.*

"Oh, Callie. I understand you not wanting to tell your mom, but your dad. He's going to feel so hurt." Brenda shook her head again.

"I couldn't tell him and ask him to keep it from Momma. That would put him in a terrible place. They don't keep secrets from each other. Besides, I've saved some money and I'll have the insurance from the business. Part of that is Alma's and I have to pay Dad back. But I'll still have some money left to see me through." Callie frowned, thinking of her tight budget.

"I think you're taking a chance, but what else have I known you to do since Joe died? I'm not sure I could do what you're doing." Brenda threw her hands up in surrender.

"You forget, I've had lots of help. Besides, I've got months of food in the pantry and freezer. I can fish and keep working the shrimp and crab pots. So, there's not much I really need to buy. I'll be able to take care of the power and phone." Callie stuck out her chin, determined to end the discussion.

Brenda shook her head again. "Honey, you seem to have a plan. I'll see if I can get Mike and his brother to help us with Alma's coop and the shed on Saturday. I know we've finished at our place, but there's still stuff to clear out of my parents."

"Even if you just help get the framing up on Saturday, that would be great. I know Alma is ready to get back here, and I was hoping to help her do that in a couple of weeks," Callie said.

"Yeah. It would be good to have her back. I miss her. Let me talk with the guys," Brenda said.

Brenda left, and Callie went about finishing her work for the evening. Kimberly followed Callie from room to room, and despite napping on the way down, she was soon ready for bed. It had been an eventful day for the little girl as she got reacquainted with her home. Callie continued putting things away for a few hours before crawling into bed herself.

The next day dawned sunny. *If I can get the rest of this stuff put away, we'll go down to the beach after Kimberly's nap.* Since she didn't get to it last night, Callie did the rest of the ironing and folded diapers while Kimberly was napping. She always wanted to help, which usually meant emptying the laundry basket onto the floor. It was cute but always made doing laundry take longer.

Once Kimberly woke up, Callie put her in the stroller and headed for the beach. She hadn't really taken the opportunity to walk on the beach during her earlier trips since she had focused on making the house livable again. She missed the renewal she always felt when she was near the ocean. Kimberly and Callie waved as they passed their neighbor's homes. Spanish moss was reappearing on the oak trees. Briar bushes were popping up in open areas. Nearing the ocean, the marshlands were recovering. The herons took wing as Kimberly called out to them.

On the beach, Callie parked the stroller and stood Kimberly on the sand. At first, Kimberly held tightly onto her mother's finger as they walked to the water's edge. Seeing the birds up ahead, the little girl let go and toddled away, chasing sandpipers. *This is the life. Warm sun, sand, and water.* As the sun dipped closer to the horizon, Callie turned her daughter toward the abandoned stroller. "Come on, baby girl. Let's go up by the pavilion."

After they got past the loose sand and onto the boardwalk, Callie put her daughter back in the stroller. "Here we go. I want to see how Pete's doing." Even though it was just late afternoon, Pete had already closed the store for the day. Except for the diner with its for sale sign, the other businesses sported signs saying they'd reopen in the spring. "Oh, well, a coke would have been good. Guess we have to catch him early in the morning."

Back at home, Callie started a seafood boil and put cornbread in the oven while Kimberly played nearby. As she waited for the food to finish cooking, Callie went through the notes she had made about her finances. It would be close, but she felt she could make it for a few months. As much as she wanted to remain in this house, she knew she needed to support Kimberly and herself without counting on the supervisors to rebuild the pier.

As usual, Callie woke up early on Saturday morning. Her only plans were to get the building projects completed and pick up the chickens if she finished the coop soon enough. She took tools and the playpen over to Alma's before Kimberly woke up. After a quick breakfast, Callie gathered her daughter and a few toys before going next door.

She met up with Mike and his brother as they backed the truck into Alma's backyard. "Did Alma want to fence in the coop? Or was she going to let them run loose?" Mike asked as he got closer.

"She didn't order any chicken wire. I think at first, she just wanted to get the coop rebuilt so I could get the chickens from her friends in Conway."

"There's some chicken wire at Brenda's parent's place we were going to scrap. We could probably use that and give Alma a good sized pen for them. Think there's some posts, too," Mike said as he leaned on his truck.

"It sure would be easier for her to gather eggs if she didn't have to go checking under every bush. And the chickens would be safer from the wildlife." Callie tossed Kimberly's toys back into the playpen.

"Alright, we'll get it. Her parents have taken everything they can use. We're down to cleaning up the property. Not sure what they're going to do with it, though. Just don't want it to become an eyesore." Mike walked away, shaking his head and muttering. "There's just so much to do."

"I hear you. Once I get Alma's coop set up, I can come help clear stuff out," Callie said. Mike turned his head and nodded to let Callie know he heard her.

Everyone had so much to do cleaning up after the hurricane, Callie felt it was only right to help her friends when she could. *Mike seems off, but I don't know why. He volunteers to help. Maybe he's just tired, like everybody else.*

Mike and his brother returned almost immediately with the fencing, and Brenda arrived with her boys. The four of them quickly built and fenced in the coop. They framed in Callie's shed before lunch time.

Callie reminded Mike to call her when he was doing the clean-up for Brenda's parents later in the week. After seeing everyone off and feeding Kimberly lunch, Callie got her daughter into the truck. She had just enough time to get the chickens and have them in the new pen before dark.

Because she had called before heading to Conway, Alma's friend had the chicken crated when Callie arrived. Knowing she didn't have many scraps at home, Callie bought a bag of feed from Alma's friend. The sun was nudging toward the horizon as Callie pulled into Alma's backyard. She unloaded the crates and set them inside the pen with the doors open.

With a small pan of feed, she and Kimberly went into the pen and closed the gate. Sprinkling feed across the yard, Callie called, "Here, chickee, chickee. Here chickee, chickee." Slowly, the chickens left the crate in search of food. Kimberly chased them around the pen. As Callie set up their water, a couple of chickens found the new coop. She had been afraid that they might resist living in the new coop at first. *Alright, that's off the list. Next weekend I'll get Alma.*

"Come on, sweetie. Let's get home. We'll come see the chickens in the morning." As Callie held out her hand, Kimberly wrapped her hand around her mother's little finger.

During the week, Callie helped clear out Brenda's parents' property and finished the shed. She also started weaving sections of fencing using limber twigs and some sturdier sticks. While in Columbia, she had read an article in a magazine about wattle fencing and thought it might work for her around the garden and her compost pit. More tightly woven along its lower section, the fence would keep the rabbits out and look good, too. If she had time this spring, Callie thought about growing some flowers along the outside of the fence line. *There's no reason the vegetable garden shouldn't be pretty. I've always enjoyed gardening, even when I didn't need to grow food. Momma and I always gardened together. She seemed so peaceful then. We were probably closer when we gardened than any other time. Be nice if we could get back to that.*

The weekend came quickly; it was finally time for Callie to drive to Columbia and pick up Alma. She would stay with her parents Friday and Saturday; Sunday, she and Alma would drive back to the island. Although she was excited to see her parents, she dreaded telling them the county wouldn't rebuild the pier.

Her Dad hadn't gotten off from work when Callie returned to Columbia and her mother was out. Using her key, Callie let herself in. After a quick lunch, she put Kimberly down for a nap and took a glass of tea out to the porch. It wasn't long before she heard a car in the driveway.

"Bobby, I didn't know you were coming this weekend," Callie called out as she ran across the yard to give her brother a hug. "Where are Susan and the kids?"

"Susan didn't feel up to the drive." Bobby said, stretching after Callie released him from her bear hug.

"Oh, I'll miss seeing them, but it's a long drive from Spartanburg, especially if she's still having morning sickness." They strolled up the sidewalk and into the house, settling in the kitchen with ice tea once Callie retrieved her glass from the porch.

"Yeah, she is and it usually lasts most of the day. I feel bad because there's not much I can do to relieve it." Bobby brushed the dark brown hair from his forehead. "Anyway, I've been promising Momma and Dad a visit. We were talking on the phone last night and they said you would be here this weekend. So, here I am. Tell me, how's life on the island? Sorry I haven't been able to help with the hurricane damage."

"It's okay. Susan's pregnant and you're getting your practice going. Things are coming along. I'm doing the winter prep for my garden. Setting up the compost pit and weaving a fence from the fallen tree limbs."

"Like those forts we used to build when we visited Aunt Sally as kids?"

"Yeah, something like that. I think they're called wattle fences. How about you? What's happening in the big city of Spartanburg?"

"The practice is getting off the ground. I have privileges at the hospital and my colleagues are sending me referrals. We're doing pretty well. Susan's due in January. We just moved into the new house."

"I'm so happy for you. You've worked hard for this."

Vehicles in the driveway heralded their parents' return. Callie and her brother went out to help unload grocery bags from the car. Once the bags were in, Bobby went to check on Kimberly who was cooing in her crib.

"Come see Uncle Bobby. It's been a long time since I last saw you." Stepping into the hall, he called out to the kitchen. "Callie, I'll change Kimberly and take her outside while you and Mom get supper going."

"Okay, Bobby," Callie called from the kitchen while she helped her mother put away the groceries. "What are we doing for supper tonight, Momma?"

"I've got a roast thawed in the refrigerator. If you'd start peeling potatoes and carrots, I can get it all in the pressure cooker. Then there's the green beans we put up earlier this year. I've got a lemon meringue pie for dessert and those oatmeal cookies Kimberly loves."

"Alright, Momma. Just thinking about it makes me hungry. I'll get started on the potatoes."

Before long, Kimberly was tired from running around the yard, so Bobby brought her inside before following their dad to the workshop out back. "Your dad always keeps a beer or two in the porch fridge. Guess it can't do any harm for them to have a beer. Not like either of them drinks every day." Her mother said.

"They'll be fine. It'll give them something to do while they catch up on man things. Neither one of them is used to sitting around."

"I knew your dad had the occasional beer when I married him but, Aunt Flo didn't tolerate any drinking when I was growing up. It's hard putting some things behind you." Callie's mother stared out the window as she spoke.

"So, Momma, what was it like growing up with Aunt Flo?" Kimberly's cries interrupted before her mom could answer.

Both women hurried into the living room. "What happened?" Callie asked calmly. An overturned step stool told the story. "You tried to climb up to get Grandma's cats, did you? Those are Grandma's pretties. Not for you. Here, let's find something in the toy box."

"Glad she's okay. I'll just get everything into the pressure cooker. We can start the green beans bit later."

Callie wanted to continue the conversation from the kitchen, but realized the mood was gone, since her mother was suddenly very busy in the kitchen. Besides, Bobby and her dad were walking toward the house. Her mother joined everyone in the living room, while Bobby regaled them with stories about moving into his new house and setting up his practice. Before long, supper was ready and by the time they had nearly finished eating, Bobby ran out of stories.

"Callie, you've been quiet. Tell me about this stand you had before the hurricane. Understand you were doing rather well. Will you be able to start again?" Bobby asked.

"I did well enough. Starting again will have to be different. I'm not sure what that will be. They're not rebuilding the pier. Apparently, it costs too much to rebuild it safely." Callie rolled her eyes, disgusted by the supervisors' decision.

Eyes narrowed; her mother turned to face her. "When were you going to tell us this? You just need to sell that place." Her mother's tea glass clattered against the table as she set it down, completely missing the bright lemon shaped placemat.

Callie closed her eyes, tried to breathe slowly and count to ten. *Why does she always make me feel like a misbehaving child when she's upset?* Silence filled the room as everyone waited for Callie to speak. After letting out a long sigh, Callie said, "We were having so much fun, I didn't want to spoil it. I planned to tell you about the pier before I left, Momma. Besides, I'm looking into setting up at open-air markets. I'm not selling the house. I'll figure this out."

"Sis, I'm sorry." Bobby reached out to rub his sister's shoulder.

"Not your fault, Bobby. Momma, I don't know why you can't trust me to do what's right for me and my daughter. Excuse me. I need to get Kimberly bathed and ready for bed," Callie said, picking her daughter up from the high chair.

She heard her mother in the kitchen after Kimberly was asleep. Instead of helping, as she usually did, Callie went out to the front porch to avoid talking to her mother. *I don't know how I'll get through this weekend. She's going to harp on this constantly, this whole visit. Maybe tomorrow I'll go see Alma. Maybe we can leave early on Sunday.*

"Sis, is it okay if I join you?" Bobby sank down into the rocker next to Callie.

"Sure, Bobby. I might not be good company right now," she replied.

"I'm your big brother. You are fine however you might be. Oh, I almost forgot. Susan found a box while she was unpacking. She said Momma gave it to us a few years ago, but felt it really belonged with you. It's full of old pictures and letters. Let me get it. I'll put it in the truck for you."

Bobby quickly returned to the porch. He and Callie talked over her plans for staying on the island and their mother's insistence on Callie staying in Columbia until they finally had to call it a night. *I'm lucky to have a brother like Bobby. Funny, he doesn't seem to understand Momma any more than I do.*

Breakfast the next morning was quiet. Nobody wanted to pick up the conversation from last night. Bobby left before lunch. Callie and Kimberly went to see Alma shortly after he left. Visiting Alma usually helped Callie regain her composure.

"Your Momma's just trying to look out for you," Alma said, trying to explain Callie's mother's behavior.

"I wish people would stop saying that." Callie threw her hands up in exasperation. "She doesn't have to be so hateful. Momma didn't even wait to hear my plan. It's confusing. She always pushes me but then tries to keep me on a short leash. When I think for myself, she's upset. I just don't know."

"Well, you've lived with her. I only know her a little. She didn't visit much once when y'all lived next door. It's still early, we could go back today instead of tomorrow. Be there by suppertime. I don't have that much here to pack. Just a matter of getting it out of the shed and onto the truck."

"Sounds good to me. I don't think I could take staying there tonight. It will blow over eventually, but right now I just want to go to *my* home. I'll go say goodbye and grab my stuff. See you in about an hour."

Callie cried quietly most of the way to her parents' house. After putting Kimberly in the crib, she tossed their things into her suitcase and set it by the door. Picking up Kimberly, she went in search of her parents. From the kitchen, she saw them on the back porch. Callie took a deep breath as she opened the back door pausing on the threshold. "I'm going back to the island tonight. Alma's got everything ready and is waiting. Just wanted to say goodbye and thanks for everything."

Her dad stated to protest, but stopped when he saw Callie's red-rimmed eyes and the determined look on her face. He shook his head and got up to give her a hug. "Sorry you have to go early."

"I'm sorry you're going too, baby." Her mother added as she stood to hug Callie and Kimberly.

"I'll call in a couple of days. I've got my suitcase already." Callie said as she picked up her suitcase and went to her truck alone, leaving her parents on the porch.

The drive to the island was quiet. Her mother's behavior still troubled Callie. Alma and Kimberly drifted off to sleep before they were out of Columbia. Back on the island, it didn't take long to unload Alma's things. Tired, Callie went home to fix supper. She put the Belk's dress box Bobby gave her on the shelf in the coat closet, not even thinking about the old pictures he told her about. Yesterday had been a hard day, and she just wanted to laze around until it was time for bed.

Mid-October 1970

Alma walked across the yard and stood for a minute watching Callie weave another section of the garden fence. "How are you doing today? That fence is looking good."

"Doing okay. Think I'll plant some flowers along the outside. Make it look prettier," Callie said and kept her head bent, focused on the task. The sun was warm even with the brisk wind. Kimberly sat playing beside her.

"Have you talked to your parents?" It had been a week since they returned to the island after cutting the visit short.

"We talked on the phone. They're doing fine. Momma acts like nothing happened. I don't understand her sometimes. Do you know why she is like this with me? Why does she think I can't figure out my life? Why does she think I have to be married to be respectable? Why does she start in on something and then just drops it?"

"Whoa, you got a lot going on there. Honey, I never knew your mother well. Like I told you, she didn't come around much, even when she lived next door. Now, your Aunt Sally eventually became like a sister to me."

"Have you had lunch?" Callie said, leaning the section of fence she was working up against the part already installed.

"Not yet," Alma replied.

"Well, come in. I'll fix lunch. Will you, please, tell me about my Aunt Sally? Maybe that will help me understand my momma." Callie picked up Kimberly.

"Alright." Alma joined Callie as they crossed the backyard.

Callie set out cold sliced chicken and other things for sandwiches. Kimberly had decided she was too big for a highchair and wanted to sit at the table. Callie sat her on the tall kitchen stool with an apron tied around her waist and the chair back to keep her in place.

"Well, come on. Momma never talks about her childhood. Come to think about it, neither did Aunt Sally. What do you know about Aunt

Sally?" Callie asked, goading her reticent friend to get on with the tale as she sat down as they each made a sandwich.

"I don't really know what to tell you. All Sally would say about her childhood was that she grew up an orphan in her aunt's home and your momma always looked out for her. Your momma was just a few years older than Kimberly when their momma died. Apparently, there wasn't a lot of money. All the kids worked from the time they could walk the rows in a field. They came to Charleston when she was sixteen and your mother was eighteen. They both worked in the mill and your momma was going to night school. Sally had a second job as a hat-check girl in a supper club. That's where she met Claude. Once she and Claude married, he taught her about the family business. His family was in shipbuilding and had Navy contracts in World War II. They still work with the Navy, but build yachts as well. Sally quickly learned how to hostess all his business dinners, cocktail parties and had a sharp business mind. She was quite the thing in Charleston's social circles from what we saw in the papers.

Claude doted on Sally and the children. Their youngest, Millicent, got scarlet fever after going to a friend's house when she was eight. Sally moved a cot into Millicent's bedroom. She stayed at Millicent's bedside, spooning broth and other liquids into the child's mouth. After three weeks with a raging fever, Millicent died in her sleep. That's why he built the house out here, so Sally could have a quiet place of her own. Sometimes, losing a child drives a wedge between a couple. But like me and Nate, Sally and Claude grew closer."

Kimberly began hitting the table with her spoon. "What is it, sweetie? Do you need more milk? Go on Alma, I'll just fill up her cup," Callie said.

After taking a few bites of her sandwich, Alma continued. "Like I said, Sally and I often walked the beach together. She wasn't handy like you and your mother, said no one ever taught her and now she was too busy to figure it out herself. Still, she helped me gather sea grasses and sat with me as I wove baskets out on the porch. Sometimes we sat in silence and sometimes we talked about our lost children, the hopes, the dreams we had for them. That's the thing about mourning. Some people think you gotta get on with life after a few months. Maybe your momma's like that. Then other people won't talk about the ones who passed. It's talking about the departed that helps you remember and helps you heal."

"So, how did we wind up here?" Callie scrunched up her face as she tried to remember living on the island. She couldn't recall a solid memory, just the feeling of peacefulness and the smell of the marshes. Absent mindedly she ate her sandwich.

"When your mother was carrying Bobby, Sally offered your parents the house. It was nicer than living in the mill houses. The mills around here weren't doing well, so the houses were pretty run down. Your mother stopped working in the mill. Like I told you before, she didn't socialize much unless she was visiting the sick. She was really protective of you kids and had your dad fence the yard. Of course, by then I was back working at the truck farm. Then you moved to Columbia when the mills pulled out.

Sally and her family kept coming back to the island during summers and holidays. They met Max and Louise at my place one weekend. When he was in his late forties, Claude had a heart attack and died. After the funeral, Sally closed up the big house and moved to the island year round. She kept a hand in the business, but their children were ready to take over once they came of age. One thing about Sally, if you saw her walking on the beach, you'd never know she had money. Anonymously, she became a benefactor for a few projects on the island. One reason they're redoing the boardwalk and pavilion is because of a trust she set up." Amla finished her sandwich and moved her plate away.

As Alma continued the tale, Callie put away the lunch remains and set Kimberly on the floor to play. After refilling their tea, Callie encouraged Alma to continue with the story. "I barely remember Uncle Claude. But go on."

"Sally, sometimes Claude, Max, Louise, and I would get together on the weekend for a fish fry or seafood boil, even after I lost Nate. We rotated through each other's homes. I'll never forget when she heard about the shameful business about the loan for Max and Louise's house. Banks wouldn't lend money to Black people to keep them out of certain communities. Of course, the government turned a blind eye. The lawyers and bankers, people with the money, did what they wanted. Even veterans like Max had trouble getting a loan. If they got a loan, it was through some shifty company and the rates were sky high. Then the loan company added clauses so the lender could take the house if they missed just one payment." The vein at Alma's temple stood out and pulsed visibly.

"This particular year, the fishing hauls were the worst in decades." Alma hung her head remembering the hard times, then she looked up at Callie. "Max was taking the boat out seven days a week, but it still wasn't enough to pay the bills, even with Louise doing hair. Louise and I were on the porch when she told me they might lose the house if things didn't turn around soon. About then, Sally came around the corner. Her face was red and screwed up in a frown. It was clear she had heard everything.

'Louise, what are you talking about---losing the house.' Oh lordy, was Sally hot. She fumed, and she fussed I can still hear her." Grinning now, Alma slowly shook her head, remembering Sally's fury. "She called lawyers and congressmen. It didn't do no good. Finally, telling no one, Sally had her business buy the loan for Max and Louise's house. They received a letter with information about the new terms of their loan, but that was all. She did that for a few other folks on the island. No one knew until after she died that Sally's company had bought up the loans. She worked with the NAACP for years. Sometimes it cost her business, but she didn't care. She felt you had to stand up for what was right."

Kimberly crawled off toward the back porch. "Alma, let's go out on the porch. Kimberly can play out there," Callie said, picking up her daughter. "Will you grab our tea?"

Alma picked up the glasses and followed Callie to the porch. Callie gave Kimberly some blocks and a couple of small trucks. Alma quietly sipped her tea.

"Come on, Alma. You can't stop here." Callie pleaded, picking up her glass.

Alma smiled and continued. "The children came to visit pretty often. As they, and she, got older, her children tried to talk her into leaving the island and coming to live with them. But she stayed on until a hurricane put a tree through the roof. She got the roof repaired and had some of the other things done. But then she had a stroke. She was still young, but had never watched her blood pressure. Always too busy trying to right the world." Alma shook her head slowly. "Eventually, she recovered except for a slight limp. Still, she wouldn't drive anymore. She sold the house in Charleston and moved to Columbia," Almas said as she gazed out toward the garden out back.

"I know Sally left Bobby money for school. He talked about being a doctor even when he was a kid. And she left me the house, so I'd always have something of my own. And I knew her kids were well off, but I didn't know about the shipbuilding business until you told me. Even Aunt Sally is a mystery and I thought I knew her. I've heard Momma mention an Aunt Flo a time or two. But other than she was her dad's sister and took care of them, Momma never said much else." Callie shrugged, frustrated that although she knew more about her Aunt Sally, she still didn't know why her mother acted like she did.

"Honey, maybe since you're grown with a child of your own, you should just ask her. Nobody else can tell you what she can." Alma said.

"Alma, I usually think you give good advice, but I'm not sure about this time, at least right now. I've got so much else to focus on, like how to make a living, to get into it with Momma. Once she gets started, it always ends with her trying to get me to move to Columbia. I'll talk to Momma sometime, but I've got to help her see we are going to be okay here," Callie said, avoiding Alma's eyes.

Shaking her head, Alma stood up to leave. "You got to make your own way. That's a given, but eventually you've got to make peace with your mother. At least get to where you're not so torn up about her all the time. Just don't wait too long. Well, I got to get some stuff done in the house. I'll see you later," Alma said as she opened the porch's screen door.

"Okay. Thanks Alma, I'll think about what you said."

Once she cleaned up after lunch, Callie walked to the beach with Kimberly. Being on the beach always helped clear her mind. Sun rays shot through the clouds as they hugged the horizon. She wanted to do some surf fishing today, but it looked like it might rain. As Kimberly grew tired, Callie put her in the stroller and went to Pete's store. *We must be quite the sight, with this fishing pole balanced across the stroller's sun shade.* When they got to the store, she parked the stroller near the door and leaned the fishing pole against the wall.

"Hey, Pete," Callie called out to let him know she was in the store, even though the bell sounded as the door opened.

"Hi, Callie. Where's that sweet girl of yours? Ah, there she is. Hello, Kimberly. How about a stick of candy?" Pete asked as he reached into his shirt pocket and unwrapped a small peppermint stick. Callie noticed he was moving slower. Grizzled gray hair and beard framed the bright eyes and a smile that made everyone an instant friend.

Kimberly waited for her mother's nod before taking the candy. "Tank you."

Callie noticed several empty spaces on the shelves as she made her way back to the milk cooler. It occurred to her she and Pete might help each other out.

Back at the counter, she asked. "Pete, how are things going?"

"Well, not so good right now. I'm not stocking much because I'm going to sell. But I hate to let the place go, so I've got a friend looking for a buyer, trying to find the right one." Pete leaned against the counter.

"Oh, I see. I was hoping to bring in some seafood and other stuff to sell but, that won't help you much."

"Wish things were different, but I'd hate for you to get something started and then have the new owner change things up on you. You did fairly good selling on the pier. Have you ever thought of owning a store?" He explained what he thought a fair price would be.

"Pete, I'm sure I can't swing a loan for that much. It would be perfect for us, though. Are you and Lyla coming tomorrow? Tell Lyla not to worry about cooking. You guys have done so much for this community. Just come and enjoy yourselves." Callie bent to pick up Kimberly as she moved toward the door.

"Well, you think about it. Let me know. And yes, we'll see you tomorrow."

On the way home, Callie kept thinking about the store. *I could make a play area for Kimberly with some rearranging.* Having now accepted that she could not work from a stand or open air market anymore, Callie had filed a claim against the insurance policy her dad had taken out. This would give her some money to help tide her over until she found a job. Half of that was Alma's. *Oh well, don't make yourself sick over it. You're not getting anywhere spinning your wheels. Besides, you're home now and you've got to get ready for the celebration tomorrow.*

5

Late October 1970

Waking early, as usual, Callie settled into her wicker rocking chair on the front porch with her first cup of coffee. A light, salt-tinged breeze wafted across the porch. Herons took wing from the nearby marsh. The island was quiet, except for the sound of the distant ocean. Callie couldn't stop thinking about the store. *The large window in the front would be perfect for displaying the artisans' wares. I know a lot of them are looking for places to sell from too. Kimberly could have a playroom in the back corner. It would be perfect for us. Enough daydreaming. I need to get ready for the celebration this afternoon. Everyone worked so hard after the hurricane. Not just in their own homes, but helping each other. That's why I love this place. Not just the ocean, but the people here. Well, I'd better get moving. There's a lot to do before everyone gets here.*

Callie drank the last of her coffee and went inside to get dressed. Once her daughter had eaten, they went outside. As soon as the toddler's feet hit the ground, she went to the sandbox under the magnolia. Seeing her occupied, Callie continued on to the shed.

Alma called over the fence. "Need a hand with anything?"

"I could use help setting up the table. It's just a sheet of plywood and a few sawhorses, but it will work." Callie stopped and rested against the saw horse she was pulling out of the shed.

"Hold on, let me put these eggs down. I can help with that." Alma set her egg basket down by the fence.

"The porches are ready if we need them, but we'll have more room outside. Let's set up under the magnolia out back here." Callie pointed to the right of the yard.

"I got this sawhorse. If you get the other one, then we can get the plywood together."

"Okay, Everyone's bringing enough chairs for their family. I've got a couple extra just in case."

"And I have a couple of tablecloths, so we can cover the plywood and it'll look like a regular table." Alma paused while she caught her breath.

"That's great. It'll be festive." Callie propped herself on a sawhorse again to give her friend a minute before they went back to the shed. The two women quickly put the makeshift table together.

"I've got my deviled eggs in the Frigidaire and a pie. What else do we need?" Alma asked as they returned to the shed for the plywood.

"I think we'll have plenty of food. Max and Louise are bringing flounder. Max is setting up his fryer by the fire pit. Louise made banana pudding. Brenda is bringing green beans and cookies. Josie's bringing potato salad and something else. I forget what, though. If anybody goes away hungry, it's their own fault. Let's go in and get something to drink. I need to get Kimberly down for a nap, or she'll be cranky this afternoon, and besides, I want to frost the cake while she's sleeping."

Callie bent down to pick up Kimberly, and they went inside. After giving Kimberly some fruit and a drink, Callie poured two tall glasses of ice tea. "Have a seat for a minute." Callie sat down at the table near her daughter.

"Nah, I'm good right here." Alma leaned against the kitchen sink.

"I stopped in at Pete's while I was out yesterday. He suggested I buy the store. It would be good since I wouldn't need a babysitter. But I don't see how I can get a loan from the bank. I don't have much of a down payment. I don't want to mortgage the house or touch Kimberly's savings." Callie brushed a few loose hairs from around her face.

"Honey, you don't know until you try." Alma crossed her arms over her chest.

"You're right. Maybe I'll talk to the bank on Monday." Callie turned to give Kimberly some more fruit.

"Think I'll head home now. I'm sure there's something else I should be doing. See you later. Call if you need anything." Alma put her glass in the sink before going home.

"Alright. I think I'm good now. Thanks for the help with the table."

Soon after she finished lunch, Kimberly was ready for a nap. Callie frosted the cake and then reviewed her budget. Looking at the figures, she shook her head. Things needed to turn around soon. *Guess I'd better find a babysitter and look for a job. I'll talk to the bank, but I'm not pinning my hopes on that. If I use the money from the insurance, then I have no working capital. I'm just not sure this will work out.*

A knock at the back door interrupted her thoughts. "Hey there, Josie. Come on in."

"Hey, do you have some room in your fridge? I'd like to keep this potato salad cold. Tom's gone to get some ice. I brought some big pans and a couple of tubs with me. Then we can ice down some of the cold stuff." Josie said as she crossed the kitchen.

"Sure. Set it down on the counter and let me make some room on a shelf. Glad you thought of ice." Callie kneeled in front of the refrigerator, rearranged the food, and then added the large bowl of potato salad.

"What do we need to do outside? I brought a table over for food. That'll be easier than passing things at the big table." Josie held out a hand to help her friend stand up.

In short order, they had everything ready: tables, chairs, dishes, and flatware. Josie sat down to enjoy the warm afternoon sun.

"Josie, I've got to get Kimberly ready. I'm sure she's awake now. Be back out in a bit."

Kimberly was playing in her crib when Callie entered the bedroom. "Hey, sweetie. Let's get you changed, and your hair combed. Then we can go outside." Kimberly's red curls defied Callie's efforts to control them. *Oh, well, at least the curls are cute.*

Alma crossed the yard while Callie was inside and joined Josie under the magnolia. Max and Louise were the next to arrive. Max worked at getting the fire started. Everyone watched out for Kimberly as she flitted from one group to another. Tom and the boys came with ice and the rest of Josie's food. Then Brenda and her brood arrived. By then, Max was frying flounder. Finally, Pete and Lyla pulled into the driveway. Callie went over to welcome them.

"Pete, Lyla, it's so good to see you." Callie gave Lyla a steadying hand as she got out of the car.

"Glad we could make it out today." Lyla smiled up at Callie.

"Come this way, Lyla. The path here is a little smoother. I've got a comfortable chair with your name on it." Callie placed a hand on Lyla's lower back.

Shortly after their arrival, the flounder was ready. The kids lined up first and fixed their plates. Once she settled her daughter with food, Callie joined the adults at the buffet table. Everyone gathered around the table. Pete said a brief prayer of thanks for the food and for everyone having made it safely through the hurricane. At that point, they all sat down and started eating. It wasn't long before conversation turned to the repairs going on for the boardwalk, pavilion area and the nearby businesses.

"Pete, do you have a buyer yet?" Brenda asked between bites of food.

"Not yet. Callie would be the perfect person for the store. It'd be nice if a local could buy it. I'd hate to see some chain store on our boardwalk. We can hold out a little longer, though." Pete smiled at Lyla and patted her hand. Lyla had terminal cancer; all her treatments were palliative at this point, and they just wanted to spend time with family.

Everyone looked at Callie in surprise. "I don't think I can swing it. Even though I know I could make a go of it. But I'm going to the bank on Monday. We'll just have to wait and see," Callie said, bowing her head, her long hair hiding her face.

Max looked closely at Callie and then changed the subject. "The diner still has the for sale sign and the sundries shop is still closed."

Max put in. "But at least they took down the plywood. That looks a little better."

"I know. Having the plywood down makes it look like the island will prosper again. Hurricanes always shake things up, even though most people stay on and rebuild," Pete said with the air of someone who'd survived many hurricanes on the island.

"Steve told me the pavilion and boardwalk should be ready by spring," Louise said, as she tried to steer the conversation to something more positive.

"Well, at least we all have our homes. I feel truly fortunate. I have my family in Columbia and my island family. I can never thank you enough for all you've done for us. Now, let's get that dessert," Callie said, smiling at her friends seated around the table.

The older children played tag football while the adults continued trading stories. As the light faded, they all gathered closer to the fire. Everyone kept going back for more food. Someone lit a few Coleman lanterns as Callie slipped away to put Kimberly to bed. Finally, as the sun sank completely below the horizon, even the older children grew tired and sank down around the fire pit. That seemed to be the cue for the adults to wrap things up for the night. Josie's husband carried Alma's things over in a galvanized tub as she headed home. "I'll set these in the kitchen. There's no hurry about the tub. We'll pick it up later," he told her.

Callie walked Pete and Lyla to their car. "I haven't had such fun in a long time." Lyla hugged Callie before getting in the car.

"I'm so glad you enjoyed yourself. I'll let you know what I hear from the bank."

As Callie returned to the backyard, she saw her kitchen chairs and most of her dishes were inside. Josie and Brenda were herding their respective families to their vehicles. With hugs, they all said good night. Joining Max and Louise by the fire pit, Callie sat down.

"So, Callie. What would you do differently if you owned Pete's store?" Louise asked, looking quizzically at Callie.

"Well, I think I would offer pretty much what I offered on the pier. I wouldn't try to be a grocery store. It's so easy to get into town now since most everyone has a car. I'd keep a few grocery items though, things that people run out of and things summer people forget to bring. There's a small kitchen downstairs. Seems I remember Lyla baking there years ago. Maybe offer cold sandwiches during the summer. I'd still like to feature Alma's baskets and some of the other local artisans' work. I feel we small people have to look out for each other. Then close off and rent the apartment upstairs." Callie shook her head. "Those are just pipe dreams. I can't-"

"But why not?" Max interrupted.

Callie told them how she felt about using the house as collateral and keeping the savings account for Kimberly. She continued. "No matter what, I have to have a home for Kimberly. My part of the insurance check from the business isn't enough for a down payment," Callie said as she slumped down in her chair.

"Sell your idea to the bank, just like that. You have no other real expenses. You have the social security check. The rental apartment would bring in regular money. Space for local vendors. Fresh produce and seafood. I'm thinking those last two will eventually bring customers from the mainland," Max said as he frowned thoughtfully.

"Wow, when you put it like that, I might have a chance." Callie straightened her shoulders.

Louise stood up. "We just don't want you to sell yourself short, going in defeated before you start. Come on Max. It's time we got home."

Over breakfast the next morning, Callie thought about last night's conversation with Max and Louise. She tried to write out costs for the business, but was having trouble focusing. The sound of Kimberly's spoon pounding on the table interrupted her thoughts. *I think I'll have to work this out later.* Callie thought while pushing the paper to the middle of the table.

"Sorry baby. Are you still hungry? How about a banana?" Callie asked as she focused on her daughter. "No?" Callie sat Kimberly on the floor after wiping off her hands. "Well, go play and after momma cleans up, we'll go to the beach."

Kimberly waddled off and soon returned with a bucket of blocks, which she promptly dumped on the kitchen floor. "Play here," she laughed.

"Okay, sweetie. You play while Momma cleans," Callie said, smiling at her daughter.

With the kitchen clean, Callie took her daughter's hand. "Come on. Let's put away the blocks and get you changed so we can go to the beach."

"Beach, beach, birdie, birdie." The toddler giggled.

It was still early, well before noon, so with Kimberly in the stroller, she walked to the beach. The seagulls whizzed through the air, shrieking loudly as another bird flew nearby. Callie appreciated the gentle breeze. Even in November, a walk could get warm. On the beach, sandpipers continued their dance with the frothy waves. Parking the stroller, Callie set Kimberly on her feet. Immediately, the toddler ran for the water and the birds. Expecting the humans to have food, seagulls joined the sandpipers in the three-way game of tag. Callie smiled as her daughter's squeals of delight scattered the birds. Finally, Kimberly plopped down at the water's edge as she tried to catch the retreating water in her hand.

"Are you tired, sweetie? You've been running hard." Callie squatted beside her daughter.

Looking up, Kimberly grinned at her mother. "Kimmie so fast."

"Yes, you are. Let's get some of the sand off. Then we'll go up to the store."

With Kimberly back in the stroller, Callie headed for Pete's. She wanted to let him know she was interested in purchasing the store. Now that she had a plan, she didn't want him to sell to someone else.

"Hey, Pete, we need a drink after running on the beach." After getting a juice for her daughter, she grabbed a Coke for herself from the red Coca Cola cooler near the counter. It was an old one, painted bright red, sporting the Coca Cola logo and the front and sides. Two sliding doors on top let the customer could reach in and get their soda.

"It's always good to see the two of you. Lyla and I sure had a good time last night," Pete said, ringing up her purchases.

"I'm so glad you came and had a good time."

"We both think you would be perfect here in the store." Pete leaned over the counter so he could see Kimberly.

"Well, I'm going to talk to the bank tomorrow. Maybe they'll think my plan is a good one."

"Let me know how it goes." Pete turned to help another customer find something.

"Of course. See you later."

Back home, Callie parked the stroller and changed Kimberly before walking over to Alma's. Going through the gate, she saw Alma out with the chickens.

"Are the chickens laying better now?" She asked as she sat Kimberly down outside the chicken coop.

"Yeah, it just took them a while to get used to being back home. I'll have more eggs than I know what to do with before long."

"Can you do me a favor tomorrow? I want to go to the bank. I'm hoping I can get a loan to buy Pete's store. Would you watch Kimberly for me?"

"Sure, but tell me about this plan of yours. Come inside while I put these eggs away."

Once inside Alma's spotless white kitchen with its black and white tile, Callie outlined her thoughts about the store. Alma's nearly black eyes were thoughtful as she said, "If you want to keep our partnership going, we could use my part of the insurance check that's coming as part of the down payment. I like having the extra money from my baskets, so it would benefit me, too."

"I'd love to keep working with you. But maybe we should keep a part of the check for operating expenses. What do you think?"

"Okay, three thousand down and two thousand for operating expenses."

"Sounds good. I'll have to talk to my dad and work out paying him back since he paid the first insurance premium."

Leaning in closer to better judge Callie's reaction, Alma asked, "Have you talked to your parents about this?"

"No, I didn't want to talk to them until after I talked to the bank. If I don't get the loan, there's nothing to talk about. Sorry to run off so quickly, but I'd better start supper." Callie gathered Kimberly up from the floor.

After her daughter was asleep, Callie sat on the porch and wrote up their plan for the business. *It would be so good if this works out. I know a lot of people would still buy seafood from me. If things go well, my few pots won't be enough. Maybe Max would want to join us. He knows most of the fishermen and his family still owns the truck farm.*

6

Monday, Late October 1970

Sunlight filtered through the curtains as Callie woke up. Pulling on a housecoat, she went into the kitchen and put on a pot of coffee. While it was perking, Callie went over the figures again. If she kept herself to the strict budget she had set up, she wouldn't have to use much of her earnings from the store. At least for the first few months, she could just turn her portion of the earnings back into the business. Alma might need to have her earnings more regularly. *This could work well for both of us. Alma could work in the store, too, and I won't get worn out.*

As Callie finished her coffee, she heard Kimberly wake up. "Momma. Momma," she called.

"Good Morning, my precious girl. Let's get something to eat before going to see Auntie Alma. Momma's got to go to the bank this morning," Callie said as she got her daughter ready for the day.

After Kimberly ate scrambled eggs and fruit, Callie sat her in the playpen. "You play right here while momma gets ready. It won't take long. I'm going to see if we can buy Pete's Market." *I'll braid and wrap my hair up and wear my blue pantsuit. Maybe it will make me look a little older to the bank manager.*

Callie dropped her daughter off at Alma's and crossed the bridge into Mt. Pleasant. She arrived just after the bank opened. Parking the truck along the sidewalk, she changed into dress shoes and took a few breaths to calm herself down. She felt herself perspiring even though the day was still cool. *Calm down. Even if you don't get the loan, it won't be the end of the world. You've written everything down, so you don't have to worry about remembering.* She told herself.

Inside the bank, Callie was thankful for the air conditioning while her heart continued to pound like a drum. The teller had Callie take a seat while she told the manager someone was waiting.

"Good morning, Mrs. Stevens. I'm Alex Taylor. Come into my office." The manager said as he approached her in the lobby.

"Good morning, Mr. Taylor." Callie stood and offered to shake hands. After a moment's hesitation, he gently took her hand before turning towards his office.

Callie followed him into a room with glass walls and blinds. As he motioned for her to take a seat, he asked, "How can I help you today?"

"I'd like to apply for a business loan." Callie's voice faltered a little, but she cleared her throat and continued. "I want to buy Pete's Market. It's on Caine's island. Pete Jenkins has been in business for years, but now that he's older, he'd like to sell and retire."

The bank manager frowned slightly and looked skeptical. Callie reached into her handbag for the budget she had worked out for the store and handed it to him. He immediately put on his glasses and began reading.

Uncertain what the bank manager expected, Callie rushed on to outline her plan. As she got to the part about renting the apartment, the manager held up his hand to stop her torrent of words. Callie held her breath. "So, you don't owe any money?" He asked, looking over his glasses.

Callie let her breath out in a small puff. "No. I inherited my house from my Aunt Sally and paid cash for my truck. My husband and I opened an account here several years before he died, but it's a small one."

"Ah, yes. I thought the name was familiar. Well, with your down payment, we could make the loan. Provided there's nothing negative in your credit history." He paused. "Did you say you were a widow?"

Callie nodded yes. Mr. Tyler frowned slightly. "Ah, do you have a male friend or family member who could cosign the loan with you?"

"Well, no. I didn't think of that. I assumed since I was a long-time customer and this was an excellent opportunity, there wouldn't be a problem. " Callie's face wrinkled with a small frown. "I'll have to talk to my dad or my brother."

"If you could meet that requirement and they have an excellent credit history, then I'd be happy to make the loan. Have you decided what to call the business?" Mr. Taylor's tone was condescending.

"No, I haven't." Callie wasn't sure whether to be angry or excited. *Would Dad or Bobby cosign for me? How is Momma going to deal with this?*

"You get your licenses and other things together. Once I have the information from your cosigner, we can have everything ready by the end of the week or Monday at the latest. You realize the loan will be in your name and the cosigner's name. I'll be happy to draw up the loan as soon as you decide on the store's name and find someone to cosign for you." Callie stood and reached out to shake his hand. He stood up and again hesitated before lightly grasping her fingers.

That's not a handshake. What's this about a cosigner? "Thank you so much," Callie said as he ushered her out of his office and left her standing alone as he rushed across the lobby to greet another customer.

Tears of happiness stung Callie's eyes as she left the bank, even though she hadn't expected the need for a man to cosign the loan. She had simply left Joe's name on the bank account and didn't realize as a woman she couldn't open an account or get a loan in her name.

Her hands were shaking so much she had trouble opening the truck's door. Sitting behind the wheel for a few minutes, she steadied her breathing before driving home. *I've done it. We can stay on the island. I want Max to join us, but I'm not sure about asking him to cosign a loan. I don't think I will. He and Louise are good friends, but cosigning a loan might be too much to ask.* She thought as she crossed the bridge to the island.

Although she was excited to tell Alma the news, Callie stopped by Pete's on the way home. Rushing to the back of the store, she found Pete restocking some shelves.

"Pete, I can't really believe it yet but, the bank will give me the loan. I have to get a cosigner though. I didn't know that was a thing." Callie scowled.

Hugging her close, Pete beamed. "Ah, well, I didn't think of that. Should have told you. Maybe your dad? I knew you could do it. When do you want to take over?"

"Well, you guys have to get ready to go to your daughter's. I've got to talk to my dad or Bobby. Alma's my partner; I don't even know what we will call the place."

"Lyla's been slowly packing for a while so moving isn't a problem. Our daughter has our area finished. She put an addition on her house in Rock Hill. Nothing fancy, just a sitting room, bedroom, bathroom, and small kitchen. This way, everyone has a space to go to. I love my grandchildren, but the four of them can get rowdy sometimes. I'm thankful that with the sale, we'll be able to pay off her construction loan and have some money left over."

"The little ones will wear you out, no matter how much fun they are. "Still, I think it might take a couple of weeks to work everything out. I'm so excited about getting started," Callie chuckled.

Hearing the door's chimes, they walked to the counter. Pete took care of a customer and then returned to the conversation with Callie. "I'll put a sign in the front window about the apartment. I'm thinking you could have it ready by the first of the year. Does that sound good to you?"

"Thanks, Pete. That sounds fine. What if we plan to take over the store in three weeks? The bank says they'll have the loan drawn up in a week. Like I said, I've got a lot to do so we before actually open. But right now, I need to get Kimberly from Alma's." She always enjoyed talking to Pete, but sometimes it was hard to get away.

"Okay. If you have questions, I'll be nearby for a couple of weeks before going to my daughter's." Pete turned toward the back of the store. "I've got to go tell Lyla."

"I'll be talking to you soon," Callie said as she left the store.

Never had the short drive from Pete's seemed so long. Pulling into her driveway, Callie saw Kimberly and Alma in the yard next door. Callie hurried across the yard, yelling, "We did it! Good news, they'll give me the loan. Bad news, I've got to get a cosigner."

Noticing Callie's excitement, Kimberly began running to her. Alma was right behind, albeit a little slower. "I knew you could do it. That's fantastic."

"I'm famished. I was so nervous I couldn't eat this morning. Let's go in and get something to eat." Callie scooped up her daughter and lightly tossed her into the air. "Are you hungry, my sweet girl?" Callie asked as she settled her daughter on her hip.

Over pimento cheese sandwiches and ice tea, Callie relayed the morning's events, including her conversation with Pete. Kimberly played nearby as the women began hashing out the details of running the store.

"I've got to ask my dad or Bobby if one of them cosign the loan. Apparently, we can't do this on our own because we're women." Callie snorted in disgust. "We've got to get the license for the business and once we have the money, we can order checks, but we need a name. I was thinking of something like Caines Seaside Emporium, but I want to ask Max to join us, so I don't want to decide right away. His knowledge of produce and seafood would be a big help. What do you think?"

"You've got a good heart, Callie. He might go for it. You know his brother's contract with the county is running out soon. Max will be looking for something. And you're right. He knows more about fishing and produce in this area than I'll ever know." Alma smiled at her friend. "The name sounds good. But will it tell people what we're selling? Maybe we could list it on bottom of the sign like in the old days?"

"Yeah, we could do that. Think I'll just ask them over for supper. I was making a pot of soup, anyway. We can ask him then." Callie paused a moment to make sure Kimberly was still happily playing. They spent an hour going over plans to rearrange the store to suit their needs. Occasionally, Callie helped her daughter build a tower of blocks as she and Alma continued their discussion. Sketches and notes littered the table. Before long, Callie put Kimberly down for a nap and started the soup before calling Louise.

"Hey, Louise. What are you guys doing for supper? I've got a few things to work out, but I'm fairly sure I'll get the loan. How about joining us to celebrate? Just some soup and cornbread, nothing big. I've got a few questions for you guys." Callie grinned at Alma sitting nearby at the kitchen table.

"That's great news. Is about five, okay? Or is that too early? Max has been pretty tired lately. He'll want to make an early night of it," Louise said. "Can I bring anything?"

"No need to do that. I'm calling at the last minute. Five is fine," Callie answered, standing by the wall phone. "Alma will be with us. I'll see you then."

Alma got up from the table. "I've got some housekeeping to take care of. Think I'll make a peach pie. I'll be back in time for supper."

Callie gave Alma a hug. "Don't know what I'd do without you. I've got stuff I need to do, too. See you later."

After tidying the porch, Callie set the table. There was more room on the porch than in the kitchen, and Kimberly would have a place to play that still kept her contained. *That girl gets more adventurous by the minute. She'll be unlocking the screen doors soon if I'm not careful.*

Even though the meal was simple, Callie set the table with the Fiesta dishware Aunt Sally had left in the house. Instead of the bright red, which was popular with many others, Aunt Sally's set had pieces in turquoise, yellow and lime green. Perfect for a beach house. Just as she finished, Max and Louise came onto the front porch.

"I'm over here on the side porch," Callie called, putting the soup tureen on the table.

"Well, isn't this something? So pretty. Sally always loved her Fiesta," Louise said as she walked around to the side porch. "It's nice to see it out again. We've got a bottle of wine and some of those cheese straws you like." Louise continued toward the kitchen door after setting a plate on the table. "Show me where your wine glasses are."

"You didn't need to bring anything." Callie shook her head. "I like the Fiesta, too. It's special without being too fancy. Alma should be here any minute." Louise was nearly as tall as her husband. Her hair formed a coal black halo offsetting her unwrinkled milk chocolate skin. Both she and Max were slender, but Louise's figure had a softness to it.

"Yeah, I'm right here. Can you give me a hand with this peach pie?" Alma called from the back steps.

"Be right there, Alma. Louise, the wine glasses are in the upper left-hand cabinet next to the sink," Callie said over her shoulder as she went to help Alma. "Let me take that, Alma. You go join Louise and Max. I'll be right out with the cornbread."

Everyone had gathered around the table when Callie returned. "Come to the table, Kimberly. Supper's ready."

Callie settled Kimberly in her booster seat with her food and a cup of milk. Max had opened the wine and poured a glass for everyone.

"So, tell me about your visit to the bank," Max said as he poured and passed a wineglass to everyone.

"I was so nervous. But I described my plan the way we talked about it Saturday night and gave him the figures I had written up. Anyway, if I find a man to cosign, he'll give me the loan. Guess I'll have to talk to my dad or Bobby. We should have the money on Friday or Monday." Callie was nearly bouncing with excitement.

"Oh girl, I knew you could do it. Dang those bankers." Max smiled from ear to ear. "So, when do you start?"

"Pete and I agreed we could take over in three weeks. Alma and I will continue our partnership. He's putting a sign up in the store advertising that the apartment will be available the first of January," Callie said, beaming from ear to ear.

"You and Alma are going to do well in the store. I just can't believe how good life can be. You've both worked so hard." Louise reached over to squeeze Callie's hand.

"Thank you, guys. But Callie and I have a question for Max." Alma waited until she had everyone's attention before speaking again. "We'd like you to join us in this venture."

"But, but—" Max sputtered, looking at each of the women sitting around the table. His eyes rested on his wife sitting next to him with a small smile on her face.

"No buts. We need your knowledge of produce and seafood. Besides, you have such a way with people." Callie nodded her head emphatically.

"Wow. I don't know what to say. Is the asking price the same?" Max ran his hand over his face. Callie and Alma nodded yes.

"Maxwell Tyler is without words. Let's mark that on the calendar." Louise laughed and playfully tapped his shoulder.

"What do you think, honey?" Max asked Louise, tilting his head, and looking up at the ceiling before looking back at his wife.

She smiled back at him. "I think it's a good thing. You should go for it."

"Alright, I'm in. What are we calling this place?" Max asked.

"We're thinking about Caines Seaside Emporium," Callie said.

"Here's to Caines Seaside Emporium," Alma raised her glass, and everyone joined in the toast.

Once everyone had eaten, and dishes were in the kitchen. Callie offered coffee and pie. "We can talk a little more over dessert. But I'll have to get Kimberly to bed soon. Alma, would you grab the folder with the sketches? It's in here on the dryer."

"Sure thing." Alma replied. "Here, let me get the pie, too."

Returning with the coffee, Callie gave her daughter a small taste of pie and her cup of milk. As both women sat back down, Max said. "Yeah, I can't stay long either. I've still got to get up early and go out with Bill tomorrow. But tell me again, how much is the loan?" He turned his head to look at his wife, who nodded imperceptibly.

Callie filled him in with the loan details. "I can cosign for that. You guys are putting up the down payment. I already know your business plan." Max grinned. "Besides, I have some history with that banker. My family has done business at that bank for years. When they started out there weren't so many Black owned banks in the area. He knows my history and won't try to pull a fast one."

"Max, are you sure?" Callie looked closely at Max and Louise. They both nodded yes. "That's fantastic. Thank you so much. I really didn't want to ask my dad," Callie said. "But I didn't want to put that liability on you either. That's why I didn't ask you to cosign."

Before the celebration broke up, they agreed Callie would update the bank in the morning and Max would talk to his brother and join him at the job site once he signed the papers. Working out a true partnership deal would wait until the weekend.

Straightening up in the kitchen after everyone left and while Kimberly was sleeping, Callie realized she needed to let her parents in on her plans, and since it had been a while since her last visit, she decided to go to Columbia. A quick phone call made sure her parents would be home and didn't have plans for the next few days.

As Callie got ready for bed, her euphoria faded as she thought about how the bank manager seemed ready to give her the loan until she mentioned Joe's death. Then she got angry about it and her thoughts were racing. *Joe and I opened our account in that bank when we first moved from Columbia nearly five years ago. Kimberly's savings account is there. Never once did I bounce a check or anything. I put the social security check in the account every month. Now, they want me to have a cosigner for a business loan. I'll show them.* It was well after midnight before she finally drifted off to sleep.

7 |

Tuesday, Late October 1970

"Good morning, baby girl. I know I'm waking you up a little early. Sorry about that. Let's get some breakfast and then we're going to Columbia to see Grandpa and Grandma."

Never a fussy eater, Kimberly ate toast, scrambled eggs, and peaches for breakfast as Callie finished cleaning up from last night. Putting away the clean dishes and packing for the trip took no time at all.

"Are you ready to take a long ride to see Grandpa and Grandma?"

"Gmpa, Gmma, go see."

"Alright, sweetie. Let's get in the truck."

Kimberly fell asleep as soon as they settled on the highway. Callie's mood swung between excitement about the store and dread that her mother wouldn't approve. *I know Dad said he wasn't worried about getting the premium for the insurance policy back anytime soon, but I can't forget about it. But to own my business! I can't believe it. Of course, I have partners, but how many twenty-five-year-old women have a business? I hope Momma sees it for the great opportunity it is.*

Her mother came down the porch steps as Callie pulled into the driveway. While her mother got Kimberly out of the car seat, Callie grabbed their suitcase from the back of the truck.

"Come here, Callie. Let me give you a quick squeeze before we go in," her mother said. While they hugged, Kimberly squirmed out of her grandmother's arms and slid down her leg. As Kimberly's feet touched the ground, she headed for the porch.

"Love you, Momma. It's so good to see you," Callie said, turning from their embrace to follow Kimberly up the walkway.

"I know. It seems like forever since I saw you last. I think she's grown an inch or two." Callie's mother laughed watching Kimberly try to negotiate the steps to the porch.

"I think you're right. She's into everything now, so we had better catch up to her real quick. Her favorite words are 'so fast'." Callie hurried to catch up with her daughter. "She's beginning to open cabinet doors at home."

Once inside, Callie took their suitcase to the bedroom while her mother gave Kimberly a drink. Joining them in the bright yellow kitchen, Callie poured a cup of coffee and sat at the table. She noticed her mother had found some new lemon patterned fabric to make placemats and coasters. The large oval wooden table had all its leaves in place, even though there was usually just her parents eating. Her mother felt it made dealing with the chairs easier if they were just around the table, instead of trying to store them somewhere.

"These new placemats are so pretty. But tell me, how are Bobby and Susan doing? Are they settling into the new house?"

"Thanks. Pretty much. Susan's mother went up to help for a few days. I think she's planning to go up again when Susan comes home from the hospital after having the baby."

"That's good. Extra help with a new baby is always nice." Callie sipped her coffee.

"It's always good to see you, but what brings you into Columbia during the week? Is everything all right?" Callie noticed her mother's white knuckles against the yellow coffee cup.

"Everything's great. I'll tell you all about it when Dad gets home. Then you don't have to hear it twice." Callie smiled mysteriously.

"Oh. If that's how you want it." Callie's mother retorted as she got up abruptly and went to the porch, slamming the kitchen door. As she returned to the kitchen, she told Callie. "I've got to drop a platter of chicken over to the Joneses. Evelyn's just home from the hospital. She had gallbladder surgery. Do you want to come with me?" Her mother set the chicken on the counter with a clatter and paused at the door leading into the living room while looking pointedly at Callie.

"No. I think we'll stay here. Kimberly's pretty mobile. She might be too much for Evelyn. Besides, she'll probably need a nap before much longer. What were you planning for supper?" Callie asked, surprised at her mother's reaction to her wanting to wait until her dad got home to share the news.

"I've got a pot roast ready to go in the pressure cooker. So, potatoes, carrots, and whatever other vegetable. Something green. Maybe biscuits. I'll just change."

Pot roast, Momma's standard for company supper. I love it though. She thought to herself. "Alright, I'll get things started if you're not home. Enjoy your visit with Evelyn. Come on, Kimberly. Let's have lunch. Then we'll go outside for a while before your nap." Callie was rummaging in the refrigerator when her mother picked up the chicken before leaving.

Callie had supper well underway when her mother returned. After greeting Callie calmly, she darted back to her bedroom to change into a house dress. *Momma's always so 1950's.* Callie thought to herself. *The only time she wears pants is if she's working in the yard. She has to do her hair and makeup before running errands. Maybe that's why she doesn't like the island. We might dress up a bit before leaving the island, but usually than means I wear my jeans and a nicer top. And forget makeup with the heat and humidity.*

"I see Kimberly's still sleeping," her mother said, joining Callie in the kitchen.

"Yeah, I woke her up early this morning. Even though she slept most of the trip, I don't think she really rested." Callie checked the setting on the pressure cooker.

"You and Bobby never slept in the car. Not that we took that many trips. Sometimes down to Caines Island to see Sally and a few times to see the Shaffers before they passed. Oh, it's time for my story. *The Edge of Night* will be on in a few minutes." Callie slipped into the bedroom and grabbed a book to read. Even when she lived with her parents, she had never watched soap operas and really didn't understand the appeal. To her, the storylines were too unbelievable. Callie sighed. *Everybody needs some kind of escape. Just give me a good book.*

Kimberly woke up as Callie's dad pulled into the driveway. Once Callie put her on the floor, the toddler waddled to the door to greet him. "Gmpa, Gmpa home."

"Hey there, sweetie." Callie's dad picked the toddler up and made his way into the kitchen. "How long before supper, Lydia? Hey Callie."

"It'll be ready in about ten minutes. Callie's got some big news for us. So go get changed," her mother answered. "The biscuits just went in the oven."

"Let me have Kimberly, then I'll get the table ready." Callie offered. She gathered plates and silverware after sitting her daughter in the booster seat with a cup of milk. Her dad always sat at the head of the table, her mother to his left and Callie on his right. Kimberly sat next to Callie.

Once everyone had served themselves, Callie's mother couldn't hold back any longer. "So, tell us this big news." Her eyes narrowed as she looked at Callie and she gripped the edge of her placemat.

Callie took a deep breath and then rushed on. "I've bought Pete's Market on Caine's island," Callie said with a huge grin. "Well, Alma, Max and I bought it." She added.

Her dad's eyes grew wide as a grin spread over his face. "Come on now. Tell us more. When did this happen? Did you have to mortgage the house?" He asked, patting her on the back.

"Pete's moving to Rock Hill. Max cosigned the loan with me and Alma. That dang bank manager was ready to give me the loan until he realized I was a widow without a credit history. But we worked that out and we will take possession in three weeks," Callie said as her eyes danced.

Her mother's mouth closed in a straight line before she said, "How did you get the money?"

"We used part of the insurance check for the down payment and the rest to have a bit of capital to start. I'll start paying you back for the first premium in January." Callie looked across the table at her parents.

"I'm not worried about that Callie-girl," her dad said, smiling with obvious pride. "What are you calling this place?"

Callie avoided meeting her mother's ferocious stare. "We're calling it Caines Seaside Emporium. Renting the apartment upstairs covers the loan payment. I'm so excited. I can hardly wait for us to get started." Callie was nearly bouncing in her seat, despite her mother's displeasure. She still couldn't get over her good fortune. *Darn it, Momma's whiter than a ghost. This isn't going well,* she thought.

"Well, that's wonderful news." Her dad looked towards his wife and gently took her hand. "Lydia, I know you really wanted them to move to Columbia, but this is a great opportunity for her."

Callie's mom looked back at him, tears glistening in her eyes. "I know. But if things don't go well, what then? Going into business is so risky." She looked back at Callie, her face flushed as she raised her voice. "You could lose everything. Then where would you be? Get your mourning done and find a husband. Be respectable. Women shouldn't be in business, anyway."

Callie sighed deeply as she shook her head from side to side. "I figured out my problem. I thought you'd be happy for me." She fought to keep her voice level and held her mother's stare as she continued. "There are things that could go wrong, but I think it's worth a shot. I might marry again someday, but not so some man can take care of me. Why are you always so negative? I should have known better than to expect you to be happy for me, Momma," Callie said, tossing her napkin onto the table.

"Callie, that's not it," her mother protested, throwing up her hands.

Kimberly's eyes got wide, her lower lip stuck out and began to quiver. Callie picked up her daughter and looked over her head to stare at her mother as she cradled the toddler to her chest. "Let's eat supper. It'll just upset Kimberly if we keep this up." She cooed softly to her daughter, coaxing a smile before settling her back in her booster seat. "Come on, sweetie. Eat your carrots."

Without conversation, supper was over soon after. Callie's mother hastily excused herself, saying she had a headache. Her dad took Kimberly outside. For a while, Callie fumed quietly at the table. *I'm so mad I could cry. Wow, I didn't think she would be happy. But this? Why do I let myself even hope she will ever be happy with my choices?* Giving herself a mental shake, Callie got up and cleaned the kitchen. *Momma and I have an argument, and somebody cleans the kitchen alone. Every time.* By the time Callie finished, her dad brought Kimberly onto the back porch and stuck his head in the back door.

"Thought a little time without Kimberly underfoot would do you some good. Is your momma still in the bedroom?" He was leaning part way through the kitchen door to the porch with one eye on Kimberly, who was trying to escape into the yard again.

"Yeah. I don't expect I'll see her until tomorrow," Callie said, drying her hands at the kitchen sink.

Shrugging his shoulders, her dad pulled two beers from behind his back. "Come sit outside with me. Kimberly can run around, and you can tell me about this store."

"Actually, a beer sounds good right now." Going onto the porch, she picked up her daughter and followed her dad outside. They sat on the wooden steps to the porch, and Kimberly played with a dump truck under the shade of a nearby pine tree.

"Tell me all about this business venture. Start at the beginning," her dad said, opening the bottles with a church key and handing one to Callie.

After a sip of beer, Callie told him how it all started when she went to talk to Pete about putting some seafood in the store on consignment.

Then Pete mentioned her buying it at their celebration last Saturday and the pep talk from Max and Louise before they went home. And then on Sunday, Alma offered to remain partners."

"That's good."

"Anyway, I wrote everything up Sunday evening. Like I'd seen you do for projects at work. Then I went to the bank on Monday." Callie looked at the label on her beer bottle, shaking her head slightly as she thought about her mother.

"So, are you going to run it as a grocery store like Pete?" Her Dad leaned forward with his elbows on his knees, turned his head toward Callie and watched her closely.

Callie's eyes brightened as she talked about the store. "No. It will be more like an indoor version of what we all sold on the pier. We'll stock a few grocery things. Stuff people run out of. Renting the apartment is a bonus. Pete's already put up a sign in front of the store that the apartment will be available January first."

"What about Kimberly?" Her dad shifted his gaze to look at his granddaughter.

"She'll be with me. There's enough room so we can set aside an area for her to play in. Alma, Max, and I will split up time in the store, so we don't have to be there all the time."

"Well, I know where you and Alma got your money. But what about Max?" her dad asked, turning back to look at her sitting beside him on the step.

"Max cosigned the loan. Can you believe that garbage? Needing a cosigner. I've been with that bank for a several years now. I wanted Max to join us anyway because he knows the local fishermen and produce. He helped me a lot when I was selling on the pier, always encouraging, or making little observations that led to me making better sales."

Max is a good man. Didn't get to know him much when we lived on the island. I worked so much overtime then." Her dad shifted his position on the step to keep his eye on both Kimberly and his daughter. Kimbelry had moved the truck closer to the steps.

"We're hoping we'll be able to draw customers from the mainland with seafood and produce. That'll take a while, though. After agreeing to join us, he volunteered to cosign the loan, since his family has dealt with that bank a long time."

"You really thought this through. I'm proud of you, sweetheart. You guys will do well, I'm sure. It'll be hard work though. But I guess it can't get much harder than carrying your baby and goods down to the pier every day. I'm especially proud you included those people who helped you when you first started out." Her dad smiled and gave her shoulder a squeeze.

"Thanks Dad, I feel much better. I think I should get Kimberly cleaned up and in bed. She's falling asleep over that truck." Callie picked her daughter up and started up the back steps.

"Are you going back tomorrow?" her dad asked, turning to look at Callie as he took the beer bottles to the trash can.

"No, I'll stay until Thursday morning like I originally planned. The bank may have the check ready Friday morning and we'll need to get the account set up. Max already has a commitment to help his brother until the contract with the county runs out. So, we can't meet until Saturday, anyway."

The rest of the visit was uneventful. Callie's mother chatted about Kimberly growing up and her neighbors, but never brought the store or marriage into the conversation. Callie wasn't surprised. It had been that way all her life. Once an argument was over, her mother avoided the topic as much as possible until the next time something pushed her over the edge. *I don't want to argue with her. I know she doesn't like the idea, but I have to live my life. She'll blow up again, I'm sure. Maybe then I can convince her I can run my own life.*

8

Early Winter 1970

Three weeks flew by as the partners worked out their agreement, ordered business checks and put ads in the local papers. Pete's word-of-mouth campaign had artisans calling for information about putting their items in the store. The neighborhood had a farewell dinner for Pete and Lyla. Before he left, Pete had cajoled the Coca-Cola rep into replacing the old sign with a new one advertising Caine's Seaside Emporium and Coca-Cola, of course.

"Morning. How are you today?" Alma said, as she walked up to the truck where Callie was getting Kimberly settled.

"Pretty good. I'm ready to get going. They're bringing the sign today. I'm so excited to actually be in the store. I know we have a lot to do, but I'm glad we can actually start doing something." Callie walked around to the driver's side of the truck before getting in.

"Even though Max won't be able to work with us until the weekend, we can start moving things around to open up that corner near the kitchen for the playroom and open up the area near the front door to display items from the vendors." Alma put her things into the back of the truck before climbing in next to Kimberly.

"It's awkward with the crib in the kitchen. Not that we'll need the kitchen much right now. It will be good for Kimberly to have a place where she can get into stuff. I think we'll have to empty the shelves before you and I can move them." Callie said pulling out of the driveway.

Reworking the layout of the store took until lunchtime, since customers frequently interrupted them. While the neighborhood would miss Pete, most people were excited that a group of locals had bought the store and were stopping in to see how things were going. Callie and Alma created an area for display in front of the large front window that spanned nearly the width of the store. Here they would feature Alma's baskets, Callie's sundresses and jewelry made by a local artisan who answered their ad. They created areas for general merchandise, produce and seafood. Of course, now, with the shelving moved, they would have to scrub the floors.

The playroom would be in the back right corner. This weekend, Max and Steve would build a half wall and top it with the tall windows Callie found at the salvage yard. This would keep Kimberly's playroom bright and give it an airy feel, even though it was in a far corner of the store.

With the change in layout completed, Callie and Alma began restocking the shelves. Kimberly helped by emptying the boxes and putting cans willy-nilly on the shelves. An adult had to rearrange things a bit, but it kept Kimberly playing happily until nap time. While Kimberly napped, the two women tackled the floors.

Kimberly was still napping when the workmen came to change out the signs. This sign was more modern than Pete's worn painted sign. Two red and white Coca-Cola logos were at each end of the white hard plastic sign with Caines Seaside Emporium in large, black capital letters in its center. Below that, in smaller letters, the sign read: Seafood, Produce and Sundries. The sign was back lit by florescent bulbs. Brenda, Josie, and a small group of neighbors stood in the parking lot watching the workmen. A cheer went up when Alma turned on the sign. Several people followed Alma and Callie inside.

"Hi, Ethel. How's your family?" Callie held the door as they entered the store together.

"We're doing good. We didn't have much damage from the hurricane. When are you going to have seafood? You always had the best."

"I'll start collecting from the pots in the next week or so when they deliver the big refrigerator. As things get going, I'd like to get flounder and maybe oysters in. We'll have fresh produce in season too." Callie pointed to the two counters in the back of the store.

"That's great. I hope you do well. I'll tell all my friends you're open." Ethel walked around the store, checking out the displays before turning to leave. "Like what you've done with the place, Callie," Ethel called out as she paused at the door.

"Thanks, Ethel."

After the last customer left, Callie joined Brenda, Josie, and Alma, who were standing near the front window. "So, what do you think about the layout?"

"I think it's great. Are you going to use the fruit crates for display here in the front?" Brenda asked as she looked around the store.

"We thought they would still be good display pieces. We'd like this part to feel like shopping on the pier. Then, too, it will give each section of the store a separate look." Alma said, pointing to the general area for each section.

"I think there are still crates up in Momma's old barn that didn't get messed up in the hurricane. Come get them," Brenda offered as her gaze returned to the group.

"Thanks, Brenda. I'll bring the truck over when we're ready for them. I think I heard Kimberly. Be right back." Callie walked toward the back of the store.

Once Callie returned with Kimberly, Josie and Brenda said their goodbyes. Alma and Callie went to the backroom and began making posters announcing their grand opening in January while the toddler played under the table. "Of course, we'll advertise in the papers. But I think putting up a few of these will help get the word out," Callie said as she picked up the poster board to do yet another sign.

"Oh yeah and these can go up anytime. Running those ads can get expensive. Have you had any calls about the apartment?" Alma got up for coffee.

"I've had a few. A woman is supposed to come by Saturday at two to fill out an application and look at the apartment. I told her we hadn't painted yet, but she said she didn't care as she wouldn't be able to move in right away."

"A young, single woman, alone?" Alma's eyebrows shot up.

"Technically, I'm a single woman living alone and with a baby. So are you. Don't you turn into Momma, thinking a woman's got to get married to be respectable. Let's talk to her and check out her references." Callie tilted her head as she pointedly looked up at Alma standing by the table.

"Callie, you're right, of course. If she checks out, we'll rent it to her. We just don't see many young single women in the neighborhood. They all either marry or move away. Anyway, you want more coffee?" Alma asked, picking up Callie's mug.

"I know they do. Yes, please, on the coffee."

The two women worked steadily for the rest of the day as they tried to make the merchandise as attractive as possible. Kimberly alternated between running through the store or playing with toys in the kitchen. That she was spending the day in a store instead of the house didn't seem to bother her. Eventually, Callie wanted to fence in the small area behind the store so she could take her daughter outside when things were quiet. Finally, it was nearly six o'clock. They hadn't had a customer since five.

"Callie, I think it's time to lock up," Alma called from behind a row of shelving.

"I agree. I'll lock up the back, grab Kimberly and my bag. Then see you up front." As she neared the front of the store, Callie said, "I'm going to have to learn how to prep supper before I come in or start having our main meal at the store. This is really too late for Kimberly to eat."

"I know you usually have supper by now. Maybe do something you can warm up easy." Alma suggested as they got into the truck.

"Good idea." Callie said, starting the engine once Alma settled in her seat.

Over her protests that she could walk across the yard, Callie pulled into Alma's driveway first. Then she went home to fix supper and get Kimberly ready for bed. With her daughter asleep, Callie prepped soup for tomorrow, cleaned the kitchen, got her own bath, and went to bed. Although she was tired, her mind raced as she thought of ways to display merchandise in the store. Unable to sleep, Callie got up and sketched out some of her ideas. After midnight, exhausted, she fell into bed.

Saturday morning, everyone was in the store early. Callie brought in a large pot of soup that could simmer on the stove until it was time to eat. Max and Steve would be there today. Max had an idea for making a small, private alcove for the apartment's entrance. Steve volunteered to help since he had learned carpentry from his dad. Callie would paint the apartment, while Alma and Kimberly waited on customers. Pete and Lydia left some of their furniture behind, thinking the new tenant might need some of it.

The prospective tenant arrived promptly at two and was filling out the rental application when Alma called for Callie to come downstairs. She hurried down from the apartment and tried to wash some of the paint off her hands before joining Max and Alma at the small table in the kitchen.

"Hi, I'm Callie Stevens. The little one running around is my daughter, Kimberly," Callie said as she joined them at the table.

"Linda Watson. She and I met earlier. She's a doll baby. I was just telling your partners; I teach third grade at Moultrie Elementary School. The school is fantastic, but I'm not fond of living in town."

"I know what you mean about living in town. Max is working on a private entrance and I'm still painting but, would you like to see the apartment? The Jenkins left some furniture, but we can remove that if you don't want it," Callie said as she quickly reviewed Linda's application.

"Sure," Linda said, following Callie to the stairs.

Linda loved the cozy two-bedroom apartment. Sunlight poured in through the large windows. She felt the second bedroom would give her a place to grade papers and sew while making it easy to keep the apartment neat. Linda already had an apartment full of furniture. When they were downstairs again, Alma promised to check her references right away as they said goodbye.

Max finished with the doors and alcove as Callie put on the last coat of paint on the stairwell. "Think we should take a break and eat. Everybody to the back room," Alma called out.

Suddenly realizing she was hungry, Callie picked up her daughter so they both could eat. Everyone gathered on stools around the worktable. The warmed-up cornbread and soup tasted good. Renovating was tiring work, but everyone was glad to take a quick break to talk to neighbors and let them know how things were progressing as people came into the store.

Over lunch, everyone agreed tackling Kimberly's area would have to wait until tomorrow and instead of a half wall, they decided that framing in an area above and below the windows would work best. For the rest of the day, they worked to arrange stock already in the store.

On Sunday, as Max and Steve set the windows, Alma and Callie started painting the inside walls a pale lavender. They would paint the trim white. Callie wanted the space to look a lot like Kimberly's room at home. By late afternoon, the windows were up, and Callie brought in a rug and rocking chair she found at a secondhand store. Of course, there was still more painting to do, but Callie wanted her daughter to know where her things would be.

"Mine, Mine," Kimberly giggled as she twirled around on the new rug.

"Yes, it's yours. Tomorrow I'll bring a few more toys and your curtains," Callie laughed while watching her daughter's antics.

The last of Linda's references called back on Monday and Linda said she would like to move in December first, instead of January, if the apartment would be ready. Everyone felt relieved since business in the store was steady, but not enough to make the loan payments without stretching things a little tightly. They agreed they would make most of their money during the summer, at least until word about the seafood and fresh produce they carried spread to the mainland.

After Christmas, preparations for the grand opening went into full swing. Max hung a couple of old wooden ladders from the high ceiling to display dresses, baskets, and scarves. Fabric screens suspended from the ceiling provided a backdrop for the front window and allowed them to create displays much like department stores. They left the store's Christmas tree up because it was so festive. Shelves made from fruit crates and simple boards held jewelry and pottery. Several artists displayed their work throughout the store.

9

10 January 1971

Finally, their Grand Opening day arrived. Callie braided her hair, wrapped the braid around her head, and pulled a loose dress over her slender frame. All her walking gave her an athletic look. No makeup, just a touch of lipstick. She threw a sweater on her bag just in case. After cutting up some fresh fruit for Kimberly, Callie took the two boxes of cookies she had made for the grand opening out to the truck. As she set the boxes in the back, Alma came up to its other side.

"Good morning. Seems like we just saw each other." Callie laughed as she and Alma met on the way to the truck.

"I know. Is there anything else to go in the truck?" Alma carefully settled her tray of peach tarts in the back of the truck.

"There's one more box on the kitchen table. If you get that, I can get Kimberly ready. I plan to feed her breakfast at the store today."

"I'll do that while you finish up with her."

Both women set a brisk pace as they crossed the yard. Inside, Alma went into the kitchen while Callie went to check on Kimberly who was playing quietly in her crib.

"Good morning, sweetie. Hope you had a good sleep. We're going to see a lot of people today." Callie spoke softly to her daughter and kept up a stream of chatter as she dressed Kimberly. Kimberly responded with smiles and her own babble.

Alma came to the Kimberly's bedroom door. "I see you've got fruit cut up for Kimberly. What else do you need?"

"I meant to put it in some Tupperware, but got distracted. The diaper bag is in the living room. I've got some dry cereal in it. If you could just put the fruit in a Tupperware and then put it in the bag then we can go."

"Got it." Alma answered as she turned to go.

The toddler caught everyone's excitement, and her red curls bounced as she twisted in her seat, trying to see everything while Callie drove to the store. Louise, Steve, and Max were already at the store. They quickly unloaded the truck and arranged the food near the coffee and other drinks. While Callie set Kimberly up for breakfast. Louise brought a big pot of oyster stew to simmer on the stove's back burner so the family would have something for lunch.

Brenda and Josie, along with their families, were among the first to arrive. "Wow, Callie. This is looking so good. Love that this section looks like your stand on the pier," Brenda said pointing to the area where they displayed Alma's baskets along with work by other artisans.

"With that small grocery area over there, it's like Pete's but better," Josie said.

"Thanks, I'm glad you like it. It took us a while to work it out, but I don't think people will be confused by all the different stuff we offer."

"No, I don't think so," Josie added. "As I came in, I could see the different sections. I think if I were looking for something I would know where to go."

"I see Dad and Momma. Let me go see to them before things get too busy. Be sure to help yourself to the snacks. And tell the boys they can go in Kimberly's room once they get bored out here," Callie said as she turned and walked over to her parents near the entrance.

Local artisans, vendors and their guests began showing up soon after. Even with the added people, Kimberly played throughout the store as usual, occasionally stopping to say hello when someone caught her eye. The Moultrie Times reporter was due to come at twelve, and everyone wanted a chance to talk to her.

Customers began coming in. Several were from the mainland. A few owners were talking with Max about supplying their restaurant. Carol, Alma's sister from Columbia, arrived just before Callie's parents arrived. She stepped away from the counter to greet them and reached her dad first.

"Hi Dad, I'm so glad you could come today. How are you doing?" she said, giving him a hug.

"That's what I should ask you. You must be exhausted. This place looks fantastic. " her dad said as he looked around the store.

"We're pretty tired. Too excited to notice right now. It'll hit us later. I'm sure. Oh, hi Momma." She stepped away from her dad to greet her mother.

Callie's mother pursed her lips, and her breathing became shallow and more rapid as she scanned the room. "Where's Kimberly?" She asked as she gave her daughter an absentminded hug while continuing to scan the room.

"I think she's over with Alma and Carol. She's fine, Momma. She's learned where not to go and we have all the cleaning supplies on upper shelves." *Oh, lord, Momma's totally strung up. Hope we all can just get through this peacefully.*

"Oh, I see her. I'll just take her to the playroom you've been talking about." Her mother said as she took off.

Before she could answer, her mother quickly crossed the room, picked up her granddaughter, and darted into the playroom. Callie shook her head. "I see she's still not at ease with my decision."

"It's going to take some time for her to adjust, sweetie." Her dad said as he gave her shoulder a squeeze. "Now, before you get too busy, show me around the place."

"Most everything out here is just the store. Someone's bought the diner, so we really don't want to serve much food. Maybe just some sweet rolls and coffee. And cold sandwiches during the summer. The main reason we wanted the kitchen was for the huge refrigerator. We've ordered another one. See, we put up a railing and gate so Kimberly can't get in here when we weren't looking. Maybe you can reassure Momma. Let me show you the alcove. Linda's already moved in, so I won't show you the apartment." She said as they walked through the backroom and out the door to the apartment's alcove.

"You guys have really done a great job here. I like the alcove and the privacy it gives your tenant," her dad said, as they came back inside.

While Callie walked her dad through the store, her mood brightened and after they had toured the public areas, she took him back to the kitchen and their work area.

"See, we put in a railing with a gate to keep Kimberly out of the kitchen. We've already rented the apartment, but let me show you the alcove," Callie said as she unlocked the back door.

"This is really great," her dad said while turning around in the entryway to the apartment. "Your tenant has some privacy and there's parking on the side of the building too. Isn't there?"

"Yeah, it's well lighted too. At first, we thought we'd add stairs outside, but that would have left the stairs inside. Such a waste of space. Not to mention expensive by the time we made a new entrance to the apartment. Since all our deliveries are smaller, we didn't need the double doors here. Max and Steve did a fantastic job," Callie said as she led the way back into the store.

Alma and Max were waving to her as she and her dad came out of the backroom. "Sorry, Dad. The reporter from the Moultrie Times is here," she said giving him a quick hug. "I've got to go up front now."

"Go do what you need to do. I'll check on your mom and Kimberly." Her dad waved a hand dismissively as he turned to go to the playroom.

For Callie, the rest of the day was a blur. She checked in on her mother and Kimberly from time to time, but her mother pointedly played with her granddaughter and didn't engage in conversation with Callie. Even when Callie brought Kimberly out for lunch, her mother remained in the playroom. Eventually, her dad brought her a mug of soup. Just before Kimberly's naptime, her parents left to return to Columbia. Although it was hard to do the round trip in a day, Callie's mother hadn't wanted to stay overnight on the island.

Everyone felt the grand opening was a tremendous success. The reporter seemed favorably impressed. Linda had spread the word among her coworkers and the ad campaign had been fruitful. Several people from the mainland came in, promising to return. All the artisans and vendors were happy with their sales for the day. The store receipts were good, and they had two contracts to supply restaurants with seafood. It didn't take long for the exhausted partners to close up.

Callie was warming supper while Kimberly played on the kitchen floor when Alma called, "Is it okay if Carol and I stop by after supper?"

"Sure," Callie answered. "Kimberly will be asleep by seven. Why don't you come over then."

"Sounds good. She just wanted to see you before she goes home in the morning."

"Alright, I'll see you then." Callie hung up the phone and sat on the floor beside her daughter.

"Hope you're not too tired to eat. We had a long day in the store today. Most days won't be so long," Callie told her daughter. Kimberly babbled happily and handed her mother a block to add to her tower. Kimberly clapped happily and promptly knocked the tower down. She erupted into giggles as the blocks tumbled.

Laughing at her daughter's antics, Callie picked her up. "Okay, let's wash up for supper now. Momma's hungry and I bet you are too. Then it will be nearly bedtime."

With Kimberly asleep, Callie had just finished cleaning up the kitchen when she heard Alma and Carol on the back porch. Drying her hands, she opened the kitchen door. "Hey there. Come on in," Callie said smiling. "Ah, you've got sweaters on. Do you want to sit on the side porch? Would you like some tea? And maybe something for dessert?"

"Just tea for me," Alma answered. "And let's sit right here in the kitchen, I'd probably fall asleep on the porch."

"I couldn't eat another bite," Carol said holding a small dish toward Callie. " I'll just have tea, but I wanted to give you this, too. Nothing much, just some of my homemade fudge. It's one thing I know you love and don't make yourself. I found the dish at a secondhand shop. I know you love your Fiesta."

"Carol, you shouldn't have, but thank you. One day you'll have to share the fudge recipe and teach me how to make it." After giving Carol a hug, Callie set the fudge on the counter, turned to get glasses, and pour the tea.

"She gave me mine in a small dish that goes with my green depression glass," Alma smiled broadly at her sister.

"I'm so proud of my little sister," Carol said beaming. "No one in our family ever owned a business before. I felt you each needed a little something to mark the occasion. She's lucky to have a friend like you."

"Alma's pretty special. I'm not sure how I would have managed without her," Callie said, smiling at her friend.

The three women talked of plans for the summer. Callie and Alma reassured Carol that Alma would still be able to visit in Columbia or take off when Carol came to the island. They were the oldest generation of their family and liked to see each other regularly. Before long, all three women were yawning.

After Carol and Alma left, Callie got a quick shower and went to bed. For once she was tired enough, she didn't think too long about her mother's actions at the store. *Maybe she'll get used to the idea and realize I've made a good choice. I hope so. If only Momma could see that this is the right thing for me. Kimberly's growing big and strong. She's so smart. I'm happy. Can't that be enough? Anyway, the Emporium's off to a good start. I've found a way to stay on the island and not live hand to mouth,* she thought as she drifted off to sleep.

10

February 1971

Callie looked out over the parking lot. If she stretched up on her tiptoes, she could see the sea oats covering the dune on the far side of the lot. Their golden stalks waved in the gentle breeze. Low-lying clouds hid the sun, but she could see the seagulls flying on their way to the water hidden by the dunes. *This is the life, being so close to the ocean.* She turned her attention to the woman approaching the counter.

"Is this everything, Ethel? I've got your shrimp right here." Callie held up the carton.

"I've got these few things in the basket, too. How's things?" Ethel pivoted as she looked around the store.

"We're all good. How's your family?" Callie rang up Ethel's purchases.

"'Bout the same. The kids are coming down for the weekend. I'll be back for flounder on Friday. You know I always do a fish fry or seafood boil when they're in town." Ethel smiled as she talked about her kids.

"Thanks for keeping us in mind. Appreciate your business." Callie handed Ethel her bag.

Ethel made her way out of the store as Max pulled into the parking lot. His face lit up with a huge smile as he opened the door. Inside, he picked Kimberly up and danced her across the store to the counter. Callie was finishing a phone call. So, with a nod to Callie, he continued the dance toward the back of the store. As Callie hung up, Max and

Kimberly made their way to the counter. The toddler was full of giggles, and Max he was a little breathless as he put her down on the floor.

"What's got you grinning like a Cheshire cat today?" Callie couldn't help but laugh as she walked around the counter.

Max held up a finger. After he caught his breath, Max continued. "Smith's trawlers have agreed to let us have the first pick, even though we'll never be able to handle their full catch. We'll be able to fill the contracts for all four restaurants. Plus, we'll have plenty for the store."

"How did you talk them into it? I knew you still had connections with the fishermen." Callie started jumping up and down with excitement. Kimberly ran to join in the fun and began twirling around the adults.

"Dizzy, dizzy," she giggled.

Callie settled down and reached out to steady her daughter. "Don't get so dizzy that you fall. The floor is hard." Kimberly stopped spinning and giggled as she wobbled toward her playroom.

"Well, you were right. Some of the old timers do remember me. Others heard about our store and remembered seeing us on the pier. Like us, they like supporting local businesses. At least right now, we can pick first, and they still have enough for the canneries. It's a win for everybody."

Brushing a few loose strands of hair from her face, Callie felt relieved. "I was a little nervous when we got the last two restaurant contracts. This will help even out our sales. Maire's coming in for a while. Your idea of having a scale for the consignment fees based on time spent working in the store was fantastic. Even in slow times it helps since it allows us to keep up with paperwork. Never thought there would be so much paperwork involved in running a store. Ah, here she is now." Callie looked toward the door. "Hiya, Marie."

"Hey Callie, Max. Anything special happening today?" Marie had a bubbly personality and made the most intricate jewelry and mobiles using beach glass.

"No, we're thinking about something around Memorial Day. That's a few months away," Max answered.

"Alright, I'll just tidy up a bit while I'm here. Maybe rework some displays up front."

"Max and I'll be in the back if you need us." Callie followed Max to the storeroom, picking up her daughter along the way.

She stopped by the playroom to change Kimberly and get her down for a nap. Max was going over the ledgers when Callie came to the backroom.

"I'm glad you know about keeping the books. The Small Business Association has helped some but, it's not the same as having someone right here to answer your questions," Callie said as she entered the back room.

"Yeah, one of many lessons I learned from my parents. 'You always need to know where your money's coming from and where it's going.' They taught me early that you can't just spend what's in the till," Max said.

After washing her hands and making a couple of sandwiches, Callie sat down at the table with Max. They had decided against a desk and set up a long table that allowed all of them to work together when needed. A wheeled, tiered cart with trays held their paperwork, so everyone had access and could easily move it. "One of these is for you. I know you didn't eat while you were out."

Max looked up. "Oh, thanks."

"I know your family has owned the truck farm in Mt. Pleasant for generations, and I don't mean to pry, but how did you become a fisherman?" Callie asked.

"That's a long story." Max shook his head, and his face became somber. "But I guess I can share it. People got to learn."

"My Uncle Phil owned a fishing boat. Sometimes during the summer, I would go out with him if he was shorthanded. I liked it a lot, much better than working in a field. Besides, being out on the open water, I felt free. Even so, my parents insisted I stay in school. All the while, I was trying to figure out what else a Black man could do besides work in a field. I'm not too good for that kinda work, but I wanted something different."

"I hear you. Definitely not the same situation, but I'd rather be doing anything here on the island than working in the mills like my parents."

"Anyway, things got bad for Black people around here. Some whites resorted to violence when they felt Black people were crossing the line, like moving into better neighborhoods or getting better jobs. A lot of Black people went up North to get away from racist activity in the south. My Aunt Mabel and her family left before the war." Max paused and brushed his hand over his eyes.

"When I was a senior in high school, Aunt Mabel came back for a visit and told Uncle Phil her husband was making good money up in Detroit. Uncle Phil started figuring out how to get to Detroit. This was in the early forties. He worked hard, and the fish were running good, so he saved enough to get his family to Detroit. He tried to sell the boat to raise more cash to help tide the family over, but everyone was trying to lowball him since they knew he was leaving. Anyway, he offered it to me. I didn't have much saved, but he trusted me to send him the rest as I earned it."

"Wow. That's a lot of responsibility. Not just making your own living, but knowing your uncle was counting on the money you sent. I understand from things Alma's told me and from what I've read, Black businesspeople really got a raw deal back then. Not sure it's much better now," Callie said, shaking her head.

"It's better, believe me, but it's still not right. Anyway, I made a living and paid my uncle for the boat. My crew kept things going while I was in the army. When I came home though, I didn't get the same breaks for buying a home as the white soldiers did. Louise and I got married anyway, and we bought a house. Even back then, Caines Island was kinda open and there weren't issues about race in the neighborhood. Probably because the island was small and it didn't attract developers. Louise and I found the island a friendly place to live. Of course, Alma and Nate, Josie's family, and Brenda's, too, were here then." Max stared off into the distance before continuing.

"Anyway, I bought another boat, thinking one day Steve would take over. But he wants to be a lawyer. That's okay, every man has his own dream. There was a bad time when I thought I would lose everything. Although I didn't find out until after she died, your Aunt Sally helped me out then. But I think you might have heard that story," Max said, pausing a minute before continuing. "Your Aunt Sally was a fine woman. I didn't know your parents well. Your momma stayed close to the house. Worked with your dad a few times on neighborhood projects."

"Yeah, Alma told me about your house. Mainly because I was asking questions about my mother and Aunt Sally. Momma never talks about the past. I really just want to understand everyone I consider family." Callie shrugged her shoulders.

"I can't blame Steve." Max continued, almost as if he hadn't heard Callie. "Fishing is hard on the body. Eventually, when my hands started knotting up, I sold the boats. It left us a little nest egg. Louise kept doing hair. I did odd jobs and sold my stuff on the pier to keep busy and have some pocket money. But I've made it a practice to help people when I can. Sometimes they just need encouragement or to be shown a different way of looking at things."

"Max, I can't imagine growing up and trying to follow all the despicable, bizarre rules like you had to. It's not right," Callie said. She was angry for her friend's sake.

"It's wrong. We did what we had to do to get by. I'm fortunate; some didn't make it." Tears glistened at the corners of Max's eyes as he brushed at his eyes with the back of his hand before going on with the story. "I worked hard, and I got some breaks. Now my son's studying to be a lawyer. There was a time I was at every protest and rally, some of them not too peaceful, now I carry on the fight in different ways. I've met some purely evil people, but I've also been blessed to meet some mighty fine ones. I prefer to focus on the good ones while fighting the evil ones." Max looked over at Callie and smiled. "Now, let's get back to these books. It's time to pay our sales tax and the quarterly income tax is due at the end of next month."

With the sales tax forms completed, the check written, and sealed in the envelope, Max went home before Kimberly woke up. Once she woke up, Callie changed Kimberly and took her for the short walk to the mailbox at the corner of the parking lot.

"Beach, beach," Kimberly called as she ran ahead of her mother to the mailbox.

"We'll take a walk on the beach after I close up tonight," she said, laughing at her daughter's early efforts to run, which made her look more like a penguin than a small human.

Returning to the store, Callie relieved Marie and thanked her for her work rearranging the displays in front of the store. Even though the artisans rotated their work periodically, just moving the displays around occasionally sparked sales. *The weather is supposed to be good this week-end. We'll probably have some people coming in for a day trip to the beach,* Callie thought.

The last few hours of the day passed quickly as people stopped in to pick up bread, milk, or something last minute for supper. After locking up the store, Callie tossed her things into the truck and grabbed the sand bucket and shovel from the back as her daughter tugged on her other arm. "Hold on Sweetie, let momma get the truck locked. We're going to the beach."

Rounding the store's building, her daughter again ran off as fast as her little legs would go. Callie broke into a trot to stay close as they neared the water. She tossed the bucket down to chase Kimberly, who, as always, was chasing the sandpipers. Within a few minutes, Kimberly grew tired of chasing the birds, and they returned to the bucket.

"Castle so high." Clapping her hands, Kimberly squealed in delight as they made a sandcastle in the damp sand.

Callie laughed distractedly as she spotted another person walking on the beach. She felt a little disconcerted as she thought to herself. *Who's here now? Linda stayed late at school. Don't be silly, this is a public beach.* Soon the walker came into view. *Oh, it's the guy that just bought the Williams' old place. I didn't think he was going to be here year round.*

As he reached Callie and Kimberly, he stopped. "Hi. I'm Mark Atkins. Just bought the Williams' old place. This is a great place to live."

Callie stood brushing off loose sand from her clothes. "Yes, it is. I'm Callie Stevens. This is my daughter Kimberly."

"Haven't I seen the two of you in the market?" Mark asked, pointing with his thumb back towards the building. Callie couldn't help but notice Mark was tall, muscular, and suntanned, even in winter. His blonde curly hair escaped his ball cap.

"Yeah, I own it with two partners," Callie said, helping Kimberly stand up.

"Oh, I see," Mark muttered. He shifted his feet, stuffed his hands into his pockets and seemed unsure about how to carry the conversation further.

And while Callie was aware of his attractiveness, she wasn't ready to even think about a relationship at this point. She picked up Kimberly along with her bucket, preparing to leave.

"Well, it's nice to meet you. We have to get home for supper," she said as she headed toward the parking lot.

On the drive home, Callie's thoughts turned to the future. *Until today, I've been so busy trying to make a living for us, I never even thought about dating or anything like that. While it would be nice to have a boyfriend at some point, I've gotten so used to making my own decisions, I don't know how well it would work. It might be the seventies but, I'm not sure how a man would feel about my keeping the store.*

11

September 1981

Rummaging in the coat closet for Kimberly's baby pictures, Callie came across the box of letters and pictures Bobby gave her while they were at her parents' several years ago. With Kimberly out of the house and things well underway for the party, she took it into the living room and sat on the couch. Lifting the box's lid, Callie found a creased black-and-white photograph. It showed a few hills with sparse pines behind the house. The yard had patches of scraggly grass but was mostly packed red clay. The little paint remaining on the house was peeling off in long strips. A young girl with stringy hair and a dirty face sat on the porch steps. She looked to be about four years old and was wearing a pair of old, patched pair of overalls. No shoes. Confused about who the girl might be, Callie held her breath as she turned the photograph over. A shaky hand had written 'Lydia 1930' on the back.

A postcard lay under the photograph. *Dear Flo, I need to bring Lydia and Sally to you for a short time. Cynthia's not well. I don't know how long they will have to stay. The doctors can't tell me how long before Cynthia will be better. I know you got 6 of your own, but I don't know nothing about raising girls. Unless I hear something different from you, I'll bring them and their stuff at the end of the month. Raymond.*

Rummaging deeper into the box, Callie found other letters. Her hands trembled as she opened a few of them. There were some from Raymond, showing he had sent a small sum of money and filled with promises to come for the girls soon. There were several letters written to Raymond and returned as undeliverable. Looking at the return addresses, Callie saw Flo had written some, asking for more money. Then there were later ones written by Callie's mother, asking him to take them home.

Further down in the box, there was a death certificate for Callie's grandmother. She had died by suicide when Callie's mother was eight years old. A yellowed newspaper clipping gave a brief account. *"Mrs. Cynthia Simmons escaped from an asylum and returned to her previous home. Authorities report neighbors said she was creating a disturbance as she knocked on doors looking for her family. They said she was distraught at not finding her husband and children. She killed herself by jumping off a bridge just outside town. The whereabouts of her husband, Raymond Simmons, are unknown. Her children were taken in by Raymond's sister some years ago, according to old Mrs. Snow."* Tears gathered on Callie's eyelashes as she squeezed her eyes closed against the mental picture of her grandmother bereft along a riverbank.

"Callie, are you in here?" She heard the screen door close, rubbed a hand over her eyes and tried to get the box out of sight before her mother got into the living room. "Hey. Kimberly out? What have you got there?" Her face mother's crumpled as she recognized the Belk's box on the floor next to the couch.

Callie jumped up and pulled her mother close. "Momma---"

Tears welled up in her mother's eyes as she clung to Callie. "I never told you before, but I guess you might as well know the entire story." Her mother dabbed at her eyes and stood back from her daughter. Callie moved the box to the coffee table before they sat side by side on the couch.

"I don't think Sally remembered Momma. She was just two when Daddy left us with Aunt Flo. Momma had red curly hair like me and Kimberly. Their wedding picture's in the box. Daddy had a small farm, part of his daddy's farm, really. From the little Aunt Flo told me, living on the farm was hard. Daddy did small engine repairs to earn extra money. I used to watch him work on things in the barn.

Momma helped in the fields. Kept the house and made our clothes. I remember being happy. Momma liked to dance and sing while doing chores. She was going to have a baby. Everyone was so excited. Daddy kept going around, saying, 'This one will be my little man. Only right since you've got your two girls, Cindy.'

Then next thing I remember, Daddy was taking her to the hospital to have the baby. Neighbors said, 'It's too soon for the baby'. We stayed with Grandpa and Grandma for a few days. Grandma fussed about 'being saddled with us at her age' the whole time we were there. One day, Daddy said Momma couldn't come home, and we had to go to Aunt Flo's for a while. He promised to get us when Momma came home."

"You grew up on a farm?" Callie asked, astonished her mother didn't grow up in town, since her mother was notorious for disliking trips to the countryside.

Her mother continued while ignoring the question. "It was a few years before Flo let slip Momma tried to kill herself when the baby boy died because he was premature. For a long time, I thought Aunt Flo lied to me. But I couldn't figure out *why* she would lie. Any more than I could understand *why* Momma would do that while she had Sally and me."

"Momma, that's awful." Callie reached out and held her mother's hand. Lydia stared off into space. A single tear made its way down her cheek. "I'll get some tissues, Momma."

When Callie returned to the couch, Lydia put the tissue box in her lap after she pulled one out. "Growing up with Flo was hard. Daddy promised to send money but didn't do it regularly and then he stopped sending it at all. Uncle Johnny worked in the sawmill, but that didn't pay much. It was the Depression.

All of us went with Flo to pick tobacco. We'd be out there ten hours a day picking tobacco. Then home to tend the garden and chickens. No matter what we did, there was never enough food. Most of the time, I was too tired to be hungry."

"No wonder you're always canning and freezing food," Callie said, taking her mother's hand again. *I've always wanted to know this and now, it's almost too much to bear and I didn't even have to live it.*

"The house only had two bedrooms. One for Aunt Flo and Uncle Johnny. We eight kids had the other. The three boys had one bed. We five girls shared the other. Aunt Flo put blankets and dressers between the beds to make it like the boys and girls had separate rooms. At least the bathroom was inside.

Aunt Flo was a teetotaler. Uncle Johnny liked a nip now and again. To be honest, I don't think Uncle Johnny drank all that much. In fact, he was home as soon as his shift ended. He always kept a bottle in the tool shed, though. Aunt Flo ranted and raved every time she felt he spent too much time out there. Uncle Johnny felt he should be able to have an occasional nip. I hated all their fighting."

"Momma, you don't have to tell me all this now." Callie gently stroked her mother's hand.

The words kept tumbling out like water over a dam. "From the time I was ten years old, Flo made it clear; Sally and I would have to leave when we got old enough to marry or get a job and live on our own. Sometimes, girls were married off at twelve and fourteen. Because girls moved away once they married, we weren't as valued as sons who would bring families to work alongside them on the farm. I always thought it was funny, because we not only worked in the fields and everywhere else, but we carried the children who grew up to be field hands." Her mother snorted and shook her head.

"Anyway, just after my eighteenth birthday, I heard the mills around Charleston needed more workers, so Sally and I bought bus tickets and went there. We found a room in a women's boarding house and got jobs at a textile mill. Sally liked to go out and meet people. Mostly, I worked or stayed in our room. Eventually, I took night classes to finish high school and learn some secretarial skills."

"Come on, Momma. Let's have lunch. You need to eat," Callie interrupted while pulling her mother up from the couch.

Her mother followed her into the kitchen, wiping tears from her face. Callie put out some things for sandwiches and the ice tea pitcher. "You don't have to talk about this anymore, if you don't want to."

"Should have told you a long time ago. Sally married at eighteen. She met Claude working her second job as a hat-check girl. I met your dad while working at the mill. He was already a section lead on the day shift, and I had moved into the office as a typist. We dated for a while and then he took me to meet his parents. As his parents asked questions about my family, I told them my parents died when I was young, and an aunt raised my sister and me.

Before we got married, I told your dad everything; he didn't care. He is such a gentle, sweet man. People think you can inherit these mental afflictions or that you're weak. I don't think they're right, but I believe when bad things happen, they do mark you somehow."

"So how did we wind up on Caine's island?" Callie asked, wondering if her mother would tell her more than Alma had.

"Sally offered us the house on Caine's island when I was pregnant with Bobby. I had quit my job at the mill; they would have fired me when they found out I was pregnant, anyway. We had a mill house, but not like the one we have in Columbia. That house was terrible. Even Flo's rundown old house was better than that place. No matter how much I cleaned, the mill house was musty.

I didn't know what to do with myself once we got here. I had worked all my life. The island house was nicer than anything I ever lived in. So, I tried to be sure that we didn't mess up anything while we lived there. Then, somehow, I got the idea that if I kept the same routine, then everyone would be okay. If I didn't, something would go wrong. I had to clean everything every day. When we came to Charleston, Sally fell in love with the beach. To me it's lovely, but there's the bugs, the snakes and all that water in the ocean. So much water a person could drown in it. The thought of something terrible happening to Bobby and later you got so strong, I could hardly get through the day. Your dad has always been a patient, caring man. He put the fence around the yard to help me feel less nervous about you playing outside. It didn't help. I kept trying to keep you and Bobby where I could see you. It doesn't make sense but if you're far away, I get nervous because I can't protect you. Sally said I should see a doctor and get a nerve pill. I didn't, at least not then."

"Momma. Please, just eat." Callie wiped tears from her own eyes. *Things about momma are making some sense now.*

With Callie's urging, Lydia began making a sandwich. "After we moved to Columbia, I talked to a doctor about being so afraid for you kids. He brushed it off and gave me a prescription for a tranquilizer." Mechanically, her mother took a couple of bites from her sandwich before continuing. "Then I was in the hospital for a while because that first prescription was too strong. I have a different one that I still take now and again." Lydia looked down at the table, avoiding her daughter's gaze before continuing.

"I get so afraid sometimes, even now. It was better for a while. You and your brother got married and seemed to have good lives with your families. After Joe died, it got worse again. I didn't want you and Kimberly living like I did---with nothing. I kept trying to make you stay close."

Callie struggled to find some way to comfort her mother. "You don't have to worry about us anymore, Momma. Bobby's practice is doing well, and so is the store. All the grandkids are healthy."

"I know everyone's okay, baby. It's not something I can control easily. But I really do try." Finishing her sandwich, she took their plates to the sink. And after splashing water on her face, in true form, her mother closed the dam and tried to put on a small smile. "No more of this. How can Kimberly be going into the sixth grade?"

"I know. Just yesterday, I was pushing her in a stroller. We're supposed to make a poster with some of her baby pictures. But I've got to find another box of pictures. Anyway, it's not due for another week,"

Callie said, taking the sandwich things to the refrigerator, her mind reeling from her mother's revelations.

"Okay, you look for the pictures and I'll start with the food. You said you were having deviled eggs, potato salad, and she wanted baked beans. I'll start boiling eggs. Then get to work on the potatoes."

"Yeah, instead of our usual seafood, she wanted to have pulled pork and burgers. She thought it would be a hit with her friends. I've got the pulled pork going in the slow cookers." Callie gave her mother a hug.

Her dad and Max came in through the back porch. "We've got the picnic tables. Where do you want them, Callie?"

Callie met her dad and Max at the kitchen door and led them across the porch to give her mother a moment to compose herself. "Thanks, Dad. Just spread them out under the trees, so we'll have some shade. It's going to be warm later. There's a box of citronella candles by the door. Would you put them out, too?"

It didn't take long for Callie to find pictures for the photo collage; she was in the living room when Alma called from the back door. "Do you have the food table up yet, or should I bring these pies into the kitchen?"

"I'm coming, Alma." Callie's mother called from the kitchen. "Callie's around somewhere getting a poster ready for Kimberly."

"Hi, Lydia. Didn't realize you guys were coming so early. I know Callie is glad for your help." Alma came into the kitchen.

"The food table is over near the shed. Let me have one of the pies and we'll see where she's at." Callie's mother dried her hands and reached for a pie.

Callie had placed a big sign, "Happy Birthday, Kimberly," on the shed. The food table had balloons tied to the back corners and flowers from the yard were ready for the picnic tables.

Hearing a car pull into the driveway, Callie went to the front porch, and she waved to Jeanie and her parents as Kimberly jumped out of the car. Their birthday present had been going to a matinee before the party

"Did you enjoy the movie?" Callie asked, hugging her daughter tightly.

"It was super. Is everything ready, Momma? When will people start coming?" Kimberly asked, bouncing with excitement.

"I think Grandma is in the kitchen where we're working on food. Grandpa and Uncle Max are in the backyard. Things are coming along pretty well. Uncle Bobby, Aunt Susan, and your cousins should be here soon. Is your room picked up? Remember, they're spending the night with us."

"I remember. I think everything is ready for them." Kimberly headed for the kitchen.

"Go check, please." Callie smiled at her daughter's enthusiasm.

Kimberly went off to check her room, and Callie returned to the kitchen to help her mother with the final food preparation. When they finished, they joined everyone on the deck. She had added the deck last summer to extend the outdoor space. It wrapped around from outside the side porch to the backyard.

"Looks like we'll have a little breather before everyone gets here." Callie sat in a lounge chair next to her mother.

"Is there anything else that needs to be done?" Her mother asked, shielding her eyes from the sun to look at Callie.

"Nothing until everyone is here. Thanks for all your help today and for talking to me." Callie studied her mother's face.

"The kitchen was nothing, and the other was long overdue. So, tell me, will you be doing your usual Halloween this year?" Her mother said to change the subject.

"Yeah. Things are coming together. We'll have a maze in the side parking lot this year. I hope to hear from a farmer about hay bales soon. Sounds like Bobby's car. Let me go give them a hand getting settled." Callie stood up.

Rapidly, the backyard filled with laughing people as parents dropped off Kimberly's friends. She and her friends formed a group around the record player. Callie, with help from family and friends, filled the food table while her dad grilled the burgers. The kids seemed to enjoy the party. Kimberly was excited about her gifts.

Later, when everyone had left, Callie and Bobby sat on the porch, enjoying the evening breeze.

"You know Kimberly's got her life planned out, Sis." Bobby said, looking closely at his sister.

"Really?" Callie cocked an eyebrow in disbelief.

"She's decided she's going to be a nurse. Before her friends got here, she was grilling me about what nurses do in the hospital and in my office. She was all ears, as I explained. She's young yet, but if she wants to go into nursing, make sure she gets into a four-year college. Don't let her enter a diploma program at one of the teaching hospitals. From what the nurses at the hospital tell me, the four-year degree will be the ticket for her."

"Well, I'll be. Good thing I've never had to touch the money I put back for her. She's talked about nurses with me, but I didn't realize she was so serious. Thanks for taking time with her. It means a lot to me." Callie reached over to squeeze her brother's arm.

"Hey, somebody's got to be the man in her life." Bobby laughed. "How about you, Sis? Are you thinking about any man in particular? I didn't see anyone tonight that wasn't attached."

"I don't know Bobby. Michael and I have been seeing each other for a while now and it's been okay. He just seems to want to remake my life and doesn't seem to hear me when I talk about continuing with the store." Callie shrugged. "I like my life. Just want someone to join in. Kimberly knows him as a friend of mine, but we don't do family things together because I'm not sure about us."

"That's a good move. Kids can get so attached. Kimberly's mature for her age, but the adult world can be so confusing to kids. You've gotten so involved with the Chamber of Commerce and such. You're bound to find the right guy."

"When you gave me that box of pictures a few years ago, did you know what was in it?" Callie turned to see her brother's face.

"No, Susan told me they were old pictures and letters. I don't think she did more than take the lid off." Bobby slid down comfortably in his chair and put his feet on the foot rest.

"Well, I saw them today and Momma talked with me about her childhood. I could hardly believe it." For a while, Callie and Bobby talked about their mother's past and her trouble with depression and anxiety. They agreed to be more understanding of their mother's moods.

"This isn't my specialty," Bobby said running his hands over his face. "Maybe I can find something out from my colleagues."

"As much as I hate it, I need to get some sleep. I've got to open the store tomorrow. The doctor hasn't released Alma to come back to work since her heart attack last month. Although she is up and around the house more." Callie stood up.

"Night, Sis. I know we're going to the beach tomorrow, so I'll see you then. Think I'll enjoy this quiet for a while longer before going back to the apartment." Bobby slid down in his chair.

12

September 1981, The Next Day

The sun's rays, well above the horizon, glinted across the water. Callie missed seeing the early morning sunrises of her first year on the island without Joe. Not that I miss worrying about every little thing and counting every penny. She still took a long walk on the beach every day. This time of day, the sun created sharp glittering diamonds instead of the multicolored, jeweled reflections of a sunrise. Now the sun beat down on her back as she made her way back to the store and a general unease settled on her shoulders. Life is good. I've got nothing to complain about. But am I missing something? Well, no time for this nonsense, whatever it is. I promised Kimberly I'd have her room at the store ready. She seemed to have a good time at her birthday party yesterday.

A few hours later, Callie stood back to view her handiwork in Kimberly's room at the store. *Where has the time gone? Seems like I was just setting this up for her with a crib. She's in the sixth grade. I think she'll like this.* The bell on the front door jingled, pulling her out of her musings.

"Oh, hi Alma. I didn't expect to see you this morning. How are you?" Callie walked toward her friend.

"I decided I might as well come on in. It's too quiet at the house. Your place is sleeping too. I'm feeling better. So, what have you been up to while I've been stuck in that house?" Alma wrapped an arm around Callie's waist. "Show me what you've done."

Together, the two women walked back to Kimberly's room. "I hung some of her posters today. We brought the couch and chairs in earlier. I've just been trying to figure out where the time went." Callie said as they entered the room.

"Funny how time flies. We've done well here. Who'd have thought I'd buy and start driving a car? I used to walk everywhere. Nothing like progress. You're going to find time just keeps speeding up as you get older," Alma laughed, shaking her head.

"When do you go back to the doctor? Have they said you can come back to work? I don't want you to come back too soon." Callie was concerned Alma may have overextended herself helping with the birthday party.

"I have an appointment tomorrow. I'm feeling good, no palpitations, pain, or anything. Of course, I've done nothing harder than feed the chickens or walk down to the mailbox or over to your place since I got home from the hospital. Today, I thought I'd get out. Kimberly will like this room." Alma continued on her way to the backroom. "Have you got the fall decorations out? I can go over those and make sure they're ready."

"They're in the back." Callie followed in her friends wake. "Talked with a farmer out near Mt. Pleasant. He'll donate some hay bales for Halloween. He'll even take them back later. Your idea of having a small maze for the kids was a good one. I'll get the decorations off the shelf for you."

"I'm glad we started this. It gives the kids something to do on the island. I heard the Jones' at the diner are doing a haunted house at their end of the building." Alma sat down at the backroom's worktable.

"That's great. Liz and some of the other artists are making larger plywood pumpkins, ghosts, witches, and such for the maze. I think the kids will have a good time this year." Callie put the box on the floor next to the table.

A few minutes later, Linda and Mark came in the front door, grinning from ear to ear. Callie laughed to herself, thinking of the first time she met Mark. *What a goof I was; thinking he wanted to ask me out. He wanted to ask about Linda.* Alma came out to see how the couple were doing.

"Hello, you two. How's it going?" Callie asked as she crossed the store with Alma in her wake.

Linda's smile got even larger. "I wanted to give you an official notice. I'll be moving out after Thanksgiving. Mark and I are getting married. I'll still be on the island since I'm moving into his place."

"I'm so happy for you guys. Linda, let me see that ring." Callie smiled as she reached for Linda's left hand.

Alma and Callie made appropriate noises over the ring. Shortly after, the couple left. "Well, I kinda saw this coming. So, tell me, how are things going with you and Michael?" Alma asked as they headed back to the workroom.

"I don't know. We always have a good time when we go out. But every time I think we are getting somewhere; he says something stupid about the store. Why is it so hard for men to understand that a woman might enjoy working outside the home?" Callie frowned with frustration.

"Some men feel threatened by strong women or else they feel like they've got to save the woman from something, be the hero," Alma said with her typical forthrightness.

"I just want someone to love me, to listen. Keep me warm at night and be a wonderful dad to Kimberly."

"At least you've got your eyes open, and you know what you want. Sometimes it takes a while to find the right one." Alma patted her friend's arm as she walked to the backroom.

The morning business was brisk, leaving Callie little time to contemplate her love life. Soon Bobby trooped in with all the kids. "They say I can't go home until I buy Cokes for everyone. You gotta save me, Sis." Bobby could be such a clown.

"Okay. Kimberly, I finished your room. Take everyone back there and I'll bring drinks." Callie took charge of the rowdy group, herding the stragglers to Kimberly's room.

It wasn't long before Susan arrived with the car to gather her family for the trip back to Spartanburg. She spent a few minutes looking through the gallery.

"Callie, I can't believe what you've done to this place." Susan called out from the front of the store. "The artists you've attracted do such great work. Bobby, come here. I think I've found the perfect painting for the dining room."

Bobby ambled over to where his wife was standing. "That's a fantastic rendition of the Angel Oak on Johns Island. I agree it's perfect for the dining room."

After they paid for the painting and Callie wrapped it for the journey, Susan and Bobby loaded their brood into the car. Kimberly had said her goodbyes inside before retreating back to her room. Callie walked out to the car with them. Bobby gave his sister a hug. "You've got to get away and come see us soon."

"We will. Love you," Callie said as she stood back from her brother's hug.

The rest of the morning went by quickly as Alma and Callie began putting up the fall decorations, maize, cornstalks, and fall colored leaves. Callie's parents stopped by on their way home to Columbia.

Around two, Max came into the store. "Hey, listen Callie. Why don't you get Kimberly and go home? You've had a busy weekend. I'll close up today."

"That actually sounds good. Normally, I'd argue with you since it's not your weekend. Not today though, I'm pooped. Don't let Alma hang out too long, either. Come on Kimberly. We get to go home early."

Pulling into the driveway, it surprised Callie to see all the picnic tables neatly stacked at the end of the driveway. *I should've known Dad and Bobby would have gotten them ready to load into the truck. Well, there's still plenty to do inside. Even with the dishwasher, there was still a stack of dishes by the sink when I went to bed.*

Entering the kitchen, Callie called out to her daughter. "Kimberly, come look at this. Grandma and Aunt Susan ran the dishwasher for us. Now you don't have a chore for this afternoon. Just the clean up after supper."

Scampering into the kitchen from her bedroom, Kimberly was full of excitement. "Oh, that's cool. Do you know what? They changed the sheets on my bed, too."

Walking through the house, Callie found the kids sleeping bags and pillows put away. Sheets were in the dryer waiting to be folded. "Okay, honey. I guess we really get a night off. Do you want to watch something on TV?"

"No, I think I'll listen to my new records in my room."

"Alright, I'll read on the porch for a while. Then we'll get something to eat."

In the morning, Callie fumed as she sat at the kitchen table and waited to get into the bathroom. Even though Kimberly was too young for makeup, she had begun a skin care routine and spent quite a while getting her curls "just right". *Even though there's a double vanity, I've been trying to respect her privacy. Why did I ever think we could get by with one bathroom? Maybe I can figure out how to fit one in without changing the house too much. I wonder if I can squeeze it in off my bedroom. Still, I can't really be mad at her.*

"I'm out now, Momma."

"Alright sweetie, I'll be right there."

Callie's routine didn't take long, and they were soon on their way to the store. Within a few minutes of getting there, the bus arrived, and Kimberly darted onboard. Callie waved from the door as the bus pulled away.

Around lunchtime, Alma stopped by to say her doctor gave her a clean bill of health and waited on a few customers while Callie tried to catch up on paperwork. Checks to the vendors with works in the gallery were due soon. Michael called, asking her to go to dinner tonight. She put him off, saying she was tired from the weekend, and suggested they get together on Friday while Kimberly was at a sleepover.

Today was an early release day, and Callie stepped outside to meet her daughter as the school bus pulled up to the door. Josie and Brenda were there to pick up their boys since they were going into town. She noticed Brenda seemed a bit overdressed for shopping in a pantsuit and heels, but didn't mention it. Brenda would explain in her own time.

"Well, I haven't seen you in a while. How's things going?" Brenda asked, pulling at a tissue in her hand. "Business is good. Kimberly's growing like a weed. How about you?" Callie said, looking a little more closely at her friend and seeing dark circles under Brenda's eyes. *That's unusual for Brenda. She usually has such clear peaches and cream skin.*

"Not so great, but it's a long story," Brenda answered, dabbing at her red nose with a tissue.

"We've got to get together soon. What are you doing tonight?" Josie asked, looking at her watch.

"Cooking supper and maybe watching TV. Hey why don't you bring the kids over after supper? The kids can hangout and we can catch up," Callie said, hoping her friends would accept.

"Sounds good to me," Brenda answered. "But I better get going. I can't be late for my appointment."

"Yeah, I'll be there too," Josie chimed in as she turned to go back to her car

Kimberly finished the last of her homework at the kitchen table while Callie cooked supper. "How was school today?"

"It was okay. I think I want to sign up to take band next year. I didn't think I would have room in my middle school schedule, but now it looks like I will." Kimberly looked up from her notebook.

"Are you talking about middle school schedules already?" Callie turned from the counter to give her daughter her full attention.

"Well, I don't think everyone is, but you know I've been recommended for AP classes next year. So, they've been talking to us about careers and stuff." Kimberly started closing her books.

"Ah, so that's why you were talking to Uncle Bobby about nursing." Callie sat at the table with her daughter.

"Yeah, well, I want to have a career and I don't want to be a teacher. Besides, I think taking care of people would be something I would like."

"Okay, baby. You still have your college savings account. Just know you can change your mind. Take your stuff to your bedroom and I'll put supper on the table," Callie said as she stood up.

"Yes, ma'am. Did I hear that Josie and Brenda were coming by tonight? Are the boys coming?" Kimberly paused in the doorway.

"Yep. They're coming after supper."

"Do we still have some of the peanut butter cookies you made for the party?" Kimberly asked as she returned to the kitchen and sat down to eat.

"Sure do. Once you unload and load the dishwasher, I'll set some out. We've got some chocolate chip ones too. We'd better get moving. I'm sure they'll be here soon."

Later, Callie lit a few candles on the side porch tables. Just enough so they could see each other. The nights weren't too cold yet, so sitting on the porch would give the adults some privacy while the kids watched TV or listened to records. Slamming car doors let her know Josie and Brenda had arrived with their broods. Walking around to the front porch, Callie opened the screen door. "Come on in. Kids, there're cookies on the kitchen table. Help yourself to something to drink."

The women went around to the side porch, giving the kids a chance to get settled before getting their own refreshments.

"So, how was shopping today?" Callie asked as they settled into chairs on the porch.

"Well, I guess you figured out I really didn't go shopping," Brenda said, biting her lower lip and balling up the tissue in her hand. "I applied for a job in the paper mill's office. I think I'll get it."

"That's great!" Callie saw her friend's eyes brimming with tears and realized there was something else to the story. "Spill the rest of it. Or do I need to get you something to drink first?"

Brenda's shoulders curved inward, and she sighed before continuing. "Mike and I are getting a divorce. Seems he found a girlfriend when they started that project in Conway last year. He said it was over, but, well, he lied. With the construction project being out of town and him only home on the weekends, the kids don't realize anything is going on yet."

"That low life. Brenda, I'm so sorry. Please tell me how I can help," Callie offered, leaning over to hug her friend.

"I think I've got things worked out, at least to start with. Josie's going to get the boys on and off the bus during school. I'll have to figure out something for the summer. I don't know exactly what Mike's going to do. It's one of the many things we're going to have to work out. I just want to keep the boys' life as normal as possible."

"Well, at least it's not the 1950's. Divorce is more common now. And the boys are going to stay in the same community. They'll do fine. You're going to do great," Josie said on her way back from the kitchen, bringing a bottle of wine and wine glasses.

"Kimberly thinks of them as brothers. So even though there's no man in this house either, our relationship won't change," Callie said, trying to reassure her friend.

"You guys are super." Brenda dabbed at her eyes with the tissue she had been mangling since she arrived. "I think I can have a glass of wine. Josie's driving, but I should be careful since we haven't settled anything in court."

"Mike's not going to try and take the boys. He'd have to act responsibly." Josie put in. "So, Callie, how's it going with Michael? I didn't see him at the party. Are y'all still sort of a thing?"

Callie shrugged her shoulders and shook her head. "I don't know what we are or if we are. We laugh. We're good in bed together—"

"So, what's the problem?" Josie interrupted with a laugh. "What else do you want? Granted, you don't know if he and Kimberly will get on."

"He keeps trying to reorder my life. Bringing up stuff like selling the store or this house. I like what I'm doing. I'd just like to have someone who wants to share what I have, not redo everything. Then, like today, he called me, at the last minute, wanting to go out tonight. I said maybe Friday," Callie said, shrugging her shoulders.

Now Brenda was laughing. "You're going to break up with him, aren't you?"

"I hadn't decided until just now. But yep, this is it. I can't see how this will turn out like I want," Callie said as she nodded emphatically.

They talked a while longer, and then Josie stood up. "I guess we should be going. Everybody's got school tomorrow."

"Let's get the kids rounded up," Brenda said as she began gathering their empty glasses.

"I'll get them later. Let's get these kids moving," Callie insisted, giving her friend an enormous hug. "We'll have to do this again soon."

"Yeah, let's not wait so long for next time," Josie said, giving Callie a hug.

"We always say that," Callie laughed as she followed her friends inside. "Let's try to do better."

13

Late Summer 1986

Callie sat on the small deck behind the store. The October sun was warm. Sea oats waved in the slight breeze. She turned her attention to the stack of rental applications Alma gave her last night. *Where did the time go? Seems just yesterday Linda was in the apartment and Kimberly was in grade school. Our last tenant was a teacher who stayed for several years before returning to Charleston to care for her parents.* Callie blew out her breath to move strands of hair from her face. *Now Kimberly's starting high school next year. Uh, oh, I'm supposed to remember to call her Kim now that she's grown up.* Callie chuckled to herself.

The partnership with Max and Alma had worked well for each of them. Callie added the bathroom she wanted and upgraded to vinyl siding. Max and Louise remodeled their house, adding an extra bathroom and bedroom, so there'd be more room when their grandchildren came to visit. Alma put in another bathroom to make it easier when her sister, Carol, came to the island. Since her husband died, Carol often came to stay for a couple of weeks at a time. Alma added a deck, too.

We're doing really well, but the slow season is coming and if we want to expand into the space next to us, we need to keep putting back money, Callie thought. They received several calls a week from artists who want to display their works in the store. Somehow, Caines Seaside Emporium had gained quite the reputation for displaying local artists and treating them fairly.

Callie went inside to make calls and set up appointments for people to come in and see the apartment. There were three she felt good about, so she started with these. Like last time, all three partners would weigh in on the decision of which person to rent to. Quickly, she had the appointments set and then called Max and Alma to let them know when the appointments were.

It wasn't long before Alma and Max came in and Callie brought them up to date on the applications. "So, you've narrowed it down to three?" Max asked, briefly looking at the applications Callie handed him and passing them to Alma as he finished each one.

"Yeah. These seem like the best in the group. I've numbered the others in case these don't pan out. They're all coming in this afternoon," Callie said, sipping her coffee.

They went through two appointments, explaining to each that there were others interested in the apartment, but they should be able to let them know by the end of the week. One was a young couple with a small baby and the other applicant was a teacher at the same school Linda taught in. They were leaning toward the teacher when the last applicant arrived.

The bell on the door jingled as a tall, lean man came through the door and wandered around in the gallery area. He paused near a couple of paintings. Shaking himself, he headed to the register.

"Hi, I'm Luke Perkins. I'm here about the apartment. Sorry I kept you waiting. I've just heard so much about your gallery," Luke said as he walked up to the counter where Callie and Alma were standing.

Alma nudged a suddenly mute Callie in the side. "Come on to the workroom." Alma waved Luke toward the back of the store. "We'll be able to talk there."

As they took their seats, Callie introduced herself and sat quietly. Alma asked Luke if he was an artist. Something about Luke reached out to Callie. He was attractive, with auburn, wavy hair, and gray eyes. He looked more like a lanky baseball player than a leading man. Still, there was something about him. Neat, self-contained. *Whoa, girl. It's been too long. Think I'll sit this one out. If Max and Alma choose him, it'll be okay. Otherwise, the teacher gets my vote. Pay attention, Alma just asked a question and he's answering.*

"Well, in my spare time." Luke ducked his head briefly. "I work as the maître de at the King's Courtyard Inn, downtown Charleston. Not glamorous, but it pays the bills. I'm looking for something with enough room to have a studio."

"Alright, Max, you want to show him the apartment?" Callie offered, backing out of her usual job, and burying her head in some paperwork. Alma sat with Callie sipping coffee. Max took Luke through the back door to reach the apartment entrance.

After the tour, Luke stopped back by the table where Callie and Alma sat to say how much he liked the light in the apartment and the second bedroom would be a great studio. As Max walked him through the store, Luke grabbed a soda before leaving. After ringing up Luke's purchase, Max came back to the worktable. He and Alma looked at Callie questioningly.

"Have you decided already?" Max laughed as Callie shifted around in her seat under their gaze.

"No, I haven't. You guys tell me what you think." Callie hedged, feeling the warmth creeping up her neck and onto her cheeks.

"Well, I'll do the reference calls, but if everything is even, I think Luke would be the one. I haven't seen that gleam in your eye for a long time," Alma said, breaking into a huge grin.

"Alma, I admit I felt something there, but let's not be hasty. Just get us a good tenant," Callie said, still struggling with the attraction she had felt towards Luke.

Several days later, while they were rearranging the window display, Alma let Callie know Luke would move in on the first of the next month. He had also discussed bringing some of his work to display in the store and how that arrangement worked.

"Well, that's not a surprise. It's hard to get gallery showings." Callie was thankful she could answer without blushing.

"Do you think we can apply for the loan? It would be great to get the renovations done in time to have a grand re-opening around New Year." Callie was happy Alma changed the subject.

"I think so. It seems like Luke will be a dependable tenant, from what you said. Let's talk to Max and see what he thinks. Remember, I'm going to Columbia to see my parents over Thanksgiving." Callie stepped back to get a better look at a group of small pottery pieces.

"Yeah, I think we'll probably close until Monday after Thanksgiving, anyway. Like before, we'll all be here to get the space together. Let's look at it from outside." Alma stepped out of the display and went outside.

"I think this time we can probably afford to have pros help with some of the renovation." Callie continued as she followed Alma outside.

Max came in a couple of hours later and the three of them worked out a rough plan for connecting the store and the space next door to create the gallery. They wanted space for a small bar area, with a few tables, for the larger events. They would cater any food for a gala. The upstairs space had enough room for two small but attractive apartments. Since the county had paved all the roads on the island a few years ago, there had been an influx of people looking for rentals. They had ten great applicants for the one apartment, so it seemed adding two more would help maintain a positive cash flow.

Callie left for the bank in Mount Pleasant to present their proposal. Max and Alma started on the phone calls to contractors between taking care of customers in the store. Max was busy with a customer when she returned. Callie started a fresh pot of coffee and Alma pulled out things for a quick lunch while waiting for Max to finish.

"I'll wait on Max finishes for the details, but is it a go for the extra space?" Alma asked.

"Yeah, we got the loan. Seems the bank wants to be seen in the community as encouraging the arts, and we've earned an excellent reputation with local artists. It wasn't as hard as I thought it would be. Not at all like the first time, when he acted like I was a silly school girl.

Apparently, the bank likes our way of doing business, " Callie said as she poured mugs of coffee for everyone.

"Am I hearing right? We got the loan without any hassle?" Max asked, getting a cup of coffee. "Oh, I left my notes at the counter. Be right back."

Seated around the small worktable, the three went through the building contractors. "It looks like Ralph or Charles will have time to do the work. They can meet with us on the first to put in bids," Max said, looking at his notes. "But I think Charles will wind up being the best choice. He has the best reputation in the area."

"What about painters?" Callie said as she put down her sandwich.

"They both have a full crew. They can do everything except--- hauling away construction debris will be an additional charge if we go with Charles," Max said, shaking his head. "I don't understand why they don't do the entire job."

"That's what I heard, too. I called your brother Bill, and he quoted us a good price for hauling the debris away. I think he lowballed himself with his price, so we should add something extra. Figured we'd keep it in the family." Alma laughed. Since there was no need for further discussion until January, Alma and Callie went home, leaving Max to cover the afternoon and close up.

A few weeks later, Callie looked up from the gallery's plans as Luke came to the counter with a sweet roll and coffee.

"What are you building?" he asked.

"We're putting a door through into the next space and expanding the gallery. Although I guess it might be presumptuous to call it a gallery. It won't compete with the ones in Charleston." Callie straightened up from the blueprints she'd been studying.

"That's so cool. What made you want to do that?" Luke looked closer at the plans.

"We seem to have more artists who want to bring in their work than we have room for. If we move bigger pieces into another space, we could bring in more without having to sacrifice the smaller things like jewelry, pottery, and baskets." Callie rang up his purchases.

"You know, it's really hard for an unknown artist to get space in a gallery. Then you have to work through all the fees and commissions." Luke handed her the money for his items.

"That's what I hear. I think we've got an arrangement that benefits us and the artists." Callie closed the register.

"If I can help, let me know. With plans like those, I figure you're using a contractor. But I might have some suggestions about lighting." Luke took a drink of coffee.

"Okay, thanks." Callie smiled as she handed him his change. "I'll keep that in mind."

"I worked out a schedule with Alma to put in some time in the store. One of you is usually here in the morning, right?" Luke asked, setting down his coffee. "What would I do while I'm here?"

"The artist usually runs the register, rearranges and dusts displays. Things like that. We come in, set up the register. Make sure the produce and seafood orders for the restaurants are right. If someone else is in, we'll make up the bank deposit, keep the books updated and handle other office stuff. That's part of what makes the arrangement with the artists so beneficial to us. We can get that stuff done during business hours."

"Yeah, that makes sense. It surprised me to see the gallery portion when I first came in. Usually, stores carry cheap souvenirs and beach towels." Luke picked up his coffee.

The morning was quiet, so when he asked, Callie told Luke how she started out selling things on the pier and how people, especially Max and Alma, helped her get started after Joe died. "The hurricane wiped out the pier. Without the pier, there was no place for us to sell. So, we opened the Emporium."

"My story isn't so interesting. I worked at a large Charleston financial firm. Bought a house. Married Myra, who worked for the same firm. Painted in my spare time. Then my wife and I found we couldn't have children. We talked about adopting, but that didn't go anywhere. Eventually, we divorced; it's been three years. I wound up as a maître de to help a friend while I figured out what I was going to do. Now, it keeps me from dipping into my savings. She stayed in the house to get herself sorted. I'm waiting for her to move on with her life. Which I think she'll do soon."

"Are you moving back to Charleston?" Callie tried not to sound too eager.

"No, when Myra moves, I'll either sell or rent the house. I don't want that lifestyle anymore. Eventually, I'd like to find a place on the island, but I hear there's usually quite a wait for properties to become available. I spent a lot of time painting here this summer. Usually, further west of here." Luke tried to take a drink of coffee, only to find the cup was empty.

"That's why I never saw you while I was walking. Oh, here comes Alma." Callie looked toward the front of the store.

"Yeah, I should get moving. Don't forget to talk to me about the lighting." Luke picked up his stuff once more.

"I won't. Refill that coffee cup before you go." Callie smiled. *Maybe there is something there besides good looks.* She hurried to the back room before Alma could start teasing her about Luke.

Callie didn't see Luke in the store again as she got ready to go to her parents' for Thanksgiving. Besides, Callie wasn't sure how to start a relationship with Luke, or even if she really wanted to.

14

November 1986, Thanksgiving

Now that they were on the road to Columbia, Luke crossed her mind a time or two, but she shook off thoughts of any relationship with him. There's just too much going on. I'm not sure Momma's doing as well as she acts from what Bobby says. A few years ago, after their mother revealed her tough childhood, he'd tried to talk their mother into changing her anti-anxiety medication. But her mother didn't think there was a problem. At least Kim will have fun with her cousins. Monica's 14, Sally's 12, and Trey is ten now. They're all growing so fast. Callie shook her head to clear her thoughts and focus on the road.

It looked like the rain forecast for the weekend was coming in early. Callie noticed the sky clouding over as she pulled into the driveway. *Why are Susan's and Bobby's cars here? They usually use Susan's car for family trips.* Her dad and Bobby came out to help with their suitcases as the rain began pelting down in fat, stinging drops. Callie felt the tenseness in her dad's muscles as he gave her a hug before opening the trunk of her new SUV. "Are you okay, Dad?" she asked quietly before he turned away.

"What? Oh yeah, I'm fine." Her dad stared into the back of the vehicle while the rain fell heavily on his shoulders.

Typical Dad, he wouldn't admit to having a rough time, Callie thought to herself. She looked at her brother, who simply flapped his hand and mouthed "Later." And then said aloud, "I've got this, Dad." Their dad waved at Kim and headed toward the house. Kim looked at her mother questioningly but followed her grandfather inside when Callie didn't answer. In a hurry to get out of the rain, Callie and Bobby were close behind. Slipping off her shoes, Callie followed her brother down the hall and into her old bedroom, where she and Kim would sleep. "What's going on? Where's Momma?" she asked.

Bobby spoke rapidly and quietly as he tried to fill his sister in on the situation.

"In their bedroom. Apparently, she started having panic attacks while she was planning Thanksgiving dinner. Dad's been trying to re-assure and help her, but I don't think it made much difference. She's been taking a lot of her Xanax lately, from what Dad says. At the very least, she needs to see a new doctor. One who won't just keep renewing the script."

"But Momma says she needs the pills." Unconsciously, Callie mimicked her brother's hushed tones.

"She probably does, but there are better ones, ones that don't make you addicted." Bobby ran his hands through his damp hair.

"Oh. I see this is more involved than I thought. Poor Dad, he's always been so protective of her. He must be really worried."

"Yeah, he tried to get her to stop the pills cold turkey earlier this month, and that didn't go well. Although he didn't really give me any details. I came down yesterday to help," Bobby added, shaking his head.

"Alright, we'll talk more later. Let me get in the kitchen to see what help Susan needs. You keep Dad and the kids on track. Susan and I will get supper finished up and go from there." Callie pulled her hair up into a ponytail with the hair tie she always kept on her wrist before going to the kitchen.

"Okay, I'll go drag out a couple of board games. That should keep the kids occupied. Holler, if you need help in the kitchen," Bobby said, as they left the room.

"Will do," Callie promised. Entering the kitchen, she took in the orderly scene. Susan was rolling out pie dough and the regulator on the pressure cooker was gently rocking. "Hey, where are you in this process? And how can I help?"

Susan smiled at Callie with obvious relief. "Well, there's a pot roast for supper tonight and that's going. I'm working on two pumpkin pies here, but there're supposed to be apple pies as well according to Mom's list," Susan said, tucking a strand of hair behind her ear.

"Alright, you finish the pumpkin pies now and I'll get the rest of supper ready." Callie washed her hands at the kitchen sink. "Then after supper we can make the apple pies and figure out the sides for tomorrow. Do we know when they wanted to eat on Thanksgiving day?"

Although her voice was light, a frown creased her forehead. "I think whenever we get it together will be alright this year."

In short order, Callie filled in their supper menu with mashed potatoes and green beans. Stepping into the living room, Callie announced. "Hey, everybody, supper's ready. Get washed up. Dad, would you see if Momma wants to eat?"

Dad returned quickly with his head bowed, his chin nearly on his chest. "Sorry, folks, Momma's going to rest a while longer. She seems to have her days and nights a little mixed up."

"Okay, Dad. It's good that she gets some extra rest, since tomorrow's Thanksgiving." Callie wanted to say something more hopeful, but kept quiet, since all she knew about the last few days was what Bobby told her in the bedroom.

Supper conversation stayed light as the adults took turns drawing the children out about school and other activities. As everyone finished, Susan and Callie handed out clean up duties to each of the kids. Kim led their chorus of groans, voicing their disappointment at having chores on a holiday. But they brightened up when they realized their grandmother had gotten a dishwasher since their last visit.

The adults headed to the front porch, out of earshot of the kids. Callie spoke up first. "Dad, don't worry about Thanksgiving. Susan and I can cover all that. But we need to figure out the best way to help Momma."

"Thanks, girls. We met the psychiatrist Bobby's colleague suggested at the hospital." Callie's eyebrows shot up. "No, she wasn't admitted anywhere. He just borrowed a room there for a few minutes since he had seen a patient in the emergency room just before. I'm hoping she and I can do this at home. Going to the hospital will be difficult for Momma, given her mother's history. Bobby, you tell them the rest." Their dad looked at Bobby hopefully.

"Momma wasn't happy about seeing him, but we were able to talk her into going. They talked for a while, he ordered labs and they drew them at the hospital. He thinks with our support she can get off the Xanax at home. But it will be hard." Bobby shrugged his shoulders and held his hands up. "It's highly addictive, and she's been taking it a long time. He called in a prescription for a different antianxiety medication to replace the Xanax, just enough to last until she sees him again. He set up a cross taper for it over the next few days. That means he'll lower the Xanax dose while increasing the new antianxiety medication." Bobby continued and explained the symptoms of psychological and physical addiction: insomnia, shaking, confusion, hopelessness, and increased anxiety.

Callie nodded her head as she took in the new information. "Wow, that sounds like Momma. Dad, I can take Kim back Saturday and come back Sunday. Alma's right next door for her. She and Max can cover everything at the store," Callie volunteered.

"Honey, I know you've got things to do." Her dad looked at the floor, not meeting anyone's gaze.

"We got the loan, so Max and Alma will just carry on like we planned. Bobby, didn't you say having someone here would be a help?" Callie looked at her brother.

'It would. I reworked my patient schedule to come yesterday and should really be back in the office on Monday. My kids need to be back in school, too. Dad, you can go back to work and Callie will be here with Momma. If she's still not sleeping, you'll be able to trade off," Bobby said as he too studied the porch floor.

Their dad held up his hands in surrender. "Okay, okay. I just hate disrupting your lives."

Callie chuckled. "Call it payback for everything you guys did as parents."

"Before we go back to the kitchen, I just want to say if you need a break, Callie, call me. I can get my mom to come stay with the kids for a few days. From what Bobby told us earlier, it may be better if you're with her at first when she's so disorganized," Susan offered.

"Okay, thanks. Let's see what else needs to be done for tomorrow," Callie said as she and Susan stood to go inside.

In no time, cornbread for dressing was coming out of the oven and two apple pies quickly took their place. Callie and Susan were washing up a few pots and pans when Callie's mother came into the kitchen. Callie turned away from the sink while drying a mixing bowl and saw her mother first.

"Hey, Momma. Are you feeling a little better?" Callie tried hard not to stare. Her mother had obviously been in the same wrinkled nightgown for several days. Her robe was unbuttoned, and she hadn't combed her hair. *I don't think Momma's been to the hairdresser for a couple of weeks. Are those coffee splatters on her gown? Oh, this just keeps getting worse,* Callie thought to herself.

"Sorry, I slept through everything. When did you get here, Callie? Is it Thanksgiving already?" Her mother looked around the kitchen.

"It's okay. You needed the rest," Susan said matter-of-factly as she brought out the plate, they'd set aside for her. "No, it's still Wednesday. Sit down and have something to eat."

"Oh, I don't know. There's so much to do." Callie's mother sat down, holding on to the table's edge as if to anchor herself. Fitfully, she moved food around on the plate, taking a bite now and then.

Callie grabbed the Thanksgiving dinner list from the other end of the table. "I think, Susan and I figured out a cooking schedule for tomorrow. You've already got everything, so there's no need to run out to the store. But let us know if we forgot something."

Perking up a little, Callie's mother took the list. Beside each menu item, the younger women had made a notation of its start time. "You seem to have the timing right. I was afraid it would be a disaster since I didn't feel well today."

"We women got to stick together," Susan laughed. "We'll be up early tomorrow and between the three of us, there'll be a fine Thanksgiving spread."

The smell of apple pies cooking brought the children into the kitchen. "Can we have some pie?" Kim asked. Trey peeked around from behind her nodding vigorously.

"That's for tomorrow. But how about hot chocolate? I saw some cocoa in the cabinet. See if Grandpa, your dad, and sisters want some," Callie said. "Kim, get the snowman mugs for me. They're in the top cabinet by the sink."

"I see them, Momma," Kim answered as she looked into the cabinet. "We have some just like this at home."

Callie stood up from the lower cabinet with a saucepan and smiled, "You and your cousins liked them so much when you were younger, Grandma gave a set to us and one to Uncle Bobby's family."

"That's cool. I like the way we still make it on the stove. I think it tastes better than the instant kind," Kim said as she placed the mugs on the counter.

Trey dashed off to the living room and returned shortly. "Everybody does. They'll be here in a minute," he said.

Everyone gathered around the table, and in a few minutes, Callie served the hot chocolate. Susan pulled the apple pies from the oven. Bobby got the kids to tell Grandma about school. Being intuitive and eager to be helpful, they repeated stories they had told just a few hours before, knowing their grandmother loved to hear about their activities. Callie smiled softly. *Momma's eaten everything and now she's working on the hot chocolate.*

"Alright, everybody finish up. It's past time for bed. You kids can sleep in, but we grownups have to be up early to cook Thanksgiving dinner." Groans from all four kids interrupted Callie briefly. A stern look from the adults silenced all protests. "Kim, you're in with me. Sally and Monica, you've got the foldout couch in the living room. Trey, you've got the sleeping bag in the living room."

"Everything for sleeping in the living room is on or by the ottoman," Bobby instructed. "Call me if you need help."

The adults lingered around the kitchen table as the children settled into bed. "How are you feeling, Lydia?" Their dad asked, rubbing his wife's shoulder gently.

"Better with food and everyone here. I think I can sleep without a pill tonight." Their mother smiled crookedly. "Maybe just half of one. Then I won't wake up antsy."

"Sounds like a good plan, Momma." Bobby put in when their dad shot him a questioning look.

Susan stretched while trying to talk around a yawn. "I'm going to bed. It will be turkey day in just a few hours. I brought some pastries, so we don't have to have a big breakfast."

"Fantastic. I brought some banana bread and yeast rolls for dinner. I'm going to turn it in too once I clean up everything from the cocoa." Calle began gathering the mugs and went to the sink.

"Here, let me help you." Callie's mother spoke up. "I'll be in to bed in just a few minutes, Bob."

"Okay. I'll see you in a little bit," her dad answered as he turned to leave the kitchen.

"Like old times. Everyone's asleep and we're in the kitchen," Callie joked as she washed the cocoa mugs while her mother dried and put them away.

"Yeah, it is," her mother said. "Everyone has grown up so much. Callie, I don't know what's wrong with me. I hope this new doctor will help."

"I hope so too, Momma. Do you think you'll sleep tonight?" Drying her hands Callie reached out to hug her mother.

"I think so," her mother lingered in the embrace.

"Okay, let's turn in then." Callie gave her mother a last squeeze before stepping away. "If you can't sleep, wake me up. And don't worry about bothering Kim. She sleeps like a log."

15

Saturday After Thanksgiving, 1986

Thanksgiving day came and went under a cloudy sky with sporadic showers throughout the day. Even though she and her family tried to keep things festive, the weather and concerns for her mother's health put a damper on Callie's mood. Now, as she was driving her daughter back to Caines Island, the rain had started up again.

"But Momma, why do you have to go back? And why can't I just stay? It would save you driving so much." Kim sighed yet again.

"Honey, your Grandma isn't well right now. She's got some appointments coming up and Grandpa needs to get back to work. So does your Uncle Bobby. Max and Alma will cover for me at the store." Callie knew Kim could sense she was holding something back.

"I can get my assignments and do them at Grandma and Grandpa's. My teachers would let me do it. I'm old enough to help," Kim insisted, turning away from her mother to stare out of the car's window.

"It's not something you can help with right now." Briefly, Callie glanced over at her daughter.

"I don't understand. What's so bad that I can't be there? Is she going to die?" Kim asked, her voice nearly a whisper.

"No, sweetie, not anytime soon. I know we've always talked about things." Seeing her daughter's sad face reflected in the window, Callie took a deep breath and continued. "Okay, I thought we could have this talk when we got home. You know, Grandma's always been kinda nervous."

"Well, yeah, that's why she takes those little pills." Kim shrugged.

Surprised Kim had picked up on her mother's medication habits, Callie took a deep breath before continuing. "Apparently, she was having more trouble than we realized. Then her doctor left her on the pills longer than he should have, and Grandma's been taking more than she should. She's found a new doctor and he will help her get off the pills."

"Is she crazy?" Kim asked softly as her brow furrowed into a frown.

"I'm not sure what you mean by 'crazy' but no, she isn't. She's still the Grandma you've always known." Callie tried to reassure her daughter.

"So why is she like this, anyway?" Kim continued to frown as she stared out the window.

"Grandma had a hard life growing up. I think it made it hard for her to accept that life can be fun and safe, so she worries all the time. From what Uncle Bobby told me, getting off the pills won't be easy. She definitely won't be herself while she's working through this, so I thought it would be better if you stayed at home." The rain fell heavier, in sheets of fat drops making it harder to see. *Lord, please get it, Kim. I need to pay attention to the road.*

Kim was thoughtful for a minute. "Momma, are you saying Grandma is an addict?"

"Yes, but no. It's not that she takes more on purpose. The more you take some things, you build up a tolerance and you need more to get the same effect and you can become addicted to it." Callie stole a quick look at her daughter. *I think she's getting it.* "It just takes more pills to help her relax. Your Uncle Bobby could explain it better than I can. It's not like she's taking heroin or something like that to get high, but the longer you take the pills, the more pills you need. I'll ask Uncle Bobby to explain it to you."

Kim looked back at her mother. "I guess I can see why it's better for me to stay home. Is this something I can talk about?"

"For right now, you can talk about it with me, Aunt Alma, Uncle Max, Aunt Louise, and Uncle Bobby. We've agreed not to keep secrets, but I don't know what Uncle Bobby has told your cousins, so let's agree not to talk with them right now. I don't want to confuse them or tell them something before they're ready to hear it." Callie reached over to briefly rub her daughter's shoulder. "And you know, Grandma keeps a lot of stuff to herself, so I don't know if she will want to talk to you about it. But if you've got questions, just ask me, okay? I'll let you know how she's doing."

"Alright Momma. Do you think Aunt Alma would let me stay at her house? I'm not sure I'm ready to stay home alone." Kim picked up her Walkman.

Callie laughed, and Kim's eyes opened wide. "Sorry baby. When we talked on the phone, Aunt Alma and I were trying to figure out how we'd talk you into staying with her. You've grown up so much recently, we weren't sure you'd agree."

Grinning, Kim rolled her eyes. "Sometimes, you're too much. I'm going to listen to music now if that's okay. Can we stop at McDonald's before we get home? I'm getting hungry." Kim paused before putting her headphones on.

"Sure, baby. I'm okay driving without someone to talk to right now. There's a McDonald's about 30 minutes down the road. I'll stop there."

When they pulled into McDonald's, Kim hopped out to order the food. When she returned, she and her mother divided up the food and started munching away on the french fries.

"These might be the best french fries," Callie said around a mouth full of fries. "But you gotta eat them while they're hot."

"Right. Hey, I think I want to go to the University of South Carolina's College of Nursing. My grades are good enough. Uncle Bobby says they have a master's program too."

"I remember you telling me about their four-year program, but what's this about a masters' degree?" Callie turned in her seat so she could see Kim. She loved the way Kim became animated as she talked about her future nursing career.

Her eyes bright, Kim continued. "I'd be a nurse practitioner then and could work more independently. There aren't enough doctors in some places. I think I'd like to work in a clinic in an area like that. Not sure how everything works, but that seems like where I could do the most good."

"Well, your savings account keeps growing and you could work summers at the store, like you have been the last couple of years.

"Sure, and my grades are good, so I'm sure I'll qualify for scholarships." Kim, like her mother, was aware a college education would be expensive.

"Got life all figured out, have you?" Callie chuckled while she began gathering the trash and putting it into a bag.

"Just this part. I don't know about the rest. I haven't met anybody like you and dad. There's nobody I like that much. They're just friends." Kim grinned.

"That's okay, sweetie. Plenty of life ahead of you. How about dumping the trash so we can get home."

"Sure, Momma." Kim hurried to the convenient trash can on the sidewalk.

Alma called shortly after they got into the house. "I thought that was you. Have you eaten? I've got some cold chicken."

"Thanks, but yes. We stopped at McDonald's on the way in. Kim's agreed to stay at your place. Actually, she asked if she could. I'll probably head out around ten tomorrow once we're packed. Bobby's waiting for me to get there before he heads back to Spartanburg," Callie said as she sat at the kitchen table.

"Alright, I'll see you in the morning, then. Get some rest," Alma said before hanging up.

After hanging up the phone, Callie went to Kim's room. Standing in the doorway, she said, "Get your stuff together for school, honey. Do you have anything that needs to be washed? I've got to wash a few things so they can go in with mine."

"No, Momma. I think most of what I need is clean. I can always come back over if I need to."

"Okay. I'll get a shower first. Then do my laundry." Callie turned and walked back to her room.

Within a couple of hours, Callie had packed for the trip back to Columbia. She felt restless, uncertain about how things would go with her mother. "Kim, there's a gorgeous full moon. I'm going for a walk on the beach. Want to come along?"

"No. I'm in pj's. Think I'll stay home." Kim continued reading.

Parking near the pavilion, Callie slipped off her shoes and walked to the water's edge. Moonlight danced across the water. Gentle waves lapped at the shore. Hermit crabs scuttled about, searching for food. Without real purpose, Callie continued her walk along the water's edge and let her mind wander. *It won't be long, and Kim will be in college. I'm going to have to get used to that idea. I'm glad she seems to have a sense of direction. But more immediately, I've got to help Momma get back on her feet. Bobby seems to think she'll have some more withdrawal symptoms since she's been on Xanax for so long. Still, he thinks the worst will be over in about a week. Of course, Momma's got some serious issues to work through.*

Without realizing it, at some point Callie had turned and was nearly back on the path to the pavilion. Laughing to herself, Callie walked back to the hard surface of the parking lot before dusting the sand off her feet and slipping into her shoes. By the time she returned home, Kim's light was out. *Time to get some sleep myself,* she thought.

Callie's return to her parents' home was quiet, and she slipped in while both of her parents were resting. Susan and the children had left Saturday shortly after Callie and Kim. As she entered the kitchen,

Bobby waved to her from the back door, urging her to join him outside once she got her coffee.

"How was your drive?" Bobby set aside his medical journal as Callie sat down.

"Not bad. How are things going here?" She murmured over her cup.

"Momma said she needed to see if she could get in to see her hairdresser before her appointment on Tuesday. That's a good sign. I didn't really expect it and was simply happy to see her up and dressed more like herself from Thanksgiving on. Dad's been handling her medication. So far, it's going well."

"Do you l think she can still get serious withdrawal symptoms?" Callie tried to talk through a yawn.

"She might get a few more headaches, have more anxiety and trouble sleeping. But the way he set up the cross taper, it looks like she'll avoid the worst symptoms from this point on."

Callie yawned again. "That's good. I hope she'll accept therapy as well. I hate to think of her suffering. But I also know how people react when someone has a mental illness. She's a private person. Hope I can convince her everyone won't know her problems. I had to explain to Kim that her grandma wasn't 'crazy'. She may call you with questions about addiction. I tried explaining, but not sure I did a good job of it."

"Sure, she can call me anytime. Susan and I haven't talked to our kids yet. Thought we'd do that at home."

"When are you headed home?" Callie was still struggling to stay awake.

"Shortly after Momma and Dad are up. I won't be here for supper." Bobby put his feet up on the footstool.

"Okay, I'll have to figure out what the three of us will eat."

"Susan took back some stuff at Momma's insistence, but there are still plenty of leftovers. I'm sure you can work some magic in the kitchen. You seem to have inherited Momma's knack there." Bobby folded his hands across his stomach and leaned back in his chair.

"Thanks, Bobby. So, tell me about these nurse practitioners. Kim says she wants to become one." She felt a little sorry about bringing up another topic. Bobby seemed as tired as she was. Still, she wouldn't be able to talk to him for a while.

Bobby spent the next hour explaining how nurse practitioners could improve care in areas where there weren't enough doctors. How they worked with a supervising physician to provide care for stable patients or those with minor illnesses.

"I see why Kim likes the idea." Callie nodded her head in understanding.

"Kim's got her future planned already?" Their dad asked as he joined them on the porch. "She's so much like you."

"It looks like it. Good thing I never needed Joe's life insurance money." Callie smiled up at her dad.

"Hey, Sis. If she needs money or anything else for school. You call me. I know you're doing well, and you never asked for anything before, but let me help, if need be," Bobby said, leaning closer to Callie.

"Okay. I promise," Callie laughed, surprised by her brother's intensity. Turning to look at her dad, she asked, "Dad, did Momma seem like she'd wake up soon?"

"She drifted off pretty easily. I'll let her rest for a little while longer before getting her up for lunch. I know Bobby needs to get back to Spartanburg, and she wanted to see him before he leaves," her dad said, as he too leaned back in his chair.

The conversation turned to football, and Callie dozed in the warm afternoon sun as their voices drifted around her. Before long, her brother was shaking her arm.

"Come on in. We've got some lunch out. Momma's up and I'll be going soon after we eat," Bobby said as he leaned over Callie.

16

A Few Days Later, November 1986

Entering the doctor's office, Callie felt she had stepped into an English gentleman's club. *Not that I've ever been in one, but it sure looks like something from a British novel.* Whoever decorated the office chose wing back chairs upholstered in a burgundy leather-like material and placed them in groups of two along with an occasional solitary chair. The look continued with heavy, dark blue draperies framing sheer burgundy panels, which muted the morning sun. Brass lamps with dark blue shades stood on tables between the chairs and offered spots of light. Thick dark blue carpet covered the floor. The only thing missing was the smell of pipe tobacco to invoke Sherlock Holmes' parlor.

A sense of calm pervaded the room except where Callie's mother sat as she shifted in her seat and rearranged her dress. The two were alone in the waiting room, out of earshot of the receptionist. *I'm glad Beth could work Momma in to get her hair done. Liking the way you look goes a long way to helping you feel better,* Callie thought to herself.

"He seemed okay when I met him at the hospital. But still, what does he think of me? A grown woman should be able to control her nerves," Callie's mother said in hushed tones as she rifled through her handbag. Finding a tissue, she snapped the handbag closed.

Callie touched her mother's arm, hoping to convey reassurance. "He's going to think you're smart to come back to see him. I hope he's easy for you to talk to."

"Maybe Bobby is right. Perhaps if I talk about these feelings I have, then I won't be so nervous all the time." Her mother began folding the tissue into tiny pleats.

"Can't hurt to try," Callie offered with a small smile.

"Lydia Shaffer? Dr. Avery will see you now."

"Coming," Callie's mother answered as she stood up.

"I'll be right here, Momma." Callie watched her mother walk stiffly through the door to the office.

A little over an hour later, Lydia's face was expressionless as she joined her daughter in the waiting room. Little twitches around her mother's left eye told Callie her mother was struggling to control her emotions, and they should leave quickly. The drive home was quiet until her mother asked her to stop at the drugstore so she could pick up her new prescription. Getting out of the car at home, Callie offered to fix lunch for the two of them.

"No, I have a headache. I'll take some Tylenol and take a nap. I'll give you my old pills and you can give them to your dad since I'm not going to take anymore Xanax. Even though I've been cutting back, Dr. Avery said I might still have some side effects." Her mother grimaced. "It needs to be done."

Lydia turned and went to her bedroom without waiting for Callie's reply. A few minutes later, she returned with a bottle of pills. Again, she simply turned and went back to her bedroom. *I guess Momma's just worn out from everything. Then too, I'm amazed she held it together on the way home. I hope she doesn't hole herself up in the bedroom. She always took such joy from doing things in the community, or did she? Maybe that was part of her trying to fit in?*

While her mother was resting, Callie straightened up the living room and then started supper. Settling with her feet up on the couch, Callie started reading. She closed her book as the crunch of tires on the gravel driveway let her know her dad was home.

"Hey, Callie-girl," her dad whispered, coming in the front door. "How did things go today?"

"Let's get some coffee and talk in the kitchen." Callie led the way. "There isn't much to tell, really. She had me drive to the hairdresser and to the appointment. I know she's nervous about what people will think about her going to a psychiatrist. She told me at least that much. I've tried to tell her she was being smart, but I don't know if it helped. Oh, here is her Xanax. She's got more of the new tranquilizer. We picked it up today."

"Well, you know she's always had this fear that her mother's mental illness was hereditary, and she would give it to you kids. I'm not saying your Momma doesn't have a problem, but I don't think it's as bad as what her mother had." Her dad stared into his coffee cup.

"I agree. From what Momma's told me, it sounds like her mother had postpartum depression and it wasn't treated properly. I hope I can reassure her on that point while I'm here. And let her know she's lost nothing in my eyes or Kim's. Momma and I have argued over the years, but a few years ago, I came to understand a lot of what she said was driven by her anxiety about not having enough as she grew up and being afraid for us kids. Then too, she never felt she fit in anywhere."

Her dad looked up from his coffee cup. "You're probably right there. She's been sleeping a little better the last few nights. For a while, she couldn't sleep and would shake without the Xanax. I don't want us to go through that again."

"I'm hoping to tantalize her with homemade vegetable soup for supper, since it's one of her favorites. Maybe I can go on some sick calls with her tomorrow, or at least get her to talk to me."

"Sounds good. I know you've got things going on at the store, but I appreciate you're being here. I'm going to go back and clean up. Maybe your momma will come out then." Her dad slipped the pill bottle into his pants pocket and shook his head. "I'll figure out what to do with these."

A few minutes later, her mother came into the kitchen. Callie looked up from the pot she was stirring. Although her mother was hesitant as she moved around the room, Callie was happy to see her eyes had lost the dazed look which had been so common since Thanksgiving.

"Ah, I thought I smelled vegetable soup," her mother said as she took a deep breath, inhaling as much of the aroma as she could. "Smells good."

"I know it's among your favorites. Do you want some coffee?" Callie asked, turning away from the stove.

"I'll get some for both of us. Come sit down for a while. Tell me about things on the island."

"Well, you know we're expanding the gallery. Work started this week. Fortunately, we don't have to do as much of the actual labor this time. Alma and Max are getting a little older, so the construction stuff is harder. One of our artists wants to do a show on New Year's Eve. He thinks the late evening show will bring people looking for a different way to start the New Year." Callie sipped her coffee.

"That sounds great. Dad and I will come down for it. I think I like Dr. Avery. He's easy to talk to, and I didn't feel he was judging me for getting into this mess. He agrees with Bobby that the headaches and sleeplessness are part of getting off the Xanax. It will get better soon." Her mother looked down into her lap before continuing. "How long are you planning to stay?"

"Things are open-ended right now. I just want to be here for you as you adjust. If nothing else, I can help with the household stuff, so you don't feel overwhelmed. Do you feel up to going out tomorrow?" Callie asked as she fiddled with her coaster. She knew she needed to encourage her mother to get out, but was afraid of alienating her mother if she pressed too hard or too soon.

"I think I'm feeling clear enough to do some visiting. Before, I often felt like I was physically shaking to pieces, so I'd take another pill. But then I was so dazed, I couldn't do anything. The new pill helps but isn't supposed to be addictive. Maybe I can learn not to need the pills." Her mother got up for more coffee.

Her dad answered the phone on his way back to the kitchen. "Callie, it's for you. A Luke?" His left eyebrow shot up as he too went for coffee. Both parents looked at her with open curiosity as Callie went into the living room to take the call.

"I'll check the cornbread," her mother said.

Picking up the receiver, Callie tried to slow down her pounding heart. "Hi, this is Callie." *What's wrong? Why is he calling?* She thought to herself.

"Hey, Callie. Hope I'm not intruding. I found out from Alma and Max that you mother wasn't feeling well. They didn't give me any details but," he paused a moment and rushed on before Callie could answer. "I just wanted to say if there's anything I can do, call me."

They talked for a while until Callie remembered supper would be ready soon. "Give me your number so I can write it down. I'll let you know when I'm coming home if I don't call before then."

Callie felt herself blushing as she went back into the kitchen and tried to cover it by looking into the oven. Closing the oven, she laughed at herself for not seeing that everything for supper was already on the table. Her parents waited with barely concealed grins.

"Come join us and tell us about this Luke person," her dad intoned. Her mother smiled behind her hand.

"Well, Luke is the new tenant in the apartment," Callie said, hoping her parents would just leave it at that.

"So, he had to call you in Columbia about a problem in his apartment?" His left eyebrow shot up again as he crossed his arms over his chest. "While you were here taking care of your ill mother?" Her dad couldn't keep the mock sternness going and broke into a grin, and her mother couldn't hold back a chuckle.

Callie had to laugh at her father's parody of his behavior when she first started dating. "We've been talking for a little while, but haven't gone out. He's an artist and seems like a good man. Let's see, he's been married but now divorced."

"I'm glad you're thinking about having someone in your life," her mother said as she reached out to rub her husband's shoulder. "As much as mothers love their children, there's something special about a good husband." Her mother looked down at her lap for a minute. Then held up her hand. "I know that's rushing things. I'm just glad you're considering this part of your life."

They finished supper as Callie told them more about Luke. The three of them made plans for the rest of the week. On Saturday, they would reevaluate the need for Callie to stay in Columbia.

The next morning dawned with heavy, dark slate gray clouds which sent sheets of rain pounding against the windows. Callie's mother decided she didn't feel well enough to go out and retreated to her bedroom. Her father went to work, but left with a worried frown. Callie busied herself around the house for a while, then went to check on her mother.

"Hey, Momma. Can I come in?" As Callie knocked, the door partially opened.

Thinking she heard a muffled reply, Callie entered her parents' room. Her mother lay on the bed, curled into a fetal position, crying. Making comforting noises, Callie curled up beside her mother and pulled her close. "It's okay. We don't have to do anything today."

In between sobs, her mother told her. "I thought I would feel ready. But just thinking of going to see anybody terrifies me. I sat up in my reading chair most of the night. Afraid I would dream again if I went to sleep. I kept seeing me and Sally when we were little girls. Sitting on the porch waiting for Daddy to come take us away. He never came. At supper time, Aunt Flo made us some inside and eat supper, such as it was, beans and fried cornbread made with water. Oh, why didn't he come?"

"It's raining too hard to go anywhere today. Just rest, Momma." Callie gently stroked her mother's arm, repeating over and over, "It's okay now. We're here with you."

Eventually, her mother's sobs quieted, and she drifted off to sleep. Callie eased herself off the bed and closed the door as she left. Feeling a bit overwhelmed, she called her brother in Spartanburg. He was with a patient, but the nurse promised to give him the message as soon as he came out of the exam room.

Within a few minutes, Bobby called back. Callie recounted the events of yesterday and this morning. "Sorry, Sis, but it may be like this for a while. Good days and bad days. I imagine Momma never grieved for the loss of her parents. Does she have another appointment this week?"

Callie looked at the wall calendar by the phone. "Yeah, tomorrow."

"Good, encourage her to keep it and to talk to Dr. Avery about losing both parents so young. Also see if she's taking any of her tranquilizer. Reassure her it's okay to take them as prescribed. What you're doing is excellent. Just hang in there. We'll all be down this weekend. Susan will stay since her mother will be here the following Monday."

Callie heard a knock at his office door. "Okay. I won't keep you. I just wanted to be sure I didn't need to get her to the doctor today. We'll be fine. I'll talk to you this weekend." Callie hung up, still feeling a bit overwhelmed.

Without really thinking, Callie called Luke. It seemed strange to talk to him about her mother's troubles, but he listened so well, no judgements or automatic solutions, just allowing her to talk through things. She learned his ex-wife was moving out of the house in Charleston and he planned to put it on the market soon. Callie was relieved to hear that news. She had been afraid that Luke might be more involved with his ex-wife than he said. He still had not found a property on the island that suited him. Before hanging up, she agreed to go out to dinner with him when she got home.

The rain had ended while she was on the phone. Callie sat at the kitchen table with a mug of coffee, looking outside at the bare black trees stretching across scattered dark clouds toward the pale December sun which was beginning to peak through the clouds. *That's the other thing about Columbia. They don't have enough of the year round green of magnolias or live oaks. Everything dies in the winter except the pine trees. Even their green is kind of dull now.*

"A penny for your thoughts," her mother said as she sat down at the table with her own coffee.

Callie shook herself from her thoughts, amazed that she hadn't heard her mother come into the kitchen and get her coffee. "Nothing too specific, just missing the island. No matter how much I enjoy being here with you and Dad, I always miss all the life on the island, except mosquitoes. I will never miss them." Callie chuckled, trying to lighten the mood.

"Even as a child, you would tell me we didn't have enough birds in Columbia. So, when are you going back?" Her mother smiled.

"I talked to Bobby while you were resting. I'll probably go home this weekend. Bobby and his family are coming then. Susan is going to stay for a while. But Bobby wanted to know if you were taking any of your new medicine?" Callie hoped she didn't sound like they were all checking up on her mother.

"Just sometimes. I'm afraid I'll get addicted to it. I don't want to go through another time like Thanksgiving again." Her mother's knuckles were white against the yellow coffee mug.

"Bobby suggested you take the medicine the way Dr. Avery prescribed it. He thinks you're being too hard on yourself by not taking any of the tranquilizer." Callie reached across the table to hold her mother's hand briefly.

"Maybe they're right, Bobby and Dr. Avery. I'll try that and see how I feel." Her mother nodded to emphasize her determination.

The rest of the week passed quietly. Her mother went to her appointments with Dr. Avery on her own and seemed more relaxed. After breakfast on Friday, they began loading the dishwasher. The worst of the withdrawal actually happened over Thanksgiving. Dr. Avery and

I will work on my fears of abandonment. And the fear I have of us losing everything. As much as I enjoy having you here, I know you have to get back home," her mother said as they loaded the dishwasher after breakfast.

"Yeah, I don't have any Christmas decorations up at the house. Kim and I usually pick out the tree and decorate it together. Fortunately, I've done most of my shopping. I know Alma and Max have decorated the store. Momma, she's growing up so fast. Just a few years and she'll be off to college. It will be so weird. So, is this what your fear's like?" Callie looked up from the dishwasher to her mother.

"Maybe a little." Her mother shrugged. "I didn't mind you growing up, except I couldn't protect you if you were far away. Like I said before, after Joe died, I was so afraid. I didn't want you and Kim to live like Sally and I did with Aunt Flo. Sometimes the fear paralyzed me. Then I would lash out. Or I took so many pills, I was in a stupor. Besides all that, I was afraid. Afraid I had what my mother had. That I gave it to you or Bobby while I was carrying you. Then, too, I didn't want people to think I was crazy." Her mother's voice faltered.

"Ah, I get it a little now." Callie closed the dishwasher and hugged her mother. "But we know mental illness isn't 'catching' and we treat it like anything else. And you're on the right path now, even though it's rocky sometimes. I'm proud of you."

Her mother closed her eyes a moment before looking at her daughter and smiling. "Thanks. Even though you've known how I came up for a while now, I wasn't sure you would understand the way it made me feel. How about we decorate for Christmas? Everything except the tree and outside lights. Dad will get the outside. Didn't you say Bobby and his family were coming down this weekend? The kids always like helping with the tree. Then you can go back tonight after supper or tomorrow morning."

"They'll be here tomorrow. I'll wait until they're here before I go home. I'll start getting boxes from the attic. After we set up the tree, we can put up the garland and redo the curio cabinet."

"I'll get something out for supper while you put the tree together." Several years ago, Callie's parents had purchased an artificial tree. Although Callie still preferred a fresh, cut tree, she could see how it made life easier for her parents.

When her mother came into the living room, they found a radio station playing Christmas music and sang along while decorating. By the time Callie's dad got home, there were stockings hung from the mantle.

"Oh, we are having Christmas," he said, smiling at his own joke.

"We got sidelined for a little while, but Callie and I made up for lost time today," her mother laughed. "Maybe you could get the lights on the tree so the children could decorate this weekend?"

"I'll do that tonight. Then I can get the outside lights up in the morning. Something smells good. What's for supper?" Her dad started digging in the box labeled 'Christmas Lights'.

"Ham and potato soup with cornbread, of course. I'll start the cornbread in a few minutes." Her mother turned back to the mantle to rearrange the Christmas stockings. A few years ago, she made a Christmas stocking for each member of the family.

"Sounds great. I'll go change and start on the tree lights," Her dad said as he headed down the hall towards their bedroom.

Later, over supper, Callie told her parents about the plans to add an apartment over the newest section of the gallery. "We'll have an alcove downstairs leading to the apartments, much like we have over the store."

"Do you think you'll be able to keep it rented?" her mother asked between bites of soup.

"When we advertised to rent the apartment Luke is in, the number of applicants was unbelievable. In the end, there were ten excellent potential tenants. We'd rather have full-time tenants, but we could do summer rentals if we need to." Callie explained around a spoonful of the thick, hearty soup. Her parents were excited about the changes in the Emporium.

After supper, the three of them spent a quiet night watching *Back to the Future*. Her dad had picked it up at Blockbusters on his way home from work. *Maybe I should get us a VCR for Christmas. I don't know why I didn't think of it before.* They laughed hilariously at the byplay between Marty and the Professor, but were stifling yawns by the movie's end. With hugs for her parents, Callie went to bed. She was asleep as soon as she snuggled into the covers.

Before Bobby and his family arrived the next morning, Callie had stripped and remade the bed she slept in. In fact, she was putting away the freshly laundered sheets when she heard their car pull into the gravel driveway. She joined her parents on the porch to welcome everyone and help bring in suitcases from the cars.

While the other adults carried the bags down the hall to the bedroom and den, Callie's mother asked, "Is anyone hungry? I fried extra bacon at breakfast so we could have BLT's for lunch."

"BLT's that sounds fantastic." "I'm starved." "Can I have mine toasted?" All the kids answered at once, as the adults nodded their heads in approval of the menu.

"Okay, let me make some toast and set up everything at the table and we can all make our own."

During lunch, they made plans for the weekend. The children were excited to be decorating another tree. It seemed no one in the family could resist helping to get ready for Christmas. Shortly after, Callie said her goodbyes.

17

December 1986

Callie couldn't remember being so excited to see her house, since she and Kim left her parents' home in Columbia after the hurricane. Her chest heaved with a tremendous sigh of relief as the white Cape Cod with its black shutters filled her vision while she parked the car. So much had happened during the last week it seemed she had been away for a month. Putting her suitcase inside the front door, Callie hurried across the yard to Alma's.

"Knock-knock. Hello, anybody home?" Callie called as she stepped into the kitchen.

"Momma, is that you?" Kim answered from the living room. Before Callie could leave the kitchen, Kim was there, wrapping her in a giant bear hug. "I'm so glad you're home."

"I've missed you too, sweetie. Where's Alma?" Callie held her daughter tightly.

"She's at the store. Usually I go with her, but I wanted to wait here for you. I'll grab my stuff. Can we to go see her and let her know I'll be at home? They've done so much work on the gallery." Breathless, Kim finally stopped talking.

"Yeah, we can go down to the store. Let's get you stuff over to the house. I've put my bag inside already. Maybe we can get a tree today." Callie laughed at her daughter's excitement.

"I'll get my bags." Kim darted from the kitchen and back to her mother.

After leaving her bags on their back porch and joining her mother in the car, Kim began an update of happenings on the island while Callie was in Columbia. "You know, Brenda is having a hard time with Matt. He's been skipping school. She was looking for you on Wednesday." Barely pausing to take a breath, Kim continued. "Are you going to date Luke? I think he's okay if that matters. He's been working with Max and Alma on the gallery extension a lot. He always asks about you. Oh, and how is Grandma? When we talked on the phone, it sounded like she was doing better." With a wide grin, Kim was about to start up again when Callie interrupted.

"Whoa, slow down. I can't answer all that at once," Callie chuckled. "Besides, we're already at the store. Short answer, Grandma's better. Luke and I talked about going out to dinner while I was in Columbia, and we'll see where it goes. I'll call Brenda. Since tomorrow is Sunday, we'll have a day to catch up before you're back at school. I've missed you, too. I've never been away from you for so long." Callie hugged her daughter again before they got out of the car. "Come on. Let's let everyone know I'm back."

Inside, they found Max and Alma looking over the remodeling plans. "Hey, everybody. I found my way back. What's going on?" Callie said, moving across the store.

"Oh, they're supposed to start on the apartments tomorrow. We were thinking about squeezing in a small laundry room," Max said, giving Callie a hug and making room for her at the counter.

"I don't know about changing the plans so late in the game. What brought this up for discussion?" Callie asked with a slight frown.

"Actually, the contractor did. He has plans that would put the laundry room in the hall next to the bathroom. It would look like a closet basically. Of course, we would put in a washer and dryer. Here, look at this." Alma said as she slid the plans closer to Callie and gave her friend a hug.

After looking at the plans for a few minutes, still frowning, Callie asked, "So how much more will this cost? I mean, it looks like a good idea, and we'll be able to charge more for an apartment with a washer and dryer. But I haven't kept up with the running costs of the remodel."

"We're still well within budget," Max put in. "Luke and the artists guild gave us the names of suppliers for the lighting and a system for hanging art on the walls. Because we're working with the artists' guild, we'll be able to get a discount. So, there's some savings there."

"Well, I guess we should go for it," Callie laughed quietly. "I thought I was just coming down to let you guys know I was back."

"What are you and Kim doing for supper?" Max asked, rolling up the plans.

"I hadn't really thought about it. Kim and I were just going to hang out at the house until Monday," Callie said, shrugging.

"Why don't you guys come over? Louise has a big pot of oyster stew on. Alma and Luke will be there. Maybe Steve and the kids." Max turned to go back to the office area.

Callie looked at her daughter's bobbing head before answering and laughed. "Alright, what time is supper? I'd like to freshen up a bit after the drive."

"Come on over when you've done that. I know you just got back, so don't worry about bringing anything. I'll call Louise so she'll know to expect you. We're about to close up here, anyway," Max said over his shoulder.

"Okay, see everyone later," Callie said as she and Kim turned to leave the store.

At home, Callie pulled a pan of yeast rolls out of the freezer. While making some to take to Columbia for Thanksgiving, she had frozen another pan to use later. "I think these will thaw while I shower and change. Guess we'll get a tree tomorrow or Monday after school."

"Momma, Max said not to bring anything," Kim insisted, while watching her mother unwrap the rolls.

"I know, honey, but it's not polite to go to supper without bringing something. You know that. We can just pop these in the oven and they'll be ready in no time." Callie went to her bedroom.

Out of the shower, Callie put the rolls in the oven while she finished getting ready. As the oven's timer dinged, Callie went into the kitchen to find Kim pulling the rolls out. "Shall I just wrap them up before putting the basket in the cooler, Momma?"

"That's my girl. I knew you'd been paying attention all these years. Let me grab my purse and we can go." Callie walked toward the front door.

Everyone seemed to reach Max and Louise's at the same time. Inside, there was a bit of shuffling to get the kids set up for video games in the living room as the adults gathered in the kitchen.

"Here you go, Louise. Just some rolls to go with supper," Callie said, handing Louise the basket.

"Girl, you don't listen. You didn't have to do that," Max laughed, shaking his head.

"They just called to me from the freezer and besides, with this crew, there can never be too much bread," Callie said.

Soon everyone gathered at the table. The conversation was lively as the kids talked about their video game prowess and the adults tried to catch up. Steve's law practice was going well, and he was doing some pro bono work with the legal aid society. Now that their children were older, his wife, Tina, had returned to the office as his paralegal. Years ago, people had thought Callie and Steve might be an item. Although they had attended several rallies and worked on community projects together, neither of them had felt any spark of attraction other than a deep friendship. Callie was glad to see her friend's happiness.

After supper, Callie slipped outside for a few minutes, breathing deeply to gather as much of the salt air in her lungs as she could while gazing at the stars shining brightly in the ink black sky. *Okay, now I can only smell home. Funny how I always have to get the smell of other places out of my nose,* she thought. The closing door let her know she was not alone. She smiled to herself as she realized Luke had followed her onto the porch.

"Hey, are you exhausted yet?" he leaned on the porch railing next to her.

"Yeah, just a bit. Being in Columbia was mentally exhausting. But I'm glad I was able to be there for my parents. It is good to be home, though." Callie tried to ignore the tingle she felt as their arms brushed. She was glad the moonless night hid her blush.

"So, what are your plans for the upcoming week?" Shifting his position on the rail, Luke turned to face her.

"Just the store and Kim. I don't think her band recital is until next week, though." Callie tried to keep her voice steady.

"Come out to dinner with me. How about Thursday?" Luke watched her face closely.

"I'd like that." Callie turned to meet his gaze.

"Where would you like to go?" Luke shifted a little closer to her.

"You have to know I don't go out much. You choose. Somewhere between jeans and evening wear. Somewhere we can just talk for a while without the waiter rushing us out," she laughed. "Not much help, am I?"

"Okay, I think I know a place. There's an inn near Mount Pleasant. On a Thursday, it should be just right," Luke suggested after a little thought and leaned toward Callie.

As he leaned even closer, Callie thought, hoped, he was going to kiss her, but the back door opened as Steve and Tina joined them on the porch. Callie and Luke laughed as they straightened up like two high school students caught making out at the school dance.

"Oh, sorry, guys," Tina chuckled. "We were just coming out to say good night before rounding the kids up."

"It's been so good to see you guys again, Tina. I suppose I should help Louise clean up and head home myself," Callie said as she gave her old friends a hug.

"Oh no. We put the kids in charge of cleanup. If I know my mom, she'll probably rearrange that dishwasher, but at least it's all in there." Steve grinned at Callie's discomfort a moment ago.

"Alright then, I'll go in and say my goodbyes." Looking back at Luke, she added, "Call me tomorrow."

The next morning, Callie woke up early. Leaving a note for Kim, she filled her Thermos with coffee, wrapped a blanket around herself like a shawl, and headed to the beach. The rising fog still cloaked much of the beach with a wispy mist. Spanish moss fluttered in the live oaks as the slight breeze rippled its way through the trees, moving on to ruffle the marsh grasses, causing the sea oats to rustle as Callie made her way across the sand. Sand pipers sought their early morning meal at the water's edge. Deciding on a spot, Callie spread her blanket before sitting down. *Ah, this is what I've been missing. Fresh salty ocean breezes. The crashing waves as the tide moves out. I'm home.* She thought as she breathed deeply.

Callie heard sand shifting before she saw him. "Hey, hope I'm not intruding. I'll move on if you want to be alone, but thought it would be rude not to speak." Luke paused near the blanket.

"No, come on, have a seat. I've reconnected with the ocean, so all is well." Callie patted a spot next to her on the blanket. *Nice he didn't walk up so close I had to crane my neck to talk to him.*

"If your parents are in Columbia, how did you wind up here?" Luke settled on the small blanket and looked out over the ocean.

"Well, we lived here before I started school. Then the mills moved to Columbia and my family went with them. My Aunt Sally left me the house when she died. Columbia was never home, so after Joe and I married, we moved to Charleston. Once we finished renovating the house, we moved here." Callie continued watching the waves.

"That's cool. Choosing where you're going to live. I've lived in or around Charleston all my life. How long were you and Joe married?" Luke turned to look at Callie.

"We were married for five years; he died shortly after Kim was born." Callie glanced at Luke's face before dropping her gaze.

"I'm sorry. I shouldn't have." Luke touched Callie lightly on the arm.

"No, it's fine." Callie shook her head before continuing. "The time Joe and I had was wonderful. We were such kids, though, renovating that old house in spurts as we saved enough money for each project. But time moves on. A part of me will always love him, but I'm not stuck in the past. It was rough for a while selling on the pier when Kim was so small. Then the hurricane took out the pier. But then we bought the store. Can't complain. Life's been good."

"So, why haven't you remarried?" Luke began playing with the sand, letting it run through his fingers.

"Wow, you're getting all the hard questions out of the way fast," Callie laughed. "I thought this would come at dinner Thursday."

"While I was out walking, you were on my mind. I didn't mean to upset you." Luke brushed the sand off his hands and turned to look at Callie.

"Oh, no. You didn't. I was just surprised." She turned her head to see his face, hoping she could judge his reaction to her next words. "I tried dating for a while. It just didn't work out. As Kim grew older, she knew I went out, but I didn't involve anyone in her life since it never became serious. I discovered I'm not casual about such things. Then too, I've gotten used to making my own decisions, especially for the business. Not always a trait admired in a woman. Then I got busy raising Kim and developing the business." Callie shrugged.

"Well, the business stuff makes sense to me. It belongs to you and your partners. And Kim's nearly grown." Luke looked away for just a moment before looking back at Callie.

"Since we're asking all the hard stuff. I know you said you and your ex couldn't have children. And that's what ultimately ended your marriage. Do you still want children?" Callie held her breath.

"Not now. For a while I did. But I never found the right person. And now, from what I understand, I'd have to marry someone a good bit younger than me and that's not what I want either." Luke paused before continuing. "Besides, I'd be an old man trying to teach them to throw a baseball. So, no children and I don't like casual either."

They stopped talking and just sat shoulder to shoulder. The wind picked up, and Callie rested her head on his shoulder as Luke pulled the blanket over their shoulders. *It's still just as peaceful as when I was sitting alone. Can this be a real thing?* With the suddenness that can happen on the coastline, clouds gathered and threatened rain.

With a shiver, Callie pulled away and stood up. "I'd better get home before the rain starts. Kim wasn't up when I left this morning."

"Did you walk or drive?" Luke stood up as well.

"I walked, but it's fine." Callie began brushing of her clothes and shaking sand from the blanket.

"Walk up to my car and I'll drive you home. Look out over the ocean; the rain is coming in now." Luke pointed eastward.

"Okay."

They were quiet on the short drive to Callie's. As they pulled into the driveway, Callie cleared her throat. "I'd really love to spend the rest of the day with you. But I promised Kim I would spend the day with her since I've been out of town."

"I get it. I'm sure I'll see you at the store. And Thursday. Is six thirty, okay?" Luke asked as Callie gathered her things.

"That sounds fantastic. I'll see you then, if not before," Callie said, getting out of the car.

Kim bounced out of her room as Callie came through the front door. "So, who was that?"

"Luke, we met up on the beach. It started raining, so he brought me home," Callie said as she made her way to the kitchen, with Kim trailing behind her.

"Why didn't you ask him in? I'm pretty sure he likes you. Don't you like him?" Kim sat down at the table.

"Slow down. Too many questions at once. He didn't come in because I promised this day to you. Even if we just watch old TV movies.

And yeah, we like each other. We're going out to dinner Thursday," Callie said as she rummaged in the pantry for a bagel.

"That's cool. I got breakfast while you were out. What do you want to do today?" Kim fiddled with the napkin holder on the table.

"It's up to you." Callie popped the bagel in the toaster before searching in the refrigerator for cream cheese.

"Let's just watch movies and eat junk food today. We haven't had one of those days in a long time."

"I like it. No need to go anywhere. We can get the tree tomorrow and then put it up."

They made Jiffy Pop popcorn and sat stretched out at either end of the couch, covered with a blanket. During commercials and sometimes over the movie, Callie updated Kim on her grandmother. Kim filled Callie in on things at school and with her friends. Then she plied Callie with questions about Luke, so Callie let her know that although it was too early to even call it a relationship, she felt this was moving the way she wanted.

"I've always worried about you being alone oncc I go to college and get out on my own. You stay busy and have friends, I know that. I just feel you need someone special. I won't be able to come home every weekend, you know." Kim sighed.

"Sweetie, don't worry about me. Just live your life like you want. Whatever happens, I'll be fine. But tell me, have you met anyone special?"

"Nah, most of the guys at school are into cheerleaders, not band members. You know I have friends; you've met them all." Kim shook her head. "I know you and Dad met in high school, but I don't think about getting married or serious dating. When I get to nursing school, I won't have time for much of a social life anyway."

"You have so many more options than I did at your age. No need to worry now about who you're going to marry or when. I think learning to be a good friend is important in relationships. If it's what you want at some point, you'll be an amazing partner and mother. Just remember to be true to yourself." Callie stifled a yawn.

Before the movie's end, mother and daughter drifted off to sleep. They didn't wake until nearly suppertime. After stretching, they both grinned sleepily.

"What an exciting pair we are," Callie said. "But it was good talking with you. I didn't realize I was still so tired. Are you hungry? We could make a pizza run."

"No. We've still got stuff for sandwiches and some chips. I'll get something in a while. Right now, home is the perfect place to be," Kim said as she burrowed back into the blanket.

18

Second Week of December 1986

Callie and Kim managed to get the tree up on Sunday. The renovations and planning for the reopening celebrations kept Callie busy. She talked with her parents to find all was well in Columbia.

Before she knew it, Callie was staring into her closet, trying to decide what to wear. *Of course a dress, but which one?* She pulled out two dresses. Holding a dress in front of her, she looked in the mirror. *No, not the navy polka dot. I look good in it but it's too dressy. I don't really like the red print for tonight either.* Putting them back in the closet, Callie rifled through a couple more dresses. A mid-length sleeveless sundress in deep royal blue with a paisley print of green and yellow caught her eye. The dress was slightly fitted through the bust and waist and the hem fell just below her knees. It really accentuated her athletic frame while still being feminine. *Ah this one.* Her wedge canvas espadrilles were nearly a perfect match for green in the dress and the rope detail along the sole made them perfect for wearing with a sundress. *The espadrilles make it look a little dressy without being too much.*

She would carry a cardigan just in case it got chilly later. Combing out her long dark brown hair, Callie debated cutting it for the millionth time. But she liked the diversity of styling long hair and tonight put it up in a loose Gibson-girl bun. A touch of mascara on the long lashes around her dark brown eyes and lipstick completed her look. Just as she finished, the phone rang.

"Hey, has Kim eaten?" Luke asked. He spoke loudly and she could hear voices in the background.

"No," Callie answered. "She just got in from practice a few minutes ago."

"Good, I picked up a pizza for her. I'll see you in a few minutes." Callie heard him thank someone for letting him use the phone as he hung up.

Luke arrived wearing a collared polo shirt, khakis, and loafers. His admiring look let Callie know she had chosen her outfit well. *We actually look good together.*

Kim came out of the kitchen. "Pizza. Thanks, but you didn't have to do that." She took the offered pizza.

"It seemed like the thing to do since I'm running off with your mother tonight," Luke said.

"Now don't you kids stay out too late. I have school and she has work tomorrow," Kim said, shaking her finger at her mother and laughing as she played the parental role.

"Yes, ma'am," Luke and Callie laughed as they played along.

Ever the gentleman, Luke opened the car door for Callie before climbing into the driver's seat and asking, "Would you like to listen to the radio?"

"No. Sometimes after a day in the store, I don't even turn on the TV when I get home—especially if it's busy like today. I'm not complaining, but we're usually quieter now. Maybe people are Christmas shopping early."

"Maybe. I was at a guild meeting last week and everyone says they're having record sales from your gallery. I know they're really excited about your expansion," Luke said as they crossed the bridge to Mount Pleasant.

"Having the artists' work displayed in the store has honestly been mutually beneficial. Most of our seafood and produce sales are commercial now. Although we still have some customers who bought from me when I was selling shrimp and crab from the pier."

"Here we are. Let me get that door for you." Luke popped out of the car.

Deftly he opened the door and helped Callie out of his low slung Porsche. "This is such a lovely setting. You could almost miss it from the road," she said.

The inn looked as if it had been standing for at least a hundred years. The yellow two story building had wide porches that swept around three sides of each level. The owner had spread wicker furniture throughout the porches. Small lanterns provided just enough light to make your way through the furniture without blinding anyone nearby. Inside, Callie found the same simple understated elegance.

The maître de guided them to a small circular booth near a large window. From there, they could look out over the ocean. Promptly, a waiter took their drink orders. After looking the menu over, Callie decided on sword fish in a lemon butter sauce with the house vegetables. Luke went with a steak and baked potato. They declined an appetizer, deciding that coffee and dessert would be in order later. That taken care of, they settled back against the booth's cushions, sipping their drinks.

"So, how did you find this place? It's elegantly gorgeous without being flamboyant." Callie looked around discreetly.

"I've been here with some of my buddies from the restaurant. You know how it is, if you work in a restaurant, you find places to go where you don't run into your customers."

"I've heard that before. Have you decided what to do about the house?"

"I'm going to put it on the market at the first of the year. Right now, I'm having it painted. I don't want to live in Charleston anymore. I've gotten used to the quiet of the island." Luke looked at Callie over his drink.

Callie studied the ice in her gin and tonic for a moment. Looking up, she saw Luke was still looking at her. Taking a deep breath, she asked. "So, what are you going to do?"

"That depends on a few things." Callie's eyes grew wide as she held her breath. Luke reached out to hold her hand lightly. "Easy there. No pressure. I meant what I said on the beach. But I want to know you better and Kim, too."

Callie took a slow breath. "That's what I want too. I know you know I've been attracted to you since we first met. Just now I was afraid you were moving off somewhere as we were just getting to know each other."

"No, not going anywhere. The apartment suits my needs for now. I'll invest the money from the sale of the house and see what the future holds. Just so you know, my investments are doing well. I'll probably sell the Porsche too. This is the first time it's been out of the garage in weeks. The Jeep is more practical on the island. I just thought the Porsche would be fun tonight." Luke grinned sheepishly.

"It definitely is fun. But what's this about working as a maître de to pay the bills?" Callie raised her eyebrows.

Luke ducked his head and nearly blushed. "A friend needed some help, and I had time on my hands. It took me a while to get in a rhythm with my painting. Besides, sometimes I enjoy being just a regular guy, not a Porsche driving investment banker."

"Ah, I see." Callie smiled.

Their meals arrived, and they spent the next few minutes enjoying their food. Conversation turned to discussions of different things they liked and Callie's plans for the store and Kim's plans for college.

"She's a smart young lady," Luke said between bites of his steak.

"She's been around so many adults all her life. I was worried, at least until she and I talked this weekend, that she would feel she had to stay close so I wouldn't be alone. I think I've made her see I'll be okay."

Luke laughed. "Now I understand why she has been not so subtly quizzing me."

Callie joined in his laughter. "Yeah, she's told me several times, 'I think he likes you. Do you like him?' Silly girl trying to play matchmaker for her mother."

Over coffee and dessert, Callie invited him to supper at the house on Saturday. "Nothing fancy. I do seafood but the old island way."

"I'd like that. Would you like anything else?" When Callie said no, Luke motioned for the check.

After Luke settled the bill and they were in the car again, he asked. "How about a walk on the beach before I take you home?"

"A perfect ending to this evening." Callie leaned back comfortably in her seat.

She slipped off her espadrilles as Luke parked near the beach. Luke took off his loafers and rolled up his pant legs. Light from the full moon sparkled like diamonds across the calm ocean. A gentle breeze tugged at Callie's dress. Soon, the incoming tide sent the diamonds flying as white-capped waves began crashing nearer to the shore. They walked hand in hand for a few minutes. Callie turned to catch something Luke said over the waves and moved into what became an embrace and a kiss. *Such tenderness and passion.* After another kiss, she stood in his embrace with her head on his chest for a moment.

"I think I should go home now." Callie stepped back and smiled at him.

"Probably for the best." Luke pulled her in for a quick kiss. "Just so you don't forget," he laughed quietly as he stepped away.

He walked her to the door, even though Callie insisted she lived in the safest possible neighborhood. "I don't even lock my doors," she laughed. After a kiss filled with longing, Luke stepped back.

"I'll see you tomorrow, I'm sure." He started down the steps.

"Yes, and don't forget about Saturday," Callie said as she stood in the open doorway.

"No way I'd forget that," Luke called over his shoulder as his long strides took him back to the car.

Inside she saw Kim curled up asleep on the couch. Covering her daughter with a blanket, Callie went to bed. *I think I'll be reading for a while tonight. So much is running around in my brain. I'm going to have to watch myself. It seems so perfect. I don't want this to turn into a thing like it was with Michael. I don't think it will.* Thinking of their kisses as she fell asleep, Callie didn't notice when her book fell across her chest.

19

Friday, December 1986

Callie was glad to see Brenda come into the store around three. "Hey, traveler. I wasn't sure you were coming back," Brenda teased.

"You know better than that. What are you up to tonight? Why don't you and the boys come by for supper?" Callie hugged her friend.

"I might come by after the boys go with Mike. Matt is giving me fits. I can't seem to get across it to him; he needs to stay in school. Oh, it's too much to go into now. I'll see you about seven." Brenda turned to leave.

"Sure, I'll see if Josie can join us. We haven't had a girls' night since the beginning of October."

Kim got off the bus, and after talking with her mother for a few minutes, went into her room at the back of the store to start her homework. Although Kim didn't hang out at the store as much these days, they still maintained "her room" there. A good student, she wanted to get her assignments done now. She was going to a movie with friends tonight after supper and there were other plans for the weekend as well.

Lord, I'm so thankful Kim's a good kid. I don't know how I'd deal with it if she had a rebellious streak. It wasn't long before the builders cleaned up and headed out for the weekend. They planned to finish the apartments next week. Hopefully, people would start calling in response to the ad placed in the paper.

"I've got everything finished for school. Do you need help with anything?"

"No. I'll be closing up soon. I've locked up, and the trash is out. Pam and Josie are coming by after supper. Are you still going to the movies with Ashley?" Callie asked as she zeroed out the register and placed the printout, along with the day's receipts, in a bank bag.

"Yeah, we're going to see *The Color Purple* for English credit. I don't know why they don't just let us read the book." Kim rolled her eyes. "Your date went well last night, I guess. I mean, he's coming over Saturday. That's never happened before."

"I had a great time, but I'd like you to meet him and tell me how you feel. Even though you're graduating next year, I wouldn't want to be with someone if you hated him."

"From what I've seen of him around here, and if you like him, I'm sure I will, too. Maybe Scrabble before dinner tomorrow?" Kim walked with her mother toward the back of the store.

"Sounds good, let's close up and get home. Oh, who's driving tonight?"

"Ashley's mother." Kim called over her shoulder as she went to grab her bag.

Josie and Brenda arrived shortly after Kim left. After exchanging hugs, the women settled in the living room, where Callie poured them each a glass of wine.

"So, what's been going on while I was up in Columbia?" Callie asked, handing a glass to each of her friends before picking up her own glass.

The conversation stalled for a few minutes as they sipped their wine. All their lives had gotten so busy. Not like the old days when they all talked nearly every day. Still, once they got together, things fell back into place.

"Matt keeps skipping school and I'm pretty sure he's smoking pot," Brenda let out in a rush. "I tried to get Mike to talk with him, but that was worthless." She stared into the glass she twirled by its stem.

"At least it's just pot," Callie offered, looking closely at Brenda seeing the dark circles under her eyes again.

"I know, but he can still get arrested. Not that I'd tell him, but it's skipping school that bothers me the most." Brenda's shoulders slumped.

"Is something new going on?" Josie asked.

"Even more than Lee, Matt never adjusted to me going to work. Hell, it's been nearly eight years. He tried to talk his dad into letting them live with him," Brenda said, scowling. "But Mike doesn't want to upset his current girlfriend. I just don't know. Half the time, Mike doesn't see them when it's his time with them. He cut their last summer visit short by two weeks." Brenda sighed and sipped her wine.

"So sorry, Brenda. How do the boys get on with your dad?" Callie asked as she over pat Brenda's arm.

"Funny, you should ask. I'm thinking about moving to Columbia. Dad and the boys get along well. Since he's retired now, he'd be able to take them hunting and fishing. I know they miss doing that with Mike. There's a house near Mom and Dad's place that I can rent for a while. We'll probably sell the house here. I always wanted the boys to have it, but with it sold, I could buy a house in Columbia." Brenda frowned in thought a minute, before continuing. "Yeah, talking about it out loud has helped me decide," Brenda added as a slow smile spread across her face.

"Well, you just tell us what help you need. You know we'll do whatever it takes," Josie offered, before turning to Callie. "So, spill it. Who are you dating? Didn't I see a Porsche in your driveway earlier this week? Don't answer yet. Does anyone want another drink?"

Brenda and Callie held up their glasses for refills. After pouring the wine and grinning from ear to ear, Josie said, "Okay, now I'm ready for all the juicy details."

"I went to dinner with Luke Branson," Callie said, purposely dragging things out to tease her friends.

"Come on, don't make me beg," Brenda giggled.

"Alright, Luke and I went out to dinner in Mount Pleasant. We seem to like each other a lot. We took a walk on the beach after dinner. He's coming over tomorrow to have supper with Kim and me." Callie really didn't like Josie's insistence on having "all the juicy details." Some things were private.

Josie especially enjoyed teasing her bashful friend. "So, have you slept together yet?"

"Oh, come on. You both know I've been too busy raising a child to get into that 'free love' stuff. I tried it a little several years ago, but it's not for me. And I just got back from Columbia. So no, there's been none of that." Callie could feel herself blushing.

"Well, if he's coming here, then you must think this is something serious. Right?" Josie said, tilting her head to look closer at Callie.

"Yeah. We've been able to have some honest conversations about what we want in life. It seems strange to date someone who's living off their investments at our age. I mean, what do you do with yourself if you don't get up for work? I know some of his paintings have sold. Do you paint every day? I don't know." Callie's voice trailed off.

"Isn't that the dream, though? Work hard and then do the thing you really wanted to do while you were working so hard?" Brenda put in as she sat her wineglass on the coffee table.

"You're right. I just can't imagine not getting up and working. But to be honest, running the store is much easier than when I started out," Callie said as she frowned thoughtfully.

"Well, I've heard that managing a portfolio takes some time," Josie giggled. "Not that I have personal experience in these things, but I've read about people who do." She held up a hand to forestall any comments.

"No, I don't think I can fault him for being smart with money," Callie said as she smiled slowly. "You know, he called me nearly every day when I was in Columbia. He'd give me news about the store or Kim, if he'd seen her during the day and make sure I wasn't overwhelmed. Luke always seems to be there when I need help with something, even if it's just to hear about home. Just being in the room with him excites me like nothing I've experienced since Joe died."

"Unless you've got a secret life somewhere, I don't think there's a lot to compare him to." Josie nudged Callie with her elbow.

"No, my love life has been a desert for quite a while now. That's the other thing for a woman of my age..." Callie's voice trailed off again.

"Don't worry about any of that," Brenda said, leaning closer to Callie. "If you're feeling chemistry already, you two will work out the rest."

"Okay, now, enough about me. Josie, how's school going? Still happy majoring in accounting?" Callie said, blushing once again as she tried to get her mind off kissing Luke.

"It's going well. I've got another year to go, but with the kids in high school, it's not too bad. It gets hectic around exams, but I manage. I daydream that when I'm a CPA, I'll make enough money to hire a housekeeper. They may say we can do it all, but there are only so many hours in a day, you know," Josie said, shrugging her shoulders.

"Oh, don't I know it. If I had more than one child, I'm not sure I would have gotten where I am now. Forget about dealing with a husband," Callie laughed.

Talk had turned to more general news about what was going on in the neighborhood by the time Kim returned from the movies. Shortly after, Brenda and Josie left. As always, they promised not to take so long to get together again.

The next morning, Callie woke up a little later than usual. Thankful not to feel hung over after last night's wine, she made her way into the kitchen for coffee. These days, she and Kim were likely to have a bagel or cereal for breakfast. The big country breakfast was a thing for holidays or when family was visiting. It wasn't long before Kim came into the kitchen.

"Morning, Momma. You guys seemed to be having a good time when I came in. Didn't mean to break things up," Kim said as she made a cup of coffee and then poured some cereal and milk into a bowl.

"You didn't. Things were winding down anyway. Not sure Brenda has told the boys, but they're going to move to Columbia. It's a shame the way things worked out between Mike and the boys." Callie sipped her coffee.

"I'm sorry to hear that, Momma. I know you guys have been friends for ages." Kim sat beside her mother at the table.

"I'll miss her. Maybe it will help Matt get turned around. They'll be close to Pam's parents. I'm so proud of the way you are growing up." Callie gave Kim's shoulder a quick squeeze.

Kim ducked her head.. "Thanks. But you're a great example. So, when is Luke coming today?"

"Probably around four. I've got to go into the store for a while. I don't think there's much to do around here to get ready. Do you need to do laundry today?"

"Yeah, I'll do that after breakfast. I could go out for a while after supper if you want some privacy." Kim smiled slyly.

Callie felt the warmth creep up her neck as she blushed. She stared into her coffee cup, trying to hide her face with her hair. "No need for that. The whole point of this is for the three of us to get together. I have to feel we'll all be comfortable together."

"Well, I already know I like him," Kim declared with all the certainty of a teenager with limited life experiences.

"Okay, give me a chance to see for myself." Callie was glad her voice sounded normal.

"Yes, ma'am," Kim laughed, giving Callie a mock salute. "I'm off to get my laundry done, Captain."

Luke arrived promptly at four. He brought poinsettias to add to the Christmas cheer. Supper simmered in the kitchen as the Scrabble tournament began. Kim finished with the high score in the last game as Callie said dinner was probably ready. Kim cleared away the game as Luke and Callie set the table.

"Do you guys always eat supper together?" Luke asked, putting napkins and silverware on the table.

"Most nights. Sometimes our schedules are different, usually because Kim has something with the band. But I try to make this our connecting point in the day," Callie answered, bring a soup tureen to the table and ladling soup into bowls.

"Momma's a fantastic cook," Kim said with a grin as she joined them at the table. "She makes a lot of stuff ahead of time. Then one of us just has to pop it on the stove when we get home."

"Well, got me sold if I can go by this gumbo," Luke said.

Callie sputtered into her iced tea and shook her head at her daughter's brazen attempt at matchmaking. "Kim, let Luke figure out things for himself," Callie said with mock sternness.

"Alright, Momma," Kim said, before turning to Luke. "When did you know you wanted to paint?"

"I've always enjoyed painting. Took a lot of art classes in high school and in my first year of college, but it didn't take long for my dad to take me aside and say painting was no way to make a living," Luke said, shrugging. "So, I started studying finance. Eventually, I went to work in an investment firm. I was lucky and did well with some investments, so now I can just paint. What else do you want to know about me?"

"Are you sad that you don't have children?" Kim asked as she studied Luke's face.

A shadow crossed Luke's face, and Callie's eyes narrowed as she stared at her daughter. "Kim, that's not—"

Luke cut her off. "Excuse me for jumping in, Callie. Normally, I wouldn't do that, but I opened myself up for that one." Luke took a deep breath before answering. "For a long time, I was sad. Now reconciled is probably a better word. Everything about my divorce is complicated. Maybe one day we can talk about it," Luke said without offense.

"Sorry. I didn't really mean to be rude. I just want Momma to be happy. And I worried you might be sad about it; I mean, I don't want her to be sad," Kim said, looking down at her plate.

"It's alright, I see where you're coming from." Then, to lighten the mood, he looked at Callie and laughed. "Wow, after this, I'm not sure about meeting your mom and dad."

"Good thing we're doing one thing at a time, huh?" Callie laughed. "How about another game of Scrabble?"

"Nah, I'm the champ tonight. I think, I have some reading to do for school," Kim said as she excused herself and began clearing the table.

Callie rolled her eyes. "Okay, I'll start some coffee."

"I'll help and it'll be done in no time." Luke joined the efforts to clean the kitchen.

Soon they had the food put away, and the dishwasher loaded. Kim went off to her room while Callie and Luke lingered at the table with coffee.

"I am sorry about Kim's question. She's usually more polite," Callie said after taking a sip of her coffee.

"I told you not to worry about it. I'd rather she ask me things instead of stewing over something," Luke said, reaching out to hold her hand. "What do you do when you're not working? It seems to me you're always in the store."

"I'm usually home. In spring and summer, I work in my garden. I'll still can and freeze food, though not as much as I once did. I design and make the sundresses you see in the store. During the winter, I take it easy. It also seems to be the time we do renovations in the store. Then there's whatever is happening with Kim at school. She's in the band. She'll get her learner's permit soon. I get together with friends. After that, I'm pretty much a homebody." Callie traced the edge of her placemat with the finger of her free hand.

"That's kinda how things have worked out for me. I do a little financial work in the morning. Work on a painting or sketch for the rest of the day. Then it's dinner and afterwards a book or movie." He gave a lopsided grin. "When I was working in Charleston, there were always drinks or dinner with clients or friends. Sometimes out or sometimes at home. I've gotten away from that over the last few years, most of my old friends are still married and don't really understand my choices lately since they're still in the business."

"I've always said once Kim is away in college, I'd like to go on a real vacation. Somewhere outside South Carolina or Georgia. Take a trip across the country to see a baseball game, maybe." Callie smiled enthusiastically as she thought about watching a ballgame in a stadium.

"You're a fan? I usually follow the Braves."

"Oh, yeah. Much to my dad's chagrin, I follow the Mets. He's a Braves fan, too. Hank Aaron was a fantastic player. We usually go to Atlanta a few times a season." Callie was enjoying the straightforward conversation and loosely holding hands at the table, but her body wanted to melt into his embrace again. Still, she didn't want to explain to her teenaged daughter why she and Luke disappeared for a time. Lost in her thoughts, Callie didn't realize Luke had spoken.

"Hey, where'd you go?" Luke asked as he squeezed her hand.

Callie smiled softly. "Thinking of things that might be, could be, but" she cleared her throat, "can't be right now." Letting his hand go, she stood up from the table.

"Ah, seems we're having similar thoughts." He sighed and stood up as well. "Perhaps I should say goodnight to Kim and head home. Will I see you tomorrow?"

"Call me in the afternoon. I'm not sure what's up tomorrow."

They left the kitchen with fingers linked and paused in the living room. "Good night, Kim. We're going to have to do a Scrabble rematch. Can't let you beat me like that," Luke called from the living room.

Kim stuck her head around the door briefly. "You're on. Goodnight. See you later."

They stopped at the door for a lingering kiss. "Okay, I really should go now. I'll call you tomorrow."

From the window, Callie watched him pull out of the driveway before going back to the kitchen. After adding the coffee cups, she started the dishwasher, told Kim good night, and went to bed. Certain she'd have a restless night, Callie started in on her book again, only to fall asleep before she finished the first page.

The morning sun woke Callie. *Guess I'm getting older,* she thought to herself. *I haven't slept this long in a while. It has been a just a little hectic around here. I'll open the store and then hang the garland and wreaths outside. Hopefully, next week we can interview some potential tenants for the apartments and finish arrangements for the gallery's opening.*

After a quick shower, Callie started the coffee. Getting her mug from the cabinet, she was happy she had invested in a Bunn coffee maker a few months ago. It brewed coffee so much faster than other drip coffee makers. Dropping a bagel into the toaster, Callie filled her coffee cup. She had made the pine garland and wreaths already, so putting them up would be a simple task later today. Finishing her quick breakfast, Callie stuck her head into Kim's bedroom to let her know she was leaving. Kim flapped her arm in acknowledgement.

At the store, Callie set up appointments for people to see the apartments on Tuesday. Everything looked on schedule to have the gala reopening on New Year's Eve. For this first event, there was a featured artist in the largest of the new rooms. The smaller rooms would have works displayed as well. Several artists and craftspeople were bustling around, changing the displays in the older section while setting up the new rooms. A few years ago, the Emporium began shortening their hours the week after Christmas. Everyone would surely be ready for the break this year.

The bell at the front door jingled, and Callie looked up to see Max. "Hey, I didn't think you were coming today."

"Well, Steve and his family are here. We're doing an early Christmas with them, since they're going to Tina's parents' Christmas Eve. You know, her parents moved to Spartanburg a few years ago. Anyway, I just needed a few minutes away from all the noise for a little while," Max said, walking behind the counter to stand by Callie.

"I know. Every time we get together with Bobby and his family, I wonder how I would have made out with more than one child," Callie laughed. "I've got interviews lined up for next week. Hopefully, we can rent the apartments before I go to my parents' for Christmas."

"Yeah, the business is doing well, but having tenants for the new apartments would be a nice Christmas present. How did things go last night?" Max watched Callie carefully.

"Things seemed to go well." Callie smiled. "He and Kim bantered throughout the evening. I don't think there's anything to worry about there. We'll just see how things go."

"Have you asked Luke to go with you to Columbia?"

"No, I don't think either of us is ready for that," Callie laughed, shaking her head. "We've only gone out once. Still since he's in the store so much and we talked on the phone while I was in Columbia, I feel like I know him pretty well. They'll probably meet at the gala. My parents are planning to come down for it. Like I said, we'll see."

"I suppose I should get back to the family. I just wanted to make sure things went well," Max chuckled.

"Max." Callie exclaimed, hugging him tightly. "You shouldn't be worrying about me. I can look out for myself."

"You're like a daughter to me; you know that. Have been since I first saw you carrying Kim on the pier. But even fierce women can be hurt," Max said as he rubbed his hand across his eyes. "I'll be in tomorrow for a regular day. See you then."

20

Christmas 1986

Christmas morning, Callie and Kim opened their presents before driving to Columbia. Kim was overjoyed to receive a Walkman with a cassette player and thought the VCR was a great family gift. She gave Callie a freshwater pearl necklace and with matching earrings. Luke called to wish them a Merry Christmas. He was visiting his sister in Charlotte. After a leisurely morning, they each packed a few clothes for the trip to Columbia.

Arriving at her parents', Callie was happy to see her brother's family was already there. The drive had been quiet since Kim had brought several tapes for the trip.

"Hi, Sis." Her brother called as he crossed the yard to the car. "Give me a hug. Hey, Kim, Monica's inside waiting for you." After they exchanged welcoming hugs, Bobby carried in their suitcases.

"I'll put these in the bedroom. Susan and Momma are in the kitchen. Think supper's nearly ready."

Joining her mother and sister-in-law in the kitchen, Callie was happy to see her mother clear eyed and energetic. "What needs to be done to get supper on the table?" Callie asked, giving each of the women a hug.

"Nothing really. The ham and mashed potatoes are just about ready. You can start putting things in serving dishes. The kids already set the table," Her mother replied as she peered into the oven. "Susan, why don't you tell everyone to wash up?" Then raising her voice a little she added, "And Bob, come carve the ham." *Good to see Momma back in charge,* Callie thought to herself.

With the ham carved, everyone gathered around the table. This year, everyone squeezed in around the large table which had been set with the Christmas china her mother had purchased on a layaway plan when Callie was a child. She had always loved the holly and ribbons along the plate's edge and the Christmas tree in its center. As she bowed her head for grace, Callie gave silent thanks for her mother's good health.

Once everyone had served themselves, the first few minutes of the meal were quiet as everyone enjoyed the food. Callie's mother was the first to break the silence. "After we open our gifts, I'd like us to visit the nursing home today. I've collected some small gifts that I'd like to deliver. We won't be but an hour or so. I visit a church member there. So many outside people come before Christmas, but not as many today."

"That's a great idea, Momma. I've often thought about doing something like that in Spartanburg." Susan smiled enthusiastically.

Bobby's eyes gleamed devilishly as he looked at his sister. "Sis, who's this Luke person Momma and Dad have been telling mc about?"

Callie surprised herself by not blushing. "He's someone I just started seeing. He and Kim seemed to hit it off well. Right now, he's renting the apartment over the store, so I've actually known him for a while. He's an artist and has done investment banking. Did it well from what I understand. I think he may become an important part of my life."

"Wow," was all Bobby could say at first, then came the inevitable. "When do we get to meet him?"

Callie smiled sweetly at her brother, knowing he was hoping for a big get together in Columbia. "He'll be at the gala, New Year's Eve, when we open the new gallery. I'm sure Mom and Dad will meet him then. As for you and your clan, I don't really know. Guess we'll just have to wait and see."

Bobby gave an exaggerated pout and dropped his head. She really couldn't blame him for wanting to meet Luke here, since Columbia was closer than the island. But that would have to wait.

After supper, the adults put away the food as the children loaded the dishwasher. In the living room, Callie's dad arranged the presents in groups, according to the recipient. Once everyone gathered, he passed out presents. Years ago, as the larger family, they began drawing a name for each adult. Each smaller family group purchased gifts for the children not in their immediate family. The practice started when Bobby was setting up his practice and Callie was a young widow. Even as Bobby and Callie became more affluent, the practice continued, as neither saw the need for the material excesses that often accompanied Christmas.

The visit to the nursing home was a big hit with the residents and the family. The highlight came when a resident, Miss Evelyn, began singing Christmas carols and the whole family joined in. Following Miss Evelyn's lead, the family continued caroling throughout the facility. As they entered the different areas, staff members paused their tasks to sing along and resident's came to their doors to join in. When they wound up near Miss Evelyn's room again, they found her grandchildren and great-grandchildren waiting for her.

Returning home, everyone settled in to relaxing activities. The kids set up the Nintendo on the den television. Adults talked quietly or watched a Hallmark movie. With the main meal over, people went into the kitchen for leftovers as the need arose. Luke called to wish everyone a Merry Christmas. Callie told him about the visit to the nursing home and how much she missed him. They agreed to call each other when they were back home.

21

End of December 1986

Even with the Emporium's shortened hours, the days between Christmas and New Year's Eve were frantic as everyone worked to get ready for the gallery's opening. Steve and Tina were taking their kids to New York for the holiday and invited Kim to join them. They left a few days before the holiday to do some sightseeing. Even before Kim left, Luke had been having supper with them most nights. He seemed to fit into their life effortlessly as he joined in whatever event was happening before going home for the night.

Callie was working in the store's back room when Luke came up behind her and wrapped his arms around her while pulling her close. "Did you put a bag in your car?" Callie asked as she turned and leaned against him.

"Yeah." Luke gave her a crooked smile. "But I've always thought of whisking you away on some romantic getaway."

"Well, we'll miss out on some of the ambiance but, it will definitely be private. And it's somewhere we can get to now." Callie tilted her head to look up at him.

"I know. Maybe I'll call the Inn later and see if they will pull together a dinner for us. They don't usually do take out, but they might make an exception for us." Hearing the bell on the front door, they stood apart.

Running her hands through her hair, Callie went out into the store, meeting the customer halfway. "Hey, Ethel. How are you today?"

"I'm doing good. Do you have any flounder? I'd like about three pounds, if you do," Ethel said as she reached Callie.

"I'm sure we do." Callie went to the back counter with Ethel in her wake.

"We were sure lucky with storms this year." Ethel loved to compare hurricane seasons. "That one in 1970 was bad, but not as bad as the one in 1955."

"That's what I remember my dad saying. Here's your flounder. That'll be four fifty." Callie placed the wrapped fish in a bag.

"Thanks, I can always count on you. Have a happy new year." Ethel counted out her money and handed it to Callie.

"You. too."

Ethel walked over to peek into the gallery on the way to the door. "You sure have come a long way from selling on the pier. I'll just head out now," Ethel said, going to the front door.

"Thanks. See you later, Ethel."

The rest of the day went by quickly. Luke helped her finish placing a few sculptures and paintings before going upstairs to his studio. Edward, the featured artist, stopped in to check out the gallery before his showing. Pleased with the arrangement of his works, he didn't stay long. As she was closing up, Luke phoned to let her know he was picking up dinner before meeting her at her place.

Driving home, Callie had to admit to herself that all the anticipation was getting to her. *It's been a long time since I've been with anyone. I'm not sure what to expect. And then what about later? I know I want this, but how do we do this as adults with lives and responsibilities? What if we aren't compatible in this way? This is silly. It's Luke. He's probably the most understanding man I've ever known. Just slow down and breathe.* Callie told herself.

Callie took a quick shower once she got home. Deciding what to wear caused another moment of near panic. Laughing at herself, she decided on a on a rose pink casual dress and sandals. She had pulled a small rectangular table and two chairs near the fireplace in the living room before going to work this morning. She was just putting candles on the table when she heard Luke's car in the driveway. Taking a deep breath, she went to the porch to greet him.

"Do you need any help?" Callie called out from the porch.

"No, I think I've got it. I'll be there in a minute," Luke said as he waved before reaching into the Jeep for several bags.

After an enthusiastic embrace, they parted after nearly falling over the bags containing dinner. "Okay. Let's see what we've got here." Luke ran a hand through his auburn hair to move it away from his forehead. "They said we should warm the main course in the oven for about ten minutes at 200 hundred degrees."

"I'll get this in the oven while you set up the appetizers and open the wine. I think I left the opener on the table," Callie said. She took one bag to the kitchen and put the main course in the oven before returning to the living room.

"I like that we're side by side here." Luke gave her a quick hug as he pulled out her chair before pouring the wine and sitting beside her.

"Well, the table's really too narrow for anything else." *Wow, that sounds silly.* Callie thought to herself.

"Here's to us," Luke said as they raised their glasses. "So, tell me. Am I being unnecessarily suspicious? Seems odd to me that Steve and his family would decide to go to New York for New Year's Eve when you guys have the gala scheduled. I figured he'd want to be here to celebrate with his dad."

"I admit it could look odd, but he promised his kids this trip months ago. Asking Kim to go along was a last-minute decision. How did you talk the Inn into doing take out?"

"Well, I didn't have to talk too hard. We have gone there a few times. Just told them an incredibly special woman and I had planned an evening in," Luke chuckled. "Even so, I had to go in through the kitchen entrance. I've also sworn us to secrecy about the source of our dinner."

Callie laughed. "Well, I don't think either of us can rival Dante's cooking, so I want to go back. The secret is safe with me. It is nice to just sit here and enjoy it rather than going out."

Occasional light touches kept their passion flaring through dinner. Although there was mousse in the refrigerator, of one accord they skipped dessert in favor of other pleasures.

Unable to stretch out fully, Callie woke up once near dawn and spooned to Luke's back. Still asleep, he reached to hold her hand. *All I could have hoped for and more. Brenda was right to say we'd work it all out.* No sooner than the thoughts drifted through her mind, she was asleep again.

Sun streaming through her bedroom window woke her up. She reached for Luke and was startled when he wasn't beside her. Noises from the kitchen gave her reassurance from the momentary doubts that her impressions of last night were mistaken. Slipping into a robe, she went into the kitchen.

"Morning sleepy head. Coffee's ready." Luke handed her a cup of the steaming brew. "I found the makings for omelets, but I'm not sure if you eat right away or need a little time first."

"Usually, it's coffee first, shower and then eat, but I today I'm feeling kind of hungry, so whenever you're ready to cook, I'll eat." Callie re-arranged the chairs at the kitchen table so they could sit side by side.

Within a few minutes, they were both enjoying their omelets. "This is fantastic."

"Why thank you, ma'am. We bachelor guys got to learn to cook or be a slave to take out or a microwave. Seriously though, what do you have to do today?" Luke looked up from his plate to gauge her response.

"Nothing really. I finished the gallery yesterday. Max and Alma have everything else covered. What are you up to?" Callie leaned her head on his shoulder.

"I don't have anything pressing. What if we just spend a leisurely day together? Maybe hang out here for a while. Maybe later go out for some lunch? And then see what happens?"

"I'd like that a lot. In a couple of days, we won't have so much alone time. My parents are staying here for the gala and, of course, Kim will be back." Callie frowned slightly.

"Let's not worry about those things. Let's just enjoy the day and see what it brings. Okay?" Luke kissed her forehead.

"Okay. Let's get this stuff in the dishwasher and then I'll get a shower."

Callie had just gotten in the shower when she heard Luke enter the bathroom. "Mind if I join you?" he said, slipping into the hot spray. The water was tepid when they finally decided it was time to consider other activities. Wrapping her hair in a towel, Callie pulled on her robe and lay across the bed. Luke wrapped a towel around his waist and joined her. Curling up to him, Callie rested her head on his chest.

"If we don't move soon, I'll be asleep again." She murmured.

"It's okay. I'm asleep myself." He pulled the covers over them.

It was nearly lunchtime when they woke up. After dressing in jeans and sneakers, they climbed into the Jeep. "Where did you want to go?" Luke asked at the end of the driveway.

"Oh, I don't know. Why not go over to the Isle of Palms? I hear the diner over there's surprisingly good." Callie looked at him and smiled.

"As you wish." Luke tipped his ball cap before turning out of the driveway.

Lunch was typical diner fare. Callie had a club sandwich and Luke had a burger. Holding hands across the table, they shared childhood stories. Callie talked about working in the mill for a few years during high school. Luke talked about studying finance when all he wanted to do was paint.

"It's not that my dad was horrible about it or anything. He just let me know 'painting pictures' was not an appropriate career choice for his son. Now that I've made some money, he doesn't complain so much, but I don't think he really likes it."

"I'm sorry, honey. Parents seem to have a way of making life tougher, all the while telling us it's because they want to see us happy."

"That's for sure, but you and Kim seem to have a good relationship."

"I've tried hard to let her be her own person and often wondered if I did her a disservice by not remarrying. Still, I felt simply providing her with a father was not a good enough reason to get married. Who knows, maybe I'm rationalizing." Callie shrugged her shoulders.

"Nah, there's some great men in her life like Max and I don't know your dad or your brother, but they seem alright to me from what you've said." Luke gave her hand a squeeze. "Have you had enough to eat?" Callie nodded. "How about a walk, then?"

"Great idea. I didn't mean to get so serious."

"That's life sometimes."

After walking along the beach and visiting a few shops, Callie and Luke went back to the house. They spent the rest of the day enjoying each other's company as they continued to explore all facets of their relationship. Around seven, they found enough leftovers to have salads for supper.

"Hey, I thought Alma was by your place most every day?"

"She usually is. She's probably just giving us space." Callie smiled and looked sideways at Luke.

"Does everyone know I'm here?" Luke smiled sheepishly.

"Probably." Callie laughed as she saw Luke's chagrin. "It's a small community, after all, and people like Josie, Alma, Max and Louise have made a habit of looking out for Kim and me over the years."

"Okay," Luke grinned sheepishly. "Just didn't want to interfere with any friendships. They're great people."

"The way they've taken to you, I don't think that will be an issue. Tomorrow my parents will be here around two and I'll have to be in the store about seven in the evening. I thought maybe an early supper with my parents. Is that okay with you? Although there will be food at the gala."

"Actually, I like it a lot. I'd rather our first meeting be when we aren't distracted by an event. Should I make a reservation at the Inn or somewhere else?"

"No, I think a fairly simple family supper would probably help keep Momma at ease. The opening gala will be challenging enough for her. Don't be surprised if she ducks off into a corner. She's come a long way, but anxiety can still get the best of her once in a while."

"So, what do they like to eat? Maybe we could do something together?"

"Well, they like simple things like pot roasts, fried chicken, soups. Meat and potato type meals." Callie's face lit up. "Can you make an oyster stew? Louise always makes for our gatherings, so I've never tried it. I've got oysters in the freezer and some rolls besides."

"I can do that."

"Momma doesn't drink, but Dad enjoys a beer sometimes. I'll have to pick some up when we go to the store. We can have wine or if you want something stronger, I have some gin and maybe bourbon."

"Wine will be fine since we'll have a long night ahead of us. We can make a list tomorrow before we go. I'll stoke up the fire once we put everything in the dishwasher, so it will be cozy in the living room." Luke got up from the table.

"That sounds nice. Turn on the TV if there's something you want to watch. I've got this here."

"Nah, just some music. Just want to relax on the couch." Luke went into the living room and Callie soon followed.

Callie woke just before sunrise. Reluctant to get up, Callie listened to Luke's slow breathing for a while. *I wish things could stay like this. I know life is real, so we can't just fall in and out of bed all day, every day. But I've enjoyed these days with Luke.* Slipping out of bed, she went into the kitchen and started the coffee.

Grabbing a cup of coffee and her small planning notebook, she sat down at the table to organize her day. As she finished her list, Luke came into the kitchen.

"I thought I smelled coffee," he said stretching and yawning as he made his way to the coffee pot.

"Do you want breakfast? I'm happy to do the cooking while you have coffee and go over this list." Callie pushed the list toward him.

"No. Maybe just a bagel and cream cheese. I thought I saw some cinnamon raisin ones yesterday." Luke looked at the list as sat down at the table.

"I'll drop them in the toaster," Callie said as she stood up.

Over a pleasant breakfast, they fleshed out the list. Luke insisted he would do the shopping while Callie was in the store. There wasn't a lot to do there today. Just double check delivery of the Prosecco order and check with the caters. In honor of Edward, everyone was dressing in evening wear for the gala. Callie had chosen a tea length semi-sheer black dress with threads of gold and silver shot through it. Black patent leather sling back heels completed the outfit. She knew Luke had a tailored tuxedo and favored a plain white shirt with black studs. Callie thought his choice was so much nicer than all the colorful ruffled shirts popularly worn with tuxedos today.

Everything at the store was in order. Restaurants promptly picked up their seafood orders for the holiday. A flurry of customers arrived near closing, but made their purchases quickly. As Callie was locking up, her parents pulled into the parking lot and she walked up to their car.

"Hey. How was the trip?" Callie said.

"Nice and smooth. We weren't sure when you'd be closing, so we stopped here first," her dad said.

"I'm heading home now," Callie said, shaking her keys with a smile.

At the house, Luke came out to help with the luggage and Callie introduced him to her parents. With introductions out of the way, Callie helped her parents settled in, being sure to hang up their clothes for tonight. Like clockwork, everyone convened in the kitchen for coffee as they finished their small tasks.

"Did you stop to eat on the road? I picked up some snacks and we'll have oyster stew about four," Luke said as he poured coffee for everyone while Callie put milk and sugar on the table.

"No thanks. We had breakfast before we left. I'm good right now," Callie's mom said.

"I'm fine," her dad said. "Will we see any of your paintings tonight?"

"I have some work displayed, but it's not featured tonight. I can show you when we get there," Luke offered as he checked the oyster stew.

With the oyster stew simmering, everyone moved to the living room. Callie's dad and Luke discussed the Braves' chances during the upcoming season. She and her mom talked about Kim's trip to New York. *Everyone seems so relaxed. I thought they would like him, but you never know. Our backgrounds are different. It's not like we're teenagers. They have to know that since I've introduced him, I'm pretty serious.* Callie thought to herself.

After their early supper, Luke left to get ready for the gallery's opening while Callie and her parents began their preparations for the night. Her mother came into the bedroom as Callie was finishing her makeup. "Luke seems like a pretty nice person. Think we'll be seeing more of him?"

"I'm in love with him, and I like him enough to carry us beyond the infatuation of early romance. He and Kim get on well. I know she graduates in a couple of years, but I wouldn't do anything to make her not feel welcome in her own home." Callie closed the case of pressed powder and turned to look at her mother.

"I'm so happy for you, baby. Have you talked about marriage? Or is it still too soon?" Her mother sat down on the bed.

"I think it's in our future. Neither one of us is the type to live with someone without marriage, even though that's more common now. But besides the ceremony, there's a lot to consider. Where would we live, for starters? But that's a long way off. Right now, I'm happy he gets along with my family and friends. And doesn't seem intent on reordering my life to fit into his."

"If you've finished with your makeup. Could you help me? I bought some new stuff at the department store. It's been years since I wore more than mascara and lipstick."

"Here, slip my other robe over your dress so we don't get anything on it." Callie helped her mother ease into the robe.

By the time her dad knocked on the bedroom door, both women were ready. "Come on in, Dad."

He whistled appreciatively as he looked at his wife and daughter. "Aren't you two gorgeous? Not that you aren't always beautiful," her dad said softly as he gave his wife a small kiss on the cheek.

"Momma. Here's a pair of ballet slippers to save your heels from the gravel. And Dad, would you drive tonight? If you guys want to leave early, I'm sure Luke or Alma will give me a ride home."

"Sure, but let's get a move on or, according to your timetable, we'll be late," her dad said.

At the gallery Callie checked on a few last-minute details, while Luke gave her parents a private showing of the new apartments and his work. The string quartet Edward hired began tuning their instruments. Edward's arrival with his family started a steady flow of guests. Callie and Max managed the sales, giving Alma time to spend with her sister, Carol. Edward was on cloud nine with the positive reception of his work.

The local press, with their photographers, made an appearance. Although Callie tried to make the night about Edward, they photographed her with Luke as she answered a few questions about changes in the store. Her mother did well with the crowd, only slipping to one of the smaller rooms a few times. Luke followed her quietly bringing her a plate of hors d'oeuvres or a soft drink. As it neared midnight, the wait staff offered glasses of Prosecco and bubbly grape juice to the remaining guests. Luke and Callie found each other just before midnight and celebrated the New Year with a kiss.

Callie's parents left shortly after midnight, which seemed to signal departure for the other guests. She and Luke sent Alma, Carol, Max, and Louise on their way, saying they would lock up when the catering crew finished. Everything else could wait until later. Professional and efficient, the catering crew was out before two.

"Why don't you wait here while I bring the Jeep around front? I don't know about you, but I'm beat. Give me your heels and I'll take them with me." Luke fished his keys from his pocket as Callie locked the front door.

"Sounds good. These last few days have been wonderful, but busy. I'll wait here."

Arriving at the house, Luke walked Callie to the door. "What's going on tomorrow, or should I say later today?"

"I think my parents are leaving after lunch. Kim will be home before supper. Other than that, I don't have any plans."

"I'll call later. There's a painting I'm working on." After a good-night hug and kiss, Luke left, telling her again he'd call tomorrow. Callie barely got into her nightgown before falling asleep thinking of all the things this new year would bring.

22

April 1987

Sitting at the kitchen table with yet another cup of coffee, Callie remembered she needed to check on Alma before relieving Max at the store. She closed her planner and tossed it into her bag. *Ordering those invitations will have to wait.* Alma's sister, Carol, had been staying with her since Alma's last heart attack. However, Carol returned to Columbia yesterday.

The flower beds along the back deck were full of daffodils, their bright yellow heads nodding in the April sun. Callie paused long enough to pick a small bouquet for Alma. As she opened the gate, she saw Alma sitting on her back porch.

"Morning. How are you doing today?" Callie asked as she opened the screen door. "I brought some flowers to bring a touch of spring inside."

"I'm doing okay. Still get a little winded walking around the house, though." Alma straightened up in her rocker.

"Did you go out to the chickens today? I can do that before I go in, if not." Callie schooled herself not to frown. The bright sun highlighted the angular shadows on her friend's slender frame. "Have you been eating?"

"I had some toast for breakfast. I'd appreciate you feeding the chickens. Now, what's the latest with this wedding?"

Callie told her about her pale gray cocktail length dress with a light rose silk band at the waist. Made from satin, it had a square neckline with full taffeta sleeves and a fuller taffeta skirt over the slimmer satin one. Luke would wear a slightly darker gray suit.

She continued, "We've got the guest list set at a solid forty people, so I'll be ordering invitations soon. Do you have physical therapy today? You've got to get stronger; you're my matron of honor."

"Yeah, they'll be here soon. We're supposed to fix some lunch as well as spend more time walking with my new friend here." Alma patted the cane resting against her leg. "I'll go into the living room while you see to the chickens."

"Okay, glad about their plans for lunch. Otherwise, I'd go in and fix it for you. Let me put these in a vase and then I'll go take care of chickens and check for eggs." Callie said as she started outside.

"Thanks, sweetie. I'll go wait in the living room."

Quietly, Callie let herself into the kitchen to put away the eggs. Alma called out as Callie closed the kitchen door. "How many eggs today?"

"Half dozen," Callie said as she came into the living room. "Look, I'll bring you a plate for supper. I know you're not an invalid, but you need to save your strength to get well. One of us will take care of the chickens in the morning and at night until you're stronger. Do you need anything from town?"

"No, at least I don't think so. You don't need to be going to all this trouble." Alma flapped a hand toward Callie.

"It's no trouble. For seventeen years, you've helped me more than I can ever say. It's my turn now. Is that a car in the driveway?" Callie looked toward the front window.

"Go let them in if you will. It's the therapy lady."

"Alright. I'll go out the front. See you at suppertime." Callie gave Alma a hug. *She has lost weight. We'll have to keep a better eye on her.* Callie thought as she felt Alma's ribs during their hug.

At the store, Callie talked over Alma's situation with Max. "I'm going to organize having members of the community pop in on Alma.

We can all make sure she has foods she can easily warm up for supper and breakfast. Going just before lunch time will also give her a chance to talk to someone and not interfere with her therapy. Luke, Kim, and I will take care of the chickens so we can check on her then."

"That's a good idea, Callie. I'll get Louise to call you. She'll help spread the word. I'd like to work it so maybe Louise and I could bring supper to her and then stay to eat with her. I know she's probably going stir crazy." Max rubbed a hand across his close cropped head.

"I've always looked at Alma like an aunt. I don't want to think about losing her." Callie blinked away her tears.

"From what Carol said, her doctors think Alma will make a full recovery. We just have to make sure she doesn't strain her heart too much. She's a strong woman. She'll be okay. On a different note, it's a good thing we have the apartments rented. Sales to the restaurants are falling off. I haven't noticed any drop off in quality when I've been making the selections at the pier. Have you seen any difference while you were putting orders together? If you come in early tomorrow, I'll make the restaurant rounds before they open. Art sales seem to be consistent for this time of year, though." Max leaned against the counter.

Callie frowned thoughtfully for a moment before answering. "No, the seafood seems as good as ever. I haven't noticed anything off when I'm cooking at home either. Maybe the trends are changing. Still, this is the Low Country, seafood is king. This afternoon and tomorrow, I'll go through the books and do some comparisons of sales over the last few years."

"Okay. We've done well over the years. If a change is coming to the market, we'd better figure it out early." Max grabbed his jacket from under the counter as he prepared to leave. "I'll get Louise to call you. See you tomorrow."

Callie started a list of friends and neighbors to support Alma during her recovery. Before she finished, Louise called, encouraging Callie to let her work out the schedule for Alma's visitors.

"With the store and the wedding, you've got a lot on your mind, honey. Me, I'm at my wit's end trying to stay busy since I stopped doing hair last winter," Louise laughed.

"Well, if that's what you'd like to do. We'll take care of the chickens since we're right next door. Max's idea of bringing supper over and eating with her was a good one."

"I think if we just do it two or three times a week, it would be good. Keep her talking to people. Don't want to wear her out though. And you know, Alma's always loved her privacy."

Within a short time, the women compared their lists. There were enough people on the list so Alma wouldn't feel she had overburdened anyone. Louise hung up, eager to arrange things to support their old friend.

As Callie began reviewing the accounts for the last few years, her mind kept drifting. *Things are happening so fast; I barely have time to think. The wedding is in July. Alma's not doing well. Heck, both she and Max are getting older. Then we're talking about remodeling the house. Kim graduates next year.* Callie puffed out her breath to move the hair from her eyes and then tucked it behind her ears. *Seems that since our picture from New Year's Eve made it into that magazine, everything's happening all at once.* Callie smiled to herself. *Shortly after the magazine was out, Luke called her, asking her to have dinner with him at his parents.*

"What will I talk about with them? What do they do?"

"It will be fine. Mom loves flowers. Talk about baseball with Dad. You've got nothing to worry about. They just feel a little left out. It's been years since they've seen my picture in print and now, I'm with a woman they don't know. They're going to love you."

He had been right, of course. They were happy to find she was a woman with her own interests and a successful business. Of course, the scale of her success couldn't rival the success of Luke and his father in investment banking, but it gave her something to talk with his father about besides baseball, even though her Mets had won the World Series the year before. That wasn't something a Braves fan would be happy about.

Callie smiled again, remembering his proposal in February. *Nothing flashy or over the top. They'd been sitting around the house in sweats, reading the Sunday papers, when he suggested the two of them take a walk along the beach. It was a beautiful day graced with warm temperatures from a false spring. The tide was running out. Even the birds were quiet today. Luke too was unusually quiet and kept fiddling with something in his pocket.*

"Is something wrong?"

He kept moving his hands to the pouch in front of his sweatshirt. "No, I think my life is nearly perfect, but one thing could make it better," he said with a slight grin as he pulled the small box from the pocket of his sweatshirt and dropped to one knee. "Callie, will you marry me?"

After the slightest pause, she said, "yes". From that moment, it's been like a whirlwind descended on us. I don't regret the decision, but I wish things would slow down.

Trying to refocus, Callie got a fresh cup of coffee. A few minutes later she was back into the accounts trying to see when the change in seafood orders occurred and by how much. After digging for a few hours, she found it was a combination of things. Callie took a few minutes to write up her notes so she could review them with Max in the morning.

Still feeling disconcerted, Callie walked on the beach before going home. As she got out of sight of the store, she sat down to watch the sandpipers dancing at the frothy water's edge. *Some things never change, the birds are always hopping near the water. I didn't feel this overwhelmed when the hurricane set my world on end. So why do I feel like I'm in a race and the finish line keeps moving? Am I afraid of starting my life with Luke? Am I afraid of facing a life without Alma and eventually Max? Or is it just because? I just wish I could put my finger on it. Wouldn't it be nice if humans had a life as simple as these sandpipers? But do sandpipers know the joys of love or the sadness of loss? I suppose not.*

Guess I should head home. I still don't know what's got me feeling so off. I'll figure it out soon.

At home, Callie went into the kitchen, intent on starting something for supper. She was happy to see Luke was making spaghetti. Everything was ready except the pasta and garlic bread.

"Hey, honey. How was everything at the store today?" Luke turned from the stove to give her a hug and kiss as she walked up beside him.

"Not too bad. Although the seafood orders have been dropping off. They're down, even for this time of year. But we'll look into it and see what we need to do. Where's Kim? I didn't see her car in the driveway."

"She should be home any minute. Kim stopped by the library after school. She is still working on that term paper for biology."

"That's right. I remember her mentioning it last night. I can't get used to her driving. If you don't need any help here, I'll go change."

"No, I'm good here. I'll have coffee ready for us when you get back."

After Callie changed, she sat beside Luke on the living room couch. They'd wait for Kim to get home to have supper. "Sorry, sweetheart. I didn't ask how your day went."

"Pretty good, actually. I finished the seascape I've been working on and started prepping a canvas for another painting. I've been thinking of doing a series of paintings, houses on the island."

"That's interesting. What brought that on?" Callie turned to look at him.

"The island's growing, not as fast as say, the Isle of Palms, but there's some new homes being built. I'd just like to record the way it is now."

"That's cool. I'm sure they will sell."

"The paintings of this house, Alma's, as well as Max and Louise's won't be for sale." When he saw how touched Callie was, Luke gave her a squeeze. And added, "but everyone else will have to pay."

"I hear Kim pulling in. Let's get supper on the table." Callie stood up from the couch.

"Hey, Momma, Luke. Sorry I'm late. I'll be back out in a minute," Kim said as she came in the front door.

Kim returned to the kitchen in time to help finish setting the vintage white enamel topped wooden table they had for years. Nowadays the two narrow leaves were left out to accommodate the three of them. As they started eating, Callie brought Kim and Luke up to date on Alma's condition and how Louise was rallying the neighborhood to look after her. Both Kim and Luke were ready to do whatever they could to help speed Alma's recovery.

"Well, that's good. I volunteered us to look after the chickens since we're right next door. I'll go over tonight," Callie chuckled.

"I'll go with you. Caring for chickens isn't something I've done before. I'm sure I'll learn quickly, though," Luke said as he finished his meal.

"I'll cover the kitchen cleanup. Think I'll start popping over to see Aunt Alma for a little when I first get home from school. Maybe I'll take my clarinet over. She always enjoyed hearing me play, especially after I learned some of her favorite jazz pieces," Kim offered.

"Thanks, sweetie. I'm sure she'll appreciate your visits. Luke, let's grab a flashlight and a plate for Alma. We won't be long, Kim. Alma's tiring out pretty quickly," Callie said, taking her plate to the counter.

Walking across the yard, Luke started laughing. "What's so funny?" Callie asked.

"Well, why do we need a flashlight? The chickens are in a pen. Anyway, I had a mental picture of us going through woods and looking under bushes for chickens and their eggs. Sorry, it's not so funny when I say it out loud, especially since they live in a coop," Luke said as they went through the backyard gate.

Callie snorted. "We need the flashlight to check the nesting boxes since it's getting dark. Also, because sometimes the hens try to hide the eggs. Then there's an off chance of a snake being in the nest. So, if you can't see clearly, take a flashlight."

By now they had reached Alma's. "Hey, Alma. It's Callie and Luke," Callie said as they opened the kitchen door.

"Here in the living room," Alma said.

"We brought supper. Did the therapist wear you out today?" Callie said, setting her flashlight on the kitchen counter.

"It wasn't too bad. They still don't want me doing much of anything outside. Except for getting winded, I feel pretty good. What's for supper?" Alma straightened up in her chair.

"The Luke special, salad, spaghetti, and garlic bread. All for your dining pleasure." Callie uncovered the tray with a flourish.

Luke set up a TV table in front of Alma's chair. "What can I get you to drink?"

"Just some iced tea. Think there's still some there," Alma said.

As Luke returned with the tea, Callie said, "I'm going to take this city slicker with me and teach him how to take care of chickens. We'll be back in a bit."

Alma giggled behind her hand. "You two beat all I've ever seen."

Several minutes later, they were back inside with two eggs. "Okay, Alma. That's two more. So, eight for today. The ladies are laying well." Callie entered the living room and was happy to see Alma had eaten most of her meal.

"Yeah, as the days get longer, they'll start laying more. Hey, why did you go getting Louise all riled up? Apparently, I'm on the sick list for meals and such." Alma frowned as she crossed her arms over her chest.

"Now, don't be that way, Alma. Who heads things up when someone dies or is ill? You, right? Allow your friends to do the same for you, please," Callie coaxed.

With a sigh, Alma dropped her hands to her lap. "Okay. Since you put it that way."

"Hey, Alma. I've got a project I'm working on. When the weather's good, could I come over and work on a painting of your house?" Luke asked.

"What you want to do that for?" Alma asked, furrowing her brow.

"I think, we need to preserve the memory of the older homes on the island. There's new construction going on, and I'd just like to have a record of the island as I know and love it." Luke told her of his plan to paint all the older homes on the island.

"Alright." Alma sat quietly for a moment. "Can you paint from a picture and include people?"

"I'm not sure I understand," Luke said as he raised an eyebrow and frowned slightly.

"I have a picture of the house with Nate, Louise, Max, Callie's Aunt Sally, and me on the front porch. Another friend had a camera that took color pictures and gave the picture to me. Do you think you could paint that picture?"

"Yeah, I can do that. I'd still like to paint your house as it is now," Luke said.

"That would be two painting." Alma's brow furrowed again. "Maybe I'm asking too much."

"Let me worry about the paintings. I'll come by tomorrow and we can look for the photograph." Turning to Callie, Luke said, "I think we'd better head home before we wear Alma out completely."

Callie got up from the couch. And after making sure Alma had finished eating, she began gathering dishes while Luke returned the TV table to its stand near the kitchen door. Giving Alma a hug, Callie reminded her one of them would be by to check on the chickens in the morning.

Once Callie got the seafood orders ready for pick up the next morning, she ordered the wedding invitations. *Okay, that's one thing off the list.* In April, there was very little foot traffic in the store, so Callie reviewed her notes on the seafood and set up a chart to better see the changes.

Luke stopped in the store before going upstairs to work in his studio. "Hello, love. How's things going?" He leaned over to give her a hug.

"Pretty quiet today." Callie reached up to Luke's embrace.

"They started working on the foundation for my studio. I saw them before I left the house. I'll be glad to let go of the apartment. Oh, by the way, I stopped over at Alma's and got the picture she was talking about. I'll probably start with it for the house series. Then go on with the sketches for the others."

"That's great. Glad they've started on the studio, too. But think about this, why don't we hold off on the house remodel? So much is happening right now. I know our space is a little tight, but Kim will be off to college after next year. There's just so much happening. You don't have to answer right now."

"Honey, are you having second thoughts about the remodel?" Luke stepped behind Callie and began gently massaging her shoulders.

"No, I like our concept of keeping the center portion of the house like it is and then adding two wings on each side, so the main rooms stay on one level. I really like adding the narrow stairs and creating a couple of rooms upstairs. With the dormer windows already there, that would be a great place for the kids when everyone's here. And I want to do it. I want it to become our house. It's just that right now, it's too much to take in." Callie turned sideways in her chair to look at Luke.

"The only time the house gets crowded is when people are in town. We're fine. And you're right, I was feeling a little pressured, too. We'll put it on a back burner until next year. I'd like Kim to have some input. I know she's going off to school, but I want her to feel she's in her home whenever she comes back." Luke kissed her on the forehead.

"You always think of everyone. I feel better already. I need to refill my coffee. Do you need anything upstairs?" Callie stood up.

"Don't think so. I'll call down when I'm ready for lunch and see where you're at with your day. I'm slipping out the back door. Be sure to lock up behind me." Callie gave him a hug and followed him to lock the door.

Callie had settled at the worktable with fresh coffee when Max came in. He joined Callie at the worktable they had moved into Kim's old room in the store. "Well, it seems like a couple of things are happening in the local market that explain what's happening here." Max said.

"Tell me what the restaurant owners said. Then I'll tell you what I found in the accounts."

"Well, it's two things, really," Mac drawled. "There seems to be more interest in swordfish, sea bass and things like squid and shark."

Callie scrunched up her nose. "Okay then. We could probably handle swordfish and sea bass. But what's the other thing?"

"Apparently, other suppliers are offering a delivery service," Max said.

"Oh." Now Callie was frowning. "That presents a few other challenges: a delivery truck, a driver, and a way to keep everything fresh until it's delivered. Even if Alma with back at work, I don't think you or I would last long making deliveries. Neither of us has done really hard work for a few years."

"I know. This getting older thing is for the birds. Anyway, what did you find out?" Max ran his hand over his forehead, across his head and down to his neck. A sure sign that the changes in the market troubled him.

"Two things really. One, we aren't making as many sales to individuals. Makes sense if you think about it. People who knew us from our days of selling on the pier made most of our in-store seafood purchases. A lot of those folks have moved or died over the last few years. And unlike us, the younger crowd eats out more. Two, there has been a downturn in our sales to restaurants. But it's the decrease from store sales that has impacted the bottom line the most." Callie slid her paperwork over so Max could look over the actual numbers.

"Man, that gives us something to think about. Tell me this. Do you ever think about selling the store?" Max's usually animated face stilled.

"No, I wouldn't know what to do if I wasn't working. I figure it's too late in life to work for someone else. I always planned to keep things going until I couldn't do it anymore. Then it turns into another question because I know Kim has no interest in the business." Callie took a sip of coffee.

"I feel the same even though my quitting time will probably come before yours. And like Kim, Steve isn't interested in the business. Okay, that being the case, we need to get with the times. I'll look into adding different seafood. If that works out, I'll look into a truck and a driver.

You've got enough on your plate with your upcoming nuptials." Max was back to his smiling self.

"Thanks, Max. I've got to plan for a meeting of the parents. Let me know if you need help with anything."

"By the way, I saw the Smitty's crew out at your place today. Are they working on Luke's studio?"

"Yes. If the weather holds, the building will be up in a couple of weeks. They've already done the tie-ins to the septic and well. The main workroom has a lot of windows. Luke's having them install tracks for the plywood for hurricanes. Hopefully, they won't get tested anytime soon."

"Like every year, we'll just cross our fingers and pray You go on now. I'll open tomorrow, just to keep myself on schedule. These days mornings are my best time to get stuff done." Max made shooing motions with his hands.

"See you tomorrow." Callie picked up her bag and paused to call Luke on her way out. "Hey, honey. I'm heading home now. Are you ready for a break?"

"No, I'll pass on lunch. The painting is going well."

"Alright, I'll see you at home."

Turning in her driveway, Callie was happy to see a neighbor's car at Alma's. *I knew Louise would get things rolling quickly.* Hanging her bag on the coat rack near the kitchen door, she pulled out her planner and started the coffee before changing into more comfortable clothes.

Feeling fortified with more coffee, Callie began the round of phone calls to determine the date for the dinner with both sets of parents. Once she had a window of their availability, Callie called the Inn in Mount Pleasant and made a dinner reservation for the last Saturday in April. She added a notation in her planner and took a walk.

On her way to the beach, Callie took special notice of the number of homes built over the last few years. Subtly, they hinted at more money coming to the island. Concrete driveways led to houses with attached garages. The landscaping near the house had a more professional air as the owner cleared the land and actually sowed grass. There were fewer woodlands in between houses. Callie shook her head. *Hope we don't turn into the Isle of Palms with hardly any natural land left, except a strip of beach. At least we don't have street lights.*

Her thoughts turned to when she met Luke's parents for the first time. They didn't live in a mansion, but the differences between their home and the island house were like night and day. The two story brick home backed up next to a golf course. Neat, regimented plantings nestled against the house's foundation. Steps flared much like a waterfall from the porch down to the brick walkway leading to the circular drive. The porch held a couple of white wrought irons chairs no one sat in and a few potted begonias. Their gardener would change them out with the seasons. Callie didn't understand their lifestyle. Still, they were welcoming to her and Kim, and they definitely loved their son.

A gentle breeze rippled through the cattails and turtle grass as Callie drew closer to the beach. Sand made small crunching noises under her feet as she walked past the pavilion. *Paved roads make driving easier, but I miss the crunch you hear when walking on oyster shells.* Sea oats undulated in the breeze as she got closer to the shoreline. Most of the birds had already completed their midday feeding, leaving only the distant sound of the ocean's crashing waves to accompany her walk. As she usually did on her walks, Callie let her mind wander without purpose and just took in the sights of nature around her. As the afternoon sun sank lower, Callie turned toward home still feeling unsettled.

Leaving the beach, she took the path that led to the store. Seeing Luke's Jeep in the parking lot, she turned to go into the apartment. He usually stopped painting about this time in the afternoon, anyway. "Hey, honey. How's it going up there?" Callie said as she climbed the stairs.

"I'm just wrapping up for the day," he answered.

"Come, look at this, since you're here," he said as Callie entered the apartment. Luke had sketched Alma's photograph onto a large canvas.

"Wow. She's going to love this."

"I'll do the others a little smaller. I wanted this one to be large enough to get details in the people, so you'd know who's who." He walked away and began cleaning his brushes after closing the tops on the acrylic paint tubes tightly. "This will just take a couple of minutes and then we can go home."

"Okay, I'll just curl up on here until you're ready. I've had my walk today, so I'm happy just to sit awhile." Callie settled in on the couch.

The few weeks before the parents' dinner, as Callie began calling it, went by quickly. Alma was recovering in leaps and bounds, although her doctors had yet to give her clearance to return to work. Max had located sources for the changes in seafood offerings, but was still looking for a truck and driver. Callie and Kim visited a few colleges, but Kim was still determined to enter USC's nursing program following graduation next year. Callie and Josie talked on the phone a few times, but since April was tax season, Josie, a newly qualified CPA, didn't have much free time. Calls to Brenda in Columbia let Callie know her friend was doing well.

Closing the store after another day of light in-store sales, Callie hurried home, hoping to get there before her parents. She had just finished changing as she heard them pull into the driveway. Looking at them as she crossed the yard to their car, Callie couldn't believe the changes in her parents. Both of them had silver strands streaking through their hair and her dad was moving slower and seemed stiffer. Her mother, however, seemed to have developed a gracefulness over the last year. *Probably the yoga Momma started a while back.*

"Hey, Momma, Dad. Let me get that suitcase for you," Callie called as she walked across the yard.

"Thanks, but I can get it," her dad said after giving her a hug. "Once we get this inside, maybe we can take a short walk. Driving makes me so stiff anymore."

"Sure. We can check on Luke. He moved the last of his stuff from the apartment to the studio out back, so I don't think he's actually painting," Callie said as she opened the front door.

After putting their luggage in their bedroom, the three went to see Luke's studio. "Hey, Luke, I've got Momma and Dad and they're ready for the grand tour." Callie said, opening the studio door.

"Come on in. I'm in the office," he answered.

Everyone was quiet for a moment as they took in the brightly lit space filled with boxes and wrapped canvases. The studio's interior was a rectangle with areas carved out for the bathroom and office. Everything else was open, including a kitchen area along one narrow wall. There were more cabinets in varying sizes than most people Callie knew had in their kitchen.

"Wow. This is more like an apartment," her mother gasped as she turned slowly to take in the space. "You've got the office, a kitchenette, a bathroom, and this really sizeable area over here. And you put in central air."

"For tax reasons, I wanted to keep everything related to my painting in one place. After using the apartment as a studio, I've gotten used to having a kitchen handy for coffee and other stuff. From a creative perspective, if I don't go into the house, I can keep my focus. The air conditioning keeps all my supplies fresh," Luke said as he came out of the office smiling.

"I know you went with tile because it's easy to clean. But don't you think you need a couple of rugs, at least away from where you're painting?" Callie asked, frowning slightly at the enormous expanse of tile.

"Yeah, you're right. As I get things arranged, I'd like you to help me come up with some simple coverings for the larger windows. So, we can coordinate the rugs, then," he said, giving Callie a hug.

"Why so many cabinets?" Her dad asked, turning to take them all in.

"Callie can tell you I get fussy about storing things and being able to find things especially while I'm working. I like to have a place for everything--"

"--and everything in its place," Callie laughed, finishing his sentence. "He cleans up so fast, he often puts something away before I've finished using it. Makes me nuts."

Luke shrugged his shoulders and smiled. "Sorry honey, I try to resist the urge to put other people's things away. Must be the banker in me, keeping all those numbers lined up. Let's close up here and go back to the house. Bob, let me show you these new tracks on the way out. They're supposed to be great for hurricane season, making it easy to slip the plywood in place. Imagine not having to drive screws into the house."

"I know Callie always fussed about filling the holes and touching up the paint. I like the way the tracks kind of blend in," her dad said as the two men walked up to the outside of a window.

Callie and her mother went into the house. "He'll be carrying on about those tracks half the night now," Callie said.

"Mom, is Grandma with you?" Kim called as she hurried across the living room and into the kitchen. "Oh, hi Grandma. I've already taken care of the chickens for tonight. Alma asked if you could stop by later?"

"Sure, we can do that after supper. How about setting the table? Momma, I made a pot roast, in your honor. I know it's one of your favorites," Callie said, smiling. "Hope it turned out okay. I haven't done it in the slow cooker before. I never got the hang of cooking in a pressure cooker and have been trying different things so that we don't have to wait so long for the main dish to finish after work."

"Callie, are you guys really going to remodel the place?" Her dad asked as he and Luke came in.

"We're going to wait a while before starting that project. Luke's made sketches, but for me it would just be too much, meeting with architects and everything, right now." Callie turned back toward the stove. "Dinner will be ready in just a few minutes."

"Are you going to add a second story to get the extra room you want?" her dad asked as he studied the wall running from the kitchen and into the living room.

Luke shook his head negatively. "Since Callie bought the corner lot next to us a few years ago, we thought we'd spread it out. The exterior of the center portion would look just like it does now, minus the screened front porch. Then we would add two wings, from the outside the elevation changes so it looks like there are two small wings on each side." Luke explained. "The kitchen would be bigger and we're thinking of adding a dining room. We just decided to build access stairs to the attic so there'll be room for the kids when everyone's in town. We'll put in the central air then. I'll show you my sketches tomorrow."

Talk turned to changes in the seafood market. Callie explained she and Max felt they could make the adjustments needed to keep their share of the market. "Max is working on finding suppliers, a delivery truck, and a driver. For the first time, we'll have an actual employee."

"Is Alma up to date on everything with the store? I don't want to say anything out of turn," Callie's mother asked.

"Not yet. We just sorted out the reasons for changes in seafood orders last week. She has a doctor's appointment on Tuesday. After that, Max and I will bring her up to date. She seems better," Callie replied.

When they finished supper, everyone helped clear the table. Luke put away leftovers, while Callie loaded the dishwasher. Kim went to her room to study for a test when the adults walked over to Alma's.

"Come on in," Alma called from the kitchen as Callie opened the screen door on the porch. "I've got coffee and pie."

"Alma, you shouldn't have," Callie's mother said.

"This was part of my therapy today. We made a pie, and I walked to the mailbox. After a little rest, I walked around the yard checking on my flowers," Alma said, beaming.

Callie grinned with obvious relief. "You *are* doing so much better."

"Y'all can't get rid of this cantankerous old woman that easily," Alma laughed as a smile crinkled the skin around her eyes. "No really, my therapist is having a hard time coming up with things for me to do. Monday, we'll come down to the store for a while."

It wasn't long before Alma and Callie's mom were trading low salt, low-fat recipes. Callie's dad had recently been having trouble with high blood pressure. Both women agreed that trying to change a lifetime of cooking and eating was hard.

"I hate to break this up. Some of those things sound really good. I hope Lydia will try them when we get home, especially the chicken," Callie's dad said. "We've got a pretty full day tomorrow."

Yawning, Callie agreed and gave Alma a hug. "See you Monday, if not before. Tomorrow, I'll be in the store until about five and then we'll be at dinner with Luke's parents. Call if you need anything."

Before going to work, Callie took a walk on the beach. Watching the sandpipers dart along the water's edge usually helped her sort out her thoughts. Not today. No matter how deeply she breathed in the salt air, Callie still felt unsettled. *What if the seafood sales don't turn around when we add the delivery service? Will the business still be viable as a gift shop and gallery? Will Alma and Max be okay if we have to close the store? I know Kim will be fine going to school, but I know Max and Alma depend on their store earnings. Oh my, next year Kim graduates from high school. Lord, I've never been away from her for more than a week. She needs to live her dreams, but I think I'll worry more than ever. Why do we have to have so much hoopla to get married? I just want to get on with our lives.* Knowing Max was waiting for her to relieve him, Callie turned back toward the store.

When she got into the store, Max told her he was going to look at a delivery truck before he went home. Callie let him know Alma would be in the store for a few hours on Monday. They felt it would be a good time to bring her up to speed, then the three of them could discuss the truck and what the wages for a delivery driver should be.

Callie came home from work to a quiet house. She read the message Kim left on the small bulletin board near the phone saying she was going to the movies with friends and wouldn't be home until eight. After checking the sewing room for her parents, she went out to Luke's studio. She found Luke and her parents knee deep in boxes as they were trying to organize the studio. Callie paused at the door a moment, enjoying the fact the three of them were working so well together.

"I'm not sure I've got these paints divided like you would. I've tried to group them by color. It's hard for me to decide about some of them.

Are they bluer or are they more purple? If I'm not sure, they're in a small box here on the counter."

Luke stuck his head out of the office door. "That's fine Mom. It's hard to figure out sometimes. I can sort it out later. Oh, Callie, you're home. I didn't realize it was so late."

They met halfway across the room for a quick hug and kiss. "You guys have gotten a lot done in here," Callie said as she slid her arm around his waist.

"I hadn't planned to work out here today, but your parents said they were bored sitting around. And we had already walked on the beach, so we just started unpacking. Dad and I got the office arranged. Glad he was here to help. Moving the desk and file cabinets was a pain."

Walking over to the doorway, Callie looked into the office. "This look's great. I hate to break up the work party, but we need to get ready for dinner. I know it's a bit early, but Momma wants to look around the inn a little before we eat."

"Okay. You ladies go ahead. Luke and I'll have a beer. That will give time for the bathrooms to open up," her dad said.

As expected, they arrived at the inn in Mount Pleasant before Luke's parents. Callie's mother was excited to see where the ceremony and reception would take place. "Callie, this will be beautiful in July. The hydrangeas will be in bloom and probably some azaleas still. And you should get a cool breeze off the water. Now, what flowers were you planning on?"

"I'm not sure, Momma." Callie frowned as she thought. "The gardens here are beautiful. I don't want a lot of cut flowers. It's just so wasteful and it's not like this is a first marriage for either of us. I just don't know. What do you think?"

"What about some potted Calla lilies? Didn't you say your bouquet was predominantly peace roses? They have a mixture of pink, white, cream, and yellow on their blossoms, right? The Calla lilies would blend in nicely and give you some understated drama without being over the top. You could plant them later, if you want, or donate them." Her mother offered. "I do like the idea of the Inn providing seating, the arch and all that stuff. Do you remember trying to put all that together when you and Joe got married?"

"Lord, yes, that's one reason for keeping it simple," Callie laughed. "The Inn does all the setup and cleanup. And their chef is out of this world. Let's go in through this side door and I'll show you the room for the reception. I think I saw Luke's parents, Tony, and Melony, pull into the parking lot."

Luke's parents were already at the table when Callie and her mother entered the dining room. Her mother paused for a moment.

"Everything okay, Momma?" Callie asked.

"I'm fine, sweetie. You know I'm not fond of meeting new people, so I just wanted to take a few breaths first," her mother said.

"Okay. They're really pretty nice, although I think Melony misses society life a little," Callie said, patting her mother's arm.

Once Luke made the introductions, everyone placed their drink orders. For her mother's sake, Callie was happy to see no one seemed to notice when her mother ordered tonic water and lime. As usual, the service was excellent. Dinner moved seamlessly through the appetizer and the entrée as they went over details of the wedding. Everyone hoped there wouldn't be rain, but the Inn assured Callie and Luke they had a large enough tent should rain be in the forecast.

"Your plans for the wedding sound great, but I haven't heard anything about a rehearsal dinner," Tony said after the waiter served their dessert and coffee.

"We weren't sure we needed one. There's only one attendant for each of us. Max and my buddy, Jake, will greet everyone and encourage them to choose a seat," Luke said. "No bride and groom sides, though. The only reserved seats will be for parents and Kim."

"Okay, I see, and you kids are paying for everything. I get that, second marriage and all, but I'd still like to do something. When are the out-of-town folks coming in?" Tony asked.

"It varies, but everyone will be here the Friday night before the wedding," Callie said.

"So, why don't Melony and I host a get together then? Nothing much, just a buffet at the house. It will be easier for those with children," Tony said, turning to look at his wife, who nodded her approval.

"Alright. I guess it would be nice for everyone to meet at least briefly before the ceremony. We've planned brunch at the house the next day before Luke and I head out. Momma, Alma, and Louise volunteered to oversee it. Although knowing Susan, my brother's wife, I'm sure she'll be in the kitchen too," Callie said, looking up from her coffee.

"I think we'll keep the menu simple. I'll call Steve's catering on Monday. I'll let you know later what they're offering now. They change up the menu from time to time," Melony said.

Over dessert, talk turned to remodeling the house and Luke's intention to paint all the old houses on the island. At first, Melony lobbied for Callie and Luke to move away from the island, but was more understanding when she realized it was a family home. She was eager to see Luke's sketches and said she'd stop by later in the week with details for the rehearsal dinner and look at those sketches.

"As much as I hate to break this up, I've got an early tee time in the morning," Tony said, reaching for his wallet.

"I've got this, Dad," Luke said, motioning for his dad to leave his wallet in his jacket pocket.

"I've got a few things to do in the morning before I go into the store, as well," Callie said as she stood up from the table.

Luke called for the check, and the three women went to the ladies' room, laughing along the way about how all three of them went at the same time. The men were waiting for them in the lobby when they returned. Walking out to the parking lot together, everyone remarked on the enjoyable food and company.

At the house, Callie's parents went to bed while Callie and Luke waited up for Kim. "I wish all this was over," Callie said, flopping on the couch next to Luke. "Sometimes I wish we had just gone to the courthouse."

"Really?" Luke asked, sitting up straighter and putting his arm around her.

"Well, sort of. First, I just want us to be married. Second, I'm already tired of all the stuff. Yeah, I want the world to know I'm your wife, but I just want to get back to living our life. No matter how much I arrange things and try to stay organized, there's always one more thing that needs to be done."

Luke pulled Callie in closer, and she put her head on his chest. "Is there something I can do? It doesn't have to be about the wedding. Is there something here at home or at the store?" He asked.

Callie shook her head as she burrowed into the crook of his arm. "Not really. We've got the invitations ready to be mailed. So, there's really nothing to do there. We just have to be sure to let everyone know about the rehearsal dinner and brunch. Hey, could you design, write up something to send to everyone? Since we're not being truly formal, we could slip it into the invitations for those people. We addressed them, but the we haven't sealed or stamped the envelopes."

"Sure. I can do that and get them mailed. Is that all you're worried about? You know Alma's recovering well." Luke leaned in closer, resting his forehead on the top of her head.

"I know she is. This change in seafood sales has me worried. I don't know anything about squid. The swordfish is just another fish. But now we need a truck and a driver." Callie sighed.

Luke gently lifted her chin so she could see his face. "Callie, you realize that no matter what happens with the store, the three of us — you, Kim, and I will still be just fine."

"I hadn't thought of that." Callie's brow furrowed while she processed the thought. "I've depended on myself for so long; it never occurred to me to bring your money into the picture."

Luke grinned. "I didn't think so. It's one of the things I love about you. You're so danged independent." Shrugging he continued, "I didn't really want to get into it before the wedding, but I can't stand for you to be worried for no reason."

Callie sat up a little on the couch and looked at him intently.

"Anyway, here are some of my thoughts about money. We should each keep the separate personal accounts we have now and open a joint account once we're married. Both of us contribute to the joint account and use it to run the household. We can talk about specifics later. I just don't want you to worry unnecessarily. And I want you to continue to have your own financial history; you worked hard for it."

"Okay, I'll just focus on what makes business sense for the store and try not to worry about everyone involved, like the artists, Alma, and Max," Callie said, settling back against his chest.

Soon after, Kim came home from the movies. She brought them up to date on things at school. Luke and Callie were particularly interested in whether she had received word about her early admission to the University of South Carolina, but she hadn't. Kim thought everyone getting together with Luke's parents the night before the wedding was a "pretty cool" idea. After a little more discussion of wedding plans, everyone said goodnight, as they knew Callie's parents would be up early since they were returning to Columbia.

Callie's mother came into the kitchen. "Morning, sweetheart. Thought I smelled bacon. Oh, you've made biscuits, too. That's so sweet. You didn't have to go through all that trouble," she said, smiling.

"We don't do the big country breakfast unless someone is visiting. It's a treat for us, too," Callie said as she turned from the stove to hug her mother.

"Dad and I will probably head home shortly after breakfast. Driving seems to tire him out so. I offered to drive this time, but he couldn't let go. He's always been our driver." Callie smiled. Everyone knew her dad was easygoing, but sometimes he dug his heels in. Driving was one of those times.

"Dad and Kim are moving around, I think. I'll put the biscuits in the oven and go out to the studio to let Luke know breakfast will be ready soon."

"I'll let everyone inside know food will be ready in a few minutes," Her mother said as she left the kitchen.

As everyone gathered around the table, Callie had already put eggs for her parents and Kim on their plates. Grits, sliced tomatoes, and bacon were already on the table. Everyone fixed their plate as Callie put out the hot biscuits. Returning to the stove, she put Luke's eggs on a bread and butter plate. She then started frying her eggs.

"Don't let that food get cold. Eat up. I'll join you in a minute," Callie said.

"Are you sure you never worked as a short-order cook?" Luke asked. Callie slid two eggs from the bread and butter plate onto his plate and laughed.

"Oh, I put a letter for you in the basket yesterday, not sure who it was from," Luke said as an afterthought.

"No, I've never been a cook. But all cooking is just a timing thing. I'll sit down in a minute." Callie returned to the stove. "I'll check the mail later today."

Of course, it always takes longer to cook a meal than eat it. Everyone lingered for a while over coffee, biscuits, and jelly. Finishing her coffee, Callie's mother began clearing the table.

"Grandma, sit down. I'll get this as soon as I finish my biscuit," Kim said.

"It's no bother. We're all family," Her grandmother said, turning from the sink to look at Kim.

"I know, but you have a drive ahead of you," Kim insisted. "I'll get it."

"Alright, I'll go check the suitcase. Bob, is there anything you need from it?" Callie's mother said before leaving the kitchen.

"No, I think I've got everything I need, but you might check the bathroom behind me," Callie's dad said.

Once Callie's parents left, Luke went out to the studio and Callie settled on the couch with a book. She was determined to relax for a while. At one point, she remembered Luke saying something about mail, but promptly forgot as she became engrossed in her book again.

Monday, Alma came into the store with her therapist. She seemed to have met all the goals set out for her and would return to work next week. Callie came in early to talk about the seafood. Alma agreed with adding sea bass and swordfish. Everyone felt the squid was a bit too specialized for most of their clients. Max told them the delivery truck he looked at was a good deal and the price was right. He had the loan paperwork for everyone to sign. No one had any idea about finding a driver.

"I guess we'll have to put an ad in the paper," Alma said.

"Suppose so," Callie agreed. "I just wish it were someone we knew at least a little. Besides making deliveries, they'll be collecting money, too. They are usually checks, though."

"I'll put the ad in the paper. With any luck, we'll be able to teach them how to get the orders ready as well," Max said, pulling the paperwork together.

A few days later, Steve came into the store. "What's got you out this way during the week?" Max asked, giving his son a hug.

"Well, Dad, I think I might have a driver for you. What kind of delivery truck did you guys buy?" Steve asked as they leaned against the counter.

"It's just a van. Don't need a commercial license. Why?"

"Okay, I've been working with this kid for a couple of years. He's twenty-one. Got into some minor trouble with the law a few years ago. That's how I met him. He wants to go back to school, but needs a job that could work around that kind of schedule. Dad, he's a good kid." Steve looked earnestly at his dad.

Max chuckled and shook his head. "You're a chip off the old block. What's the kid's name?"

"Danny. Danny Tucker. His mother moved the family to Charleston for work, but it didn't pan out. She took a position as a nursing assistant and had to take a night shift. That's when Danny got in with the wrong crowd for a while. I represented him pro bono in his court appearance. Tina and I helped his mother get some services and an apartment in a better neighborhood. He finished high school with good grades and has worked a few odd jobs. I've stayed in touch, trying to keep him headed in the right direction."

"You know he'll be collecting checks for us? You trust him like that?" Max tilted his head and looked closely at his son.

"Yes. He got into trouble because older kids were using him as a get-away driver. He didn't even know they were planning a robbery." Steve shrugged.

"Have him come in on Tuesday, at one o'clock. He's got to interview with all of us, just like anybody else."

"Thanks, Dad. I'll go let him know he's got an interview. He's living with his mom, but they don't have a phone right now." Steve stood up from the counter.

"You're welcome. Now when are you bringing my grandkids to see me?" Max laughed.

"If you're home, we'll be by this weekend." Steve grinned.

"Alright. I'll let your momma know. Sure am proud of you, son," Max said, hugging Steve and clapping him on the back.

23

Early July 1987

Danny turned out to be the best person for the job. He quickly learned the routes to the restaurants and was already coming in earlier to help Max fill the day's orders. He let everyone know he had applied to the community college for the fall semester, but planned to continue working, as his mother still needed his help financially.

"Hey, guys," Callie called as she came into the store.

Max and Danny looked up from the register. "Hey there," Max said. Danny stood quietly behind Max. "I've just been showing Danny how we ring things up and keep track of the consignment items. He's catching on real fast." Max grinned.

"Good." Callie smiled. "Have you guys talked about Danny coming in to work with Alma?"

"Yes, Miss Callie. I plan to work my school schedule around my hours here," Danny said as he stepped beside Max.

"Fantastic. But you can drop the Miss. Just Callie, please."

"Yes, ma'am. If that's all today, I'll go home now," Danny said.

"Sure. We've done a lot today. Just don't forget your timesheet," Max said, pulling a clipboard from under the counter. Max watched Danny walk through the store after filling in his hours.

"You know he's already picked up most of my cleaning routine in the morning. He'll come back after class to help Alma. I think this will be better overall and easier on her ego than you overlapping your schedule with hers."

"You're definitely right there. By the way, did Edward bring in his new stuff?"

"Yeah, I went over completing the initial form with Danny since he was here with me. And because I was training him on the register, I never went back to log them in or display it."

"That's cool. It's important he understands the front side of things. I can easily get that taken care of this afternoon."

When she got home, the house was quiet since Kim was out with friends and Luke was at an Artist Guild meeting. After warming some leftovers in the microwave and pouring a cup of coffee, Callie picked up the mail basket. Setting everything on a tray, Callie went out to the side porch, where she would catch the evening sun.

Most of the mail was innocuous junk mail, utility bills and a few wedding RSVPs . One letter caught her eye. The return address read Raymond Simmons. It's postmark was from two months ago. *How did we miss this? Oh, the parents' dinner. And the name wouldn't have meant anything to Luke. This can't be my grandfather. Surely, he's dead and buried already. But why write to me now? I never knew him.* she thought.

Opening and reading the letter, Callie's confusion continued. According to the letter, Raymond was feeling regret at having left his daughters with his sister, Flo. He said he had another family in Missouri, but wanted to meet Callie and her mother. An old friend visiting in Charleston had seen Callie and Luke's engagement picture and sent it to him. Somehow, he had traced Callie from the announcement. Now he wanted her to put him in touch with her mother.

Jumbled thoughts filled her mind as she put the letter back on the tray. *Why didn't he just write Momma? If he found me, he could have found her. I can't believe he would do this to her after all this time. Why didn't he just keep quiet? What am I supposed to do? Do I tell Momma? Do I keep quiet? I don't know what's best.*

Gathering everything, she went back into the kitchen, leaving the open mail on the counter and tossing out the junk. Absent-mindedly, she put the dirty dishes in the dishwasher. She curled up on the couch with a book and tried reading for a little while, but her mind kept returning to the letter. Exasperated, she left a quick note on the message board and went for a walk.

Unusually, Callie paid little attention to the seagulls and sandpipers moving through their dinner dance. As she walked along the water's edge, letting the foam wash over her bare feet, Callie accepted the fact that she would have to tell her mother about the letter. *She has a right to know and decide how we go on from here. I don't think I can tell her over the phone. I'll have to tell her in person,* she thought. Turning back towards home, Callie saw Luke's familiar form walking towards her. Waving, she quickened her pace to meet him.

"Hey, glad you came out to meet me." Callie rested in their embrace.

"I saw the letter in the kitchen. Figured you might need to talk this out. Do you want to keep walking?" Luke brushed the windblown hair from her face.

"No, let's just sit here for a few minutes." Callie settled on the sand. "So, you read the letter? Is it still in the kitchen?"

"Yes, and no. I put the letter in your nightstand drawer. I thought we'd talk to Kim together. So, what do you want to do?" He put his arm around her shoulders.

"What I really want to do is throw it away, or burn it, but Momma deserves to know the truth. Then whatever she decides is what we'll do. She's done so well with therapy. I'd hate for this to send her into a tailspin. Maybe we can go this weekend. I'll have to see if Alma and Danny can cover for me at the store. Guess we should get home so I can make sure Momma and Dad will be home." They got up and began brushing the sand from their clothes.

"You tell me when you want to go, and we'll do it," Luke said, reaching out to take her hand.

Kim was home when Luke and Callie returned. They filled her in on the situation. Kim decided she would stay home this trip and help at the store. Callie's dad answered the phone when she called. After she told him about the letter, he agreed with Callie's plan. Her brother would be there with his family, but "the more the merrier" her dad insisted.

Callie's brother and his family were already at her parents' house when she and Luke arrived. By this time, Luke had met all of Callie's family. All the adults came out to the porch to greet and hug the latest arrivals. Once everyone made it inside, Callie's mother tried plying Callie and Luke with lunch, even though it was well past noon. As usual, the adults gathered in the kitchen. Callie usually felt comforted by her mother's lemony kitchen, but this time, all the bright yellow fruit was jarring. *I'm just out of sorts, but man, this room is bright.* Callie thought to herself.

"There's some soup; I can warm up for you, Callie. Or would you rather have a sandwich?" Her mother asked, looking at Callie and Luke expectantly.

"No, I'm good, Momma," Callie said, looking at Luke.

"No thanks, we ate on the way up, but coffee would be nice," Luke smiled at Lydia.

"Alright, I'll get coffee going," Lydia set up the coffeemaker as Callie brought out sugar and milk. "Okay, I know you two are really busy. So why the visit today?" Callie's mother asked after the coffee was brewing.

Leaning against the counter, Callie looked nervously at her dad, who nodded imperceptibly for her to continue. "I wanted to talk to you about a letter I received. Thought it would be better in person."

Lydia squinted, looking closely at Callie. "Well, go ahead. Spill it."

Callie shifted her feet, trying to find an easy way to tell her mother and wondering about privacy. "Let me get my coffee. Then you and I can go out on the porch." Callie picked up her mug and moved towards the coffee pot.

Looking at her husband, Lydia tilted her head. "No. I think we can sit here in the kitchen. The kids are playing video games in the den.

If this is family business, we can all talk about it here. I said no more secrets, and I meant it."

Callie poured coffee for everyone and brought it to the table where the family had gathered. Spouses sat next to each other from habit. Callie sat between her mother and Luke.

"Well, I---" Callie hesitated. Reaching for her mother's hand, she started again. "I got a letter from someone claiming to be your father. I've got it in my purse."

Lydia's face froze for a moment with her mouth open. It then formed a tight line. Her knuckles were white as she carefully sat her mug on a lemon shaped coaster.

"Why? When did you get it?" Her mother asked incredulously. Callie's dad leaned closer to his wife, resting his hand on her arm.

"I don't know why. Apparently, I've had it for a while. It got stuck in the back of my mail basket at home." Callie looked from her mother to Luke. "Honey, would you get it from my purse?"

"Sure, sweetheart." Luke was up and back quickly. Everyone else hardly breathed during the brief interlude.

Callie handed the letter to her mother. "I haven't answered him. Whether we do is up to you." Callie's eyes filled with tears as she saw her mother's hands tremble as she read the letter.

When she finished reading, Lydia dropped the letter on to the table and covered her face with her hands. "How many times did I pray for some sort of word from him? How many?" She put her hands on her lap and clasped her husband's hand. "And now that I have it, I'm not sure I care." Looking at her family, she gave them a tight smile.

"Whatever you want." The family chorused, nervously looking at each other.

"I'll talk to my therapist. Part of me just wants to burn the letter. We'll see." Her mother shuddered. "Right now, I'd like to show Callie this year's garden." Lydia stood up from the table and gave everyone a wane smile. "Now don't go worrying. I'm much stronger now. But I will admit, I don't feel much like cooking tonight."

Looking down at her husband, she continued. "Bob, if you don't mind too much, when it's time, find out what kind of pizza everyone wants."

"Sure. Pizza's fine, honey. We'll take care of it," Callie's dad answered, gazing intently at his wife. "We've got plenty of tea and sodas, too."

Callie followed her mother outside. They walked silently to the vegetable garden. Reaching the garden, Callie's mother put an arm around Callie's shoulder. "After sixty-odd years, I'm not in a rush to answer him. Like I said inside, I'll talk to my therapist. Either way, we won't answer until after your wedding."

"Before or after the wedding, it doesn't matter. You do what you think is best." Callie gave her mother a quick hug. "Now show me these beans you've been telling me about."

The two women walked companionably along the garden rows. Each verbally encouraging the plants to flourish or commenting on a new variety Callie's mother was trying. Callie smiled. *Funny, I always feel closest to Momma in a garden. But then she's the one who taught me about plants, and I love being in a garden almost as much as I love the ocean.*

Turning back toward the house, Callie's mother paused. "Do I need to say anything to the grandkids?"

"I don't think so. I doubt any of them took notice since they were in the den playing video games. Once you've decided, we can figure out how to explain things to the kids. If we need too," Callie said thoughtfully. "Are you ready to go back inside? Maybe there's a movie on TV."

"Yeah, let's go in," her mother agreed.

Even though the adults were a little subdued over the weekend, the kids didn't take much notice. Everyone enjoyed a laid back visit without all the work the huge dinners caused as they rotated through video games, board games and simply reminiscing. Bobby and his family were on the road by nine the next morning. Callie and Luke left around noon. Callie was determined to let her mother sort out the business with Raymond Simmons herself. Still, she felt uncomfortable about waiting since she always liked to find a solution as soon as possible.

24

Mid-July 1987

After closing the store on a scorching hot afternoon, Callie took a walk on the beach before going home. Callie laughed as a sandpiper hopped away from the water's foamy edge and after nearly being caught by the water. "Silly bird, flying would have been easier." She said as the bird rushed back to forage in the same place as the water retreated. She mentally went over her to-do list. *Okay, tonight it's just Kim, Luke, and me for dinner. Momma and Dad will get into town on Wednesday. Bobby and his family get in on Thursday. We've done all the prep work for the wedding, meals, and such. Now that we're on the home stretch, I should just be checking things off the list.* Turning back toward the parking lot, she noticed Luke heading towards her. *Lord, I hope everything's okay. There's been so much going on, I'm not sure if I've covered everything.* She thought as he got closer.

Soon they were side by side. "Hey, love. What's going on?" Callie asked as she moved closer for a hug.

"Nothing. I finished a bit early and since you weren't home. I thought I'd walk down to meet you." Luke brushed the hair away from her face.

"That's a lost cause." Callie laughed as the wind blew her hair back onto her face. "You'd think I'd learn to keep a hat at the store. How was your day?" Loosely holding hands, they began the walk back to Callie's car in the parking lot.

"Not bad. I finished the second painting of Alma's house. Maybe we can give them to her tomorrow if nothing else is going on." The wind coming in from the ocean ruffled his hair.

"Yeah, I think we can. Do you want to have her over for dinner?" Callie glanced sideways at his face, trying to read his intent.

Luke shook his head. "No. I don't want it to be a big deal. I just want to give them to her before the wedding."

"Pretty sure that tonight and tomorrow night are our last free nights. You know, she asked me the size of the paintings and cleared wall space for them a while back." Callie smiled, thinking of how happy Luke's gesture had made Alma.

Luke chuckled. "I noticed she had moved some things around, but didn't really think about it. I'll be sure to bring along some hardware so I can hang them for her."

Callie fished her car keys from her pocket and unlocked the car. "Whew. It's hot in there still. I'll turn the AC on for a minute before we get in."

Luke opened the door on his side. "We'd cook in there before we got home, for sure." Looking over the roof of the car, Luke asked. "Did Bobby book rooms at the Inn?"

"No, they're going to stay in your old apartment. He liked the idea of being closer to us. Besides, the kids will all be here, so it's not like it would be a getaway for him and Susan. They're old enough now they can go to the beach when nothing else is going on."

"I actually like that better. I always enjoy Bobby's company. My sister is staying with my parents. I reserved our room at the Inn quite a while ago." Luke ducked and stuck his head in the car. "I think we can get in without dying from heat stroke now."

The next morning, Luke and Callie gave Alma the pictures of her house. She had tears in her eyes as she hugged Luke. "Thank you so much. You did such a great job capturing the spirit of us from the old picture, even though it was fading. It's like looking at us from the front yard."

"You're a remarkable woman. You've been through a lot in life. I'm glad I could do it for you," Luke said nonchalantly.

"Sure you guys don't want some coffee? It's a while before I have to go into the store," Alma asked as she watched Luke hang the pictures.

"No, I've got a few errands to run. But I will be by later to hang my dress in your spare room, if that's still okay," Callie said as she steadied the old wooden ladder for Luke.

"Of course, just let yourself in if I'm still at the store," Alma said, still beaming.

"Alright, that does it. I'll take this ladder back out. See you at home, Callie," Luke said, climbing down the ladder.

"I'm right behind you, honey," Callie said, giving her friend a hug. "Momma and Dad are coming Wednesday. Why don't you join us for supper? I know they'd love to see you before all the hoopla begins. We'll eat on the porch."

"Okay, I'll see you then." Alma walked Callie to the door.

Once through the gate, Luke went to the studio while Callie went inside to find her daughter. "Hey, Kim. You ready to go?" Callie called as she entered the living room.

"Yeah, Momma. I'll be right there," Kim answered from her bedroom.

Today, they were going to pick up Callie's dress and the combs for her updo. Although Callie had finally cut her hair, it was still long enough to put in a French twist. She also thought they might choose a nice piece of jewelry for Kim. Since Kim's sixteenth birthday, Callie had given Kim a special piece of jewelry for her birthday, and while it wasn't her birthday, Callie wanted Kim to feel special as well.

With shopping done mother and daughter went to lunch. Kim talked about her plans for next year. When Kim had stopped taking band last year, she had started volunteering at a free clinic attached to a shelter in Charleston after school once a week. It was part of an independent study program she had coordinated between the high school and USC's College of Nursing. Once the school year finished, Kim started volunteering in the clinic twice a week.

"Momma, I love working in the clinic," Kim said once they ordered their chef salads. "I can't do much nursing stuff now, but they taught me how to do vital signs so I can help room patients. Of course, I still do the clerical stuff." Kim grinned and gestured with her hands.

Callie smiled at her daughter's animated expression. Whenever Kim talked about nursing, her deep blue eyes became even brighter. "I'm glad you're getting this experience. I know you have a lot to learn, but this is where you said you wanted to work."

"Yeah, it is." Kim became serious. "I know we didn't have much when I was younger, but we always had enough food and a home. I've always had you. So many of our patients at the clinic don't have those things."

"At least, you know what it's like at the clinic, the things you'll see, how other people live." Callie took a sip of coffee. Initially, she had worried about what the clinic might expose Kim to. She agreed with the concept of making healthcare more available, but also realized that her daughter had led a protected life.

"I'm so lucky." Kim made one of her mercurial topic changes. "Those pearls are beautiful. I'm glad I settled on the shorter strand. They're almost a choker."

"I like your choice too. It'll be more versatile." Callie paused as the waitress served their food and continued after she moved away. "You know you could cut back your hours at the store. So, you'd have more free time."

"Maybe next year since I didn't get the early admission. I'd like some time to visit with family and a couple of friends before going to USC next fall. Right now, I'd like to save as much money as I can. They don't like for nursing students to work during the school year," Kim said matter-of-factly while putting dressing on her salad.

"I know. Our financial situation has changed a bit since you first started talking about nursing school. Luke and I can help," Callie offered, taking a bite of her salad.

"I realize things are better. The savings account you started for me way back when should cover just about everything and I should get a couple of scholarships. I don't want to be asking you to send me spending money."

"You are definitely my daughter. So independent." Callie sighed and shook her head. "I—Luke and I just want you to know we're willing and able to help you. Even your Uncle Bobby has made it clear he would help."

Laughing, Kim rested her fork against her salad bowl and threw up her hands. "Okay, okay, Momma. I promise to ask for help if I need it."

"Do you want to order dessert? Maybe split one of their decadent hot fudge brownie sundaes?" The sundae had been one of their special treats when Kim was growing up.

"Unless you really want one, I think I'm good today. Those salads got larger."

"Alright, let me get the check and we can go. I'm kinda full myself. I need to get my dress to Alma's before Luke comes in from the studio. He's heard me talk about it, but hasn't seen it."

After Callie tucked a tip under the edge of her coffee cup, she and Kim made their way to the register. "Looks like we made it just in time. The lunch crowd is coming in." Kim watched the tables fill up.

"Glad we missed the rush. Once we're home, I'll take my dress to Alma's first. Then I can fiddle around with my small bag to take to the Inn."

"Mom, what else do you have to do today?" Kim put on her sunglasses as they walked across the parking lot and got into the car.

"Not too much. Just take my dress to Alma's. Then I have to get the things together that I'll need to get ready at the inn and I have to pack for our trip." Callie started the car. "Otherwise, I plan on being lazy for a couple of days."

"When are Grandma and Grandpa getting here?" Kim began fiddling with the air conditioning vents.

"They'll be here Wednesday." Callie adjusted the air conditioning. "I forget how much hotter the city is than the island. All that concrete. We'll cool off in a minute. What are you doing today?"

"I think I might call a few friends and go to the movies. Unless there's something you need me to do." Satisfied with the airflow, Kim fastened her seatbelt.

"Not really. I'm just packing and checking things off my list. Sure, go have fun." Callie pulled out of the parking space. "I'm really just trying to relax for the next couple of days. Once your grandparents get here, it's going to be pretty busy until after the wedding."

"We'll get some pizza while we're out, so don't worry about dinner for me. Not sure what the group has going on tomorrow. You know Allison got an early acceptance at Charleston University, so we're trying to get together a few times before she has to travel with her parents. I'll be sure to be home to see Grandma and Grandpa." Kim looked out over the bridge toward the ocean.

"Yeah, I'm good for the next few days. Are you okay?" Callie gave a quick glance at her daughter.

"I'm fine, Momma. Really." Kim turned sideways in the seat to look at her mother. "It's weird; people are going off on their own. We've gone to school together since junior high. You hope you'll stay friends, but you don't know. I mean, how often do you get to see Brenda since she moved to Columbia?"

"I know, honey. It is hard when you're used to sharing experiences with someone every day." Callie reached over to briefly rub Kim's shoulder. "Ah, we've made it home."

"I'll take the bags in before I call people." Kim offered as Callie unlocked the SUV's hatch

"Okay. I'll get the dress next door and see you in the house." Callie took her wedding dress from the hook above the back window.

When Callie came in through the kitchen, Kim let her mother know she and her friends were going to an early movie in Mount Pleasant and she would be home around ten tonight. "Thanks again for the necklace. Love you, Momma." Kim hugged her mother and left to join her friends.

Luke was still in the studio, so Callie started packing her things for Saturday and then for their honeymoon. Smiling, she remembered how excited Luke was to take her somewhere she hadn't been before and where she didn't have to do anything. She chuckled as she thought to herself, *I'm not sure how well I'll do with that. Even though things are so much easier now, I'm usually pretty busy with the store. Although, he said there were different activities, like hiking, boating, and archery.*

It wasn't long before everything was ready, so Callie took her tea and a book out to the side porch. With her feet up, she soon fell asleep. She was still sleeping when Luke came in from the studio.

"Hey, sleepyhead," he whispered, leaning over to give her a kiss.

"Oh, hey love." Callie sat up and shook her head to clear the cobwebs. "What time is it?"

"It's four thirty." He answered as he sat next to her on the loveseat and loosely twined his fingers with hers.

"Dang, I haven't done anything about dinner." Callie flipped her hair over her shoulder. "Fish will thaw quickly. I can do that."

"If you want seafood, why don't we go to Kelly's on the Isle of Palms? You must be beat to fall asleep out here in this sweltering heat." Luke stood to turn on the ceiling fan. "Where's Kim? We'll all go."

"She's out with Allison and some others. Pizza and a movie. Allison's leaving in a few weeks on a trip with her parents."

"Isn't that her friend who got an early admission?" Luke frowned slightly.

"Yeah, Kim's realizing the old gang will soon part ways." Callie rubbed her eyes. "I know she still has her senior year with most of her friends and she'll make new friends in college. But I can't tell her that; figuring that out is part of growing up. Besides, there's nothing like the people who've known you your whole life." Callie shrugged. "Anyway, I think Kelly's sounds good. Let me get some shoes on."

Callie watched the raindrops splatter and run along the windshield as they drove into Charleston on their way to Luke's parents on Friday. Kim was riding with her grandparents to help make sure they didn't get lost. *I'm glad we had those quiet days at home. Wish I could think of this as a big family get together. I like Luke's parents well enough, and I've met his sister Stacey before. She seems nice. I'd just like to be married and be done with all this. It's not that his parents intimidate me. I just don't understand a life where people take care of your yard and clean your house while you play bridge and golf. But Luke sure seems excited to see everyone together.* Callie thought to herself as she watched the clouds disappear.

"You're awful quiet." Luke took his eyes off the road briefly to glance at Callie.

"Just thinking. I would rather stay home until tomorrow. I'm excited about our wedding ceremony, but the other stuff is extra. Of course, people want to celebrate with us and I'm grateful for that. Anyway, I'm fine. I've just really turned into a homebody." Callie smiled as she rubbed his shoulder. "But look, the stars are out now. They were calling for this to be just a quick shower. Everything will be perfect for tomorrow."

"Is your dad still behind us?" Luke peered into the rearview mirror. "We'll turning off into Mom and Dad's neighborhood soon. Ah, there he is."

As they were getting out of the cars, Bobby and his family pulled in. "Hey, Bobby." Callie walked over to give her brother a bear hug.

Bobby let out a low whistle. "Didn't realize we were going to the big house tonight."

"It'll be fine." Callie chuckled. "His parents aren't as stuffy as the house might make them seem. Come on. I imagine everyone else is here. I see Max and Louise's car and I know Alma was riding with them tonight."

Callie took a deep breath as they entered the foyer with its crystal chandelier and thought. *I just don't feel comfortable. Everything looks like it belongs in a magazine. I can't imagine putting my feet on the couch, even in the game room. Oh well, they want to celebrate Luke and me, so let's go do this.*

Melony and Tony were gracious hosts. After serving drinks, they encouraged everyone to eat and mingle throughout the living room and den. Warm seafood pastries and simpler fare like tiny ham sandwiches on pumpernickel dotted the buffet. There were miniature hamburgers in case the kids preferred those. Potato salad, coleslaw and a fruit salad rounded out the meal. For dessert, there were bite size pecan tarts and peach tarts. Younger members of the family quickly ate and followed Stacey's children to the game room upstairs.

Callie found Stacey to be the most down-to-earth member of the family, besides Luke. She taught high school English. Her husband was in banking, but had never been an investment banker like her father and brother. Callie and Stacey talked about balancing work and raising children. They also shared a great love for reading. Callie's mother talked with Melony about the wedding and gardening, with Alma and Louise joining them. Turned out Melony loved flowers. Before long, the talk turned to cooking, with all three women sharing their favorite ways to prepare different seafood dishes. Max and Callie's dad hung out together and talked about sports and home repairs. Luke and Callie were among the first to leave. The rest of the island people soon followed.

As predicted, the next day was sunny without a hint of clouds. The Inn's hydrangeas sported full blossoms of blue, white, and pink. The minister's pulpit stood under the natural wicker arbor, flanked by rows of Calla lilies. Callie was radiant and content as she joined Luke at the arbor. Luke's face plainly revealed his adoration of her. With vows exchanged, the minister introduced them as a married couple, and Callie and Luke turned to face their guests. *Now it's done. The reception and then it's regular life here on out,* Callie thought as she smiled at her friends and family.

25

September 1987

Once they returned from their honeymoon in the Bahamas, Luke and Callie slipped back into the comfortable groove of their life. Luke continued his work on what they came to call "the house paintings". Callie fell into her routine at the store, but with Danny picking up a lot of Max's duties, Callie rarely came in before nine and was usually home by five. Max and Louise went on a vacation to the mountains. They were talking about slowing down. Alma came in three or four afternoons for a few hours. She never fully recovered her strength after her second heart attack and was learning to pace herself.

Ethel came into the store late in the afternoon. "Hi, Callie. Do you have any shrimp and flounder left? I usually like to get it early, but Jack's not doing so good, and it sometimes takes me longer to get out of the house these days. You know he had that stroke a couple of months back."

"I was sorry to hear about Jack. Yeah, I've still got shrimp and flounder. Is there something I can do to help out?" Callie turned and walked back to the seafood coolers.

"No, but thanks. The ladies from church have been coming in a lot and he has an aide to help with the things I can't do. The kids are coming for the weekend." Leaning on her cane, Ethel slowly followed Callie across the store.

"Lord, Ethel, with all that you're got going and you're doing a fish and shrimp fry?" Callie looked up from weighing the flounder. "How much did you want?"

"Four pounds of each, please. Well, the kids and Jack love it. He's lost so much weight." Frowning, Ethel began digging in her purse.

Callie wrapped the shrimp and flounder and noticed Ethel's frown as she fumbled with her wallet. "Here you go. This one is on the house, Ethel. A get well present for Jack."

"You don't have to do that, Callie. You've got a family, too." Ethel looked up from her wallet and stretched to her full five-foot height.

"Ethel, you've been a loyal customer for years, ever since I was selling on the pier. It's my way of saying thank you, too." Callie bagged the items and walked around the counter. "Did you drive up today? I can take you home."

"I did. Don't walk as much as I used to. Guess these old bones are just getting tired. They're calling for terrible storms this year. I hope not. I'm not ready for that. Thank you for the seafood." Ethel turned to leave.

"I hope we'll have another slow storm season. You call me if there's anything we can do, Ethel. Take care of yourself." Callie watched as the older woman made her way to the parking lot. Her thoughts were melancholy. *I wonder how much longer Ethel will be with us. Ethel must be nearly eighty now. If Jack goes, she'll probably move upstate with her kids. Won't be long before Max, Louise, and Alma will be the old-timers on the island. Odd to think we've been in business for nearly seventeen years.*

Within a few minutes, other customers came in and broke up Callie's thoughts. Most of it was gallery business, as tourists were purchasing new artwork for their home or doing early Christmas shopping. Before long, it was time to close up and drop off the deposit on her way home. She usually did this in the morning before the morning person went home, but tomorrow she and Luke were meeting with a builder about renovating the house.

After supper, Callie, Luke, and Kim went over Luke's sketches of changes they wanted to make in the house while sitting around the kitchen table. At first, Kim was hesitant to express her opinion. "I won't be living here all the time. Do what you guys want," she said. After much reassurance from Luke and Callie that this would always be her home, Kim let them know she'd like built-in storage to include bookshelves and a writing desk in her bedroom. Other than that, she wanted to keep the furniture she grew up with and the same color scheme, lavender and white.

Their plans included adding two additional bedrooms upstairs. They would reconfigure Callie's sewing room to include her home office. They enlarged the kitchen by extending it into the back porch area. The plans called for widening the doorway leading into Luke and Callie's bedroom and creating a small dining room. They would enter their bedroom from the dining room. The bathroom would be accessible from their bedroom and the dining room.

"Sure you won't mind giving up privacy in the bathroom?" Luke asked, looking up from his sketches and sliding them over so Callie could have a closer look.

"No, it's not like we have a house full all the time." Callie said, taking a sip of coffee before peering at the sketches again. "Mostly, it's just the three of us. It will be handy to have a bathroom at this end of the house without having to go through the bedroom. And we're making the bathroom bigger. I'm going to love having a soaking tub and the shower. I like the bigger kitchen, but I'm not sure about the island with the stools. The table we have in the kitchen is from the 1950's. It was Aunt Sally's."

"Alright. We can decide on that a little later. What time is our appointment tomorrow?" Luke asked as he closed the sketchbook.

"Our appointment is at ten. Kim, what do you have going on tomorrow?" Callie asked as she stood up from the table.

"Just classes. I should be home about four." Kim asked as she stood as well. "I like the changes you guys are making. It seems like it will still feel like home—but better. I've got some reading to do for tomorrow. See you in the morning. Love you both," Kim said before going to her room.

"Luke, do you want to watch a show?" Callie added the last few dishes and started the dishwasher.

"I'm not sure what's on now. I'll check it out after I've changed." Luke paused in the doorway of their bedroom. "But I don't think I'll be up too late tonight."

"Okay, I'll change; grab my book and join you in a few minutes."

Up early the next morning, Callie left a note on the kitchen table and went for a walk. With the appointment this morning, today's walk would be short. The early morning fog was lifting, its elongated wisps rising through the tall grasses made her think of the ghost stories from her childhood. *It's no wonder the south is full of ghost stories between this fog and all the shipwrecks along the coast,* she thought.

When Callie returned home, Kim was ready for school, and Luke was in the shower. "Hey, sweetie. Did you sleep well?" Callie poured herself a cup of coffee.

"Pretty good. Had little trouble getting to sleep. I'm so excited about next year, at the same time I keep thinking about not seeing my friends every day." Kim frowned.

"I know it's got to be hard. Try to enjoy one thing at a time. I'm sure you'll make new friends at USC." Callie put an arm around her daughter's shoulder.

"I know Momma." Kim leaned into her mother's hug before standing up and grabbing her bookbag. "Well, I'd better get going. Love you. See you after school."

The meeting with the contractor went well. They would begin work next week, extending the kitchen and removing the living room wall around the fireplace. The builder also suggested they reinforce parts of the house to make it better able to withstand hurricanes. Some changes wouldn't be visible, like adding hurricane wraps to joists in the roof and under the floor. Other things like impact resistance windows and upgrading to fiberglass doors for the entries and the new garage would be more visible. Luke was as determined as Callie to "hurricane proof" the house as much as possible.

To prepare for the renovations, Callie began packing things like Aunt Sally's Fiesta, and the pictures and books in the living room. The contractor had reassured her they would hang heavy plastic to cut down the amount of dust getting into the rest of the house. Still, Callie felt having things in boxes would keep the house more organized now and later make it easier to arrange things when contractors finished the work in the kitchen and living room.

Feeling she had accomplished as much as she could before going into the store, Callie went outside to check her garden. She still kept a vegetable garden with tomatoes, melons, and squash. In the fall, she grew cabbages, beets and winter squashes. Callie fussed over each plant as if it were a child. This garden wasn't as extensive as in the past. She still canned her tomato and spaghetti sauces and made jellies and jams because they all preferred them. For several years, the store had bought its produce from Max's family in Mt. Pleasant. There was talk the family might sell the truck farm this year. The wattle fence was holding up well, though it usually needed repairs each spring. Callie loved walking among the vegetables, irises, rose campion, and cone flowers almost as much as she enjoyed walking on the beach. They both gave her a sense of hope and peace.

This weekend, Brenda was coming into town. Matt was away at college and Lee had a job at the mill, working with Callie's dad. Brenda was spending the weekend at Josie's. Even with the renovations, the women would get together at Callie's on Saturday. Josie's oldest was going to community college and the twins would graduate this year with Kim. After some adjustments, both Matt and Lee seemed to flourish in Columbia. *It will be good to get together with Brenda and Josie. We don't see Brenda much these days, even though she and I talk on the phone. Okay, time to get ready and get on with the rest of this day.* Callie thought as she walked towards the house.

26

October 1987

By early October, it seemed Ethel was on cue with her prediction for a severe storm this hurricane season. The National Oceanic and Atmospheric Administration (NOAA) was predicting the current storm would make landfall near Charleston and was gaining strength fast. Already the tides and winds were stronger.

NOAA hadn't issued an evacuation order, but Callie and her friends didn't want to wait until the last minute. Alma, Max, and Callie were busy trying to contact artisans with works on display in the gallery so they could move their work to higher ground. At home, Luke and Kim were loading a U-Haul truck with Luke's supplies and other things they wanted to keep out of the hurricane's path. As they finished there, they would move on to Alma's and then help Steve at his parents, if needed. Alma's chickens were already in Conway again.

"Come on Edward, pick everything up now." Callie pleaded. She was having a hard time convincing him to pick up his works from the gallery. "I know it's been years since a major hurricane hit the island, but between the warnings from Ethel and NOAA, I'm not willing to take any chances." Callie nodded her head as she listened to Edward and interjected a "Yeah" or "No" periodically. Shaking her head wearily, she hung up the phone.

"Is he coming or not?" Max set a fresh cup of coffee in front of Callie before sitting down next to her at the office worktable.

"He's coming. Although he thinks we're overreacting. He has a friend with a truck to help him. I'll let Danny know Edward will be here around two," Callie said between sips of coffee. She dialed the intercom for the gallery and let Danny know when Edward was coming and that he'd have help to load his paintings. Now, more than ever, Callie was glad they upgraded the phone system a few years ago so they could reach different areas of the store through an intercom system.

"I'll take over the phones for a while and give your ear a rest," Max laughed as he watched Callie rub her beet red ear. "Maybe Alma needs some help with the seafood."

"Alright, once we get things portioned, we'll take it to the shelter in Charleston." Callie stretched as she stood up. "By then, Luke and Kim should be finished at our place. I'll drop Alma at home before coming back here."

Max was already on the phone. He nodded and waved her away. Callie joined Alma wrapping the seafood in smaller portions so the shelter could choose to either cook it or distribute it. They finished the job quickly, and Callie soon loaded the coolers into her SUV. Alma let Max know he and Danny would be alone in the store.

Even without an evacuation order, people trying to buy food or supplies to secure their homes had traffic around Charleston snarled and moving at a snail's pace. "If traffic is this bad now. Imagine what it'll be like when the storm is closer," Alma said, staring at the line of cars beside them in the westbound lane.

"I know. I've always been afraid of being stuck in traffic when a storm hits. That's why I'm glad we're all packing up early." Callie looked in the rearview mirror at the line of cars behind them and then at the east bound traffic. "Our turn off comes up pretty soon. Going home should be easier."

"I hope so." Alma kept staring out the window as if she could will good sense into the other drivers. "When we get back to the island, don't forget to go by the store so I can get my car. I plan to leave for Columbia at first light. Figure I'll miss these fools by getting an early start."

At the shelter, there were enough helpers present to carry the coolers. Back on the road, both women were relieved that the eastbound traffic was moving steadily. Soon Callie pulled up beside Alma's car in the store parking lot. Max was just going to his car.

"Hey Max," Alma called as she got out of the car. "Were you able to get hold of everyone?"

Max walked over and stood between Callie's and Alma's cars. "Yeah, I finally got everybody. After we boarded up everything here, Danny went home to help his mother get ready. They're going to stay with their family west of Conway. There are several folks coming at eleven tomorrow, but they're bringing help to load things."

"That's great, Max." Callie stood beside her car. "Do you and Louise need help?"

"No, when I talked to Louise, she said they had everything ready. Just waiting for me to get home to board up the front door," Max said, rocking back and forth on his heels. Callie knew he was impatient to get home to his wife. "You get home then. I'll be here in the morning."

During the multiple hugs and good wishes which make up a Southern good bye, Alma let Max know she was leaving to go to her sister's in Columbia early in the morning. Max and Louise would go to her sister's outside Rock Hill. Steve would get his parents' things into a storage unit next to Callie and Luke's west of Charleston before taking his family to Spartanburg to stay with Tina's parents. Callie promised she, Luke, and Kim would leave after everyone picked up their work from the gallery tomorrow. Once they unloaded the truck at the storage facility, they would go to Callie's parents' home in Columbia. Luke's Jeep was already in the long-term lot there. Everyone pulled out of the parking lot anxious to get out of the storm's path.

Before going home, Callie parked by the pavilion. The rough waves of high tide roared as they crashed onto the beach. Except for the sounds of the ocean and wind, everything was quiet. The birds had already retreated. Trees swayed in the wind and the sea oats looked as if they would be pulled up by their roots as the wind bent them nearly parallel to the ground. *Better get on with it. Nothing to be gained by standing here,* Callie thought.

Luke and Kim were at Alma's when Callie got home. She grabbed her work gloves and went over to help them load the truck. "Now you take care of those paintings of yours. I've got them wrapped really well." Alma cautioned as she tapped Luke on the shoulder.

"Kim and I've got this down to a science. We saved a special place for the paintings," Luke said as he continued on his way to the truck.

With the truck loaded and everything boarded up but the entrances, they sat around Alma's table sharing a meal of leftovers from the two families' refrigerators. Exhausted from the day's work, they ate in friendly silence.

Luke shook his head as if to clear his mind. He looked asleep in the chair. "Alma, I'll come over first thing to turn off your breakers and close up the entrances. How early are you leaving again?"

"Soon as I've had some coffee. I'll get something to eat down the road. I want to get away from Charleston before taking a break."

"Come over to the house for coffee. I've got Styrofoam cups so you can take some with you," Callie offered. "I'm sure we'll be up. The wind seems louder already." Outside, the Spanish moss was flying off in large clumps and floated away in the powerful winds which was already separating leaves and smaller branches from the live oak trees.

"Okay, I'll get my suitcase in the car and drive over in the morning. Don't mean to be rude, but I got to sleep now to be ready for the drive tomorrow." Alma hid a yawn behind her hand.

"Me too. Come on. Let's grab this trash and get home." Callie began picking up paper plates and cups from the table and putting them in a trash bag.

Bleary-eyed, Callie got up and started coffee after a fitful night's sleep. Clouds hid the morning sun, but the winds continued to rage. Luke and Kim soon joined her in the kitchen. Everyone moved awkwardly as they tried to stretch out muscles overworked in the rush to get their prized possessions loaded onto the truck.

"I've got some bagels and cream cheese here if you two need a little something before we get started." Callie poured three cups of coffee. "I can pop them in the toaster oven and put the oven in the car before we leave."

Luke nodded yes, as Kim said, "Thanks, Momma. That sounds good."

By the time everyone finished their bagels, Alma pulled into the driveway. Callie went to the porch to greet her. "Come on in. Get out of the wind."

When she made it to the porch, Alma wrapped her arms around Callie. "You and yours are a blessing to me."

"Aw, Alma. My early years on the island would have been so much harder without you next door." Callie stepped back and brushed her hand over her eyes to hide the tears that threatened to form in their corners. "Come on in here and get your coffee. Looks like Luke and Kim have already gone to finish at your house."

Alma fixed her coffee and turned to Callie. "I hate to drink and run but—"

Callie waved a hand at her friend. "No, get going. You've got a drive ahead of you. I'll call you at Carol's when we get to Momma's. We probably won't be there until suppertime."

Callie picked up her work gloves and gave Alma one last hug before going to help Kim and Luke. She had the plywood up to the front door as Kim rounded the front of the house and sprinted up the steps. "Let me help you, Momma."

"I'm not decrepit yet," Callie laughed.

"No, but it's easier with two." Kim grinned back at her mother.

In short order, the houses were as secure against the hurricane as they could make them. Walking to the vehicles, an argument ensued between Callie and Luke. She didn't want them to wait for her at the store. In the end, Luke convinced her it would be better for them to travel together. Everyone with work still in the gallery came early, much to Callie's relief.

Traffic wasn't too bad as they skirted Charleston. Arriving at the storage facility, they put Kim's car in long-term storage with Luke's Jeep, quickly unloaded the truck, and dropped off the keys in the office. Callie plopped into her seat and kicked off her sneakers as Luke started the car.

"These darn shoes make my feet so hot." Callie wiggled her toes.

"Hey, remember. I've got snacks back here." Kim leaned toward the front seats. "None of your beloved coffee, Momma. But I've got Cokes, chips, and some fruit too."

Callie smiled as she turned back towards Kim. "I guess I can stand being without coffee until we get to your grandparents. Good thinking, though, grabbing stuff to eat in the car. Hand me a Coke, please." Turning to Luke, Callie asked, "You want something, honey?"

"Yeah, give me a Coke too, please," he answered.

"Okay, it's open for you." Callie put the coke in a cupholder. "Are you sure you don't want me to drive?"

"No, I'm good right now," Luke replied.

"Okay, I'm going to doze off for a while, then. I didn't sleep too well last night." Callie took a few sips of her coke and replaced the top. "I really like these new screw-on caps. Now wake me up if you get tired."

Callie reclined her seat and was soon asleep. *Oh, no. Here it goes again,* she thought. *The same dream as last night and the same one as seventeen years ago. I know what's going to happen and I still can't wake up. Winds howl over the island, whipping trees back and forth like seedlings. Towering waves crash into our home. Powerful tides pry away boards, sweeping them out to sea. The ocean surges over the island, swallowing it in a series of waves. Nothing living visible, just the pounding waves.*

Callie jumped as Luke touched her arm gently. "You okay over there?" He asked, placing his hand on her thigh. "You were muttering. Must have been dreaming. We'll be at your parents' in half an hour."

Rubbing her eyes and running her hands through her hair, Callie sat up. She readjusted her seat and stared into her lap. "Yeah, I'm alright. I had that dream about the island being gone. I had it last night too.

Funny thing is, I had the same dream seventeen years ago when Kim and I left the island because of a hurricane."

"Honey, that had to be awful," Luke said, giving her leg a pat before he had to go back to driving with two hands.

"It's pretty scary while I'm dreaming, but the island was okay then, it will be okay now," Callie said, lifting her chin determinedly as she stared through the windshield at the torrential rain.

27

December 1987

It was nearly two months before officials allowed residents back on the island. The hurricane had made landfall at Mount Pleasant. Roads and bridges took a horrible pounding. Unlike bridges leading to some islands surrounding Charleston's waterways, the bridge crossing over to Caines Island remained sound. Callie and Luke were on their way to assess the damage to the house and take a preliminary look at Alma's house, too.

"Are you having déjà vu all over again?" Luke asked after they had been on the road for about an hour. "You're pretty quiet over there."

Callie groaned and rolled her eyes at Luke's attempt at humor, and turned away from the window to look at him. Sometimes he said the corniest things, just to make her smile. "A little. I'm worried we won't be able to save the house, but the overall situation isn't as desperate as it was when Kim was a baby."

"You know I want the house to be salvageable, too. But from what we saw on the news, you know it may not be."

"Yeah, we'll just have to see." Callie went back to staring out the window and thinking. *Please let our houses be okay. I'm sure the store's severely damaged, at the very least. We've got more money now, so while I can't not work indefinitely, I know financially we'll be okay. But the house—the house is my anchor.*

They saw the effects of flooding much further inland than the previous hurricane Callie experienced. Some homes stood like isolated islands waiting for the water to recede, for their inhabitants to come home to the chairs abandoned on rooftops. Mud had stained walls where the water receded. Some trees still held debris snagged in their limbs during the storm. Others looked as if a giant came along lopping them off, splintering their trunks nearly in half to leave them like arrows pointing skyward. Mud was everywhere.

"This is proof this hurricane was much worse than the one back in seventy. Dad and I didn't see this much damage until we were just outside Charleston." Callie blew her hair from her face and took a deep breath. "It's going to be real ugly on the island. I'm glad Alma and Kim didn't come with us today."

Luke shrugged. "They'll have to come back sometime, you know."

"Yeah, but I want us to have a plan first and then prepare them for what they'll see." Callie forced herself to stop looking at the devastation and focus on Luke. "By the way, has anyone gone to see your parents' home?" Callie placed her hand on his shoulder. She knew he didn't have the attachment to his parents' house she had to Aunt Sally's, but he grew up in Charleston. *Funny, I always think of it as Aunt Sally's house or home. I think I'll have a plaque made "Aunt Sally's Place",* she thought to herself.

"I don't think so. They're planning a trip down soon. Maybe we can go by for a quick look after we've been to the island."

"For sure. Kim is fine with Momma and Dad. If things run too late, we can always find a room somewhere outside of Charleston. It'll be good to have a night with just us," Callie said, trying to bolster their spirits.

"It might at that." Luke smiled. "Everyone is pretty close together at your parents' place."

As they got closer to Charleston, the devastation became more severe. The storm had pushed boats inland several miles away from the waterways and left them stranded willy nilly on the shore. Thirty miles from the marina, they passed a yacht stranded in a parking lot. The hurricane had lifted cars into trees. Tilted houses looked like a group of drunken partygoers careening their way through neighborhoods. Roofs were missing shingles or were holding up trees that had crashed into them. Some roofs were simply gone.

By the time they crossed the bridge, Callie felt she was growing numb to the hurricane's destruction. *Fat chance,* she thought to herself. She had given up on the radio several miles back since they kept interrupting the music for newscasts. *Why didn't I remember to put the CD's back in the car?*

"Hey, at least there's still a bit of asphalt in between the potholes." Callie laughed as Luke artfully dodged the larger holes. "Last time, Dad thought he might get stuck in the mud just trying to avoid them."

"Do you want to go by the store first or the house?" Luke slowed the car to a crawl and took a moment to glance at Callie.

Callie blew out her breath. "Let's go by the store first. Then to the house. I'm thinking the house stood a better chance than the store. That way, we'll end on a high note."

"We might not be able to get too close. We'll see, sweetheart." Luke patted her thigh and drove a little more quickly.

As they suspected, after ripping off most of the roof, hurricane Henry folded the strip mall like a house of cards. None of the storefront windows were intact. Henry had tossed aside the protective plywood in some places. Officials had cordoned off the parking lot and posted large keep out notices along the lot's perimeter. Callie closed her eyes tightly against the tears which threatened to fall.

"Callie, I'm so sorry."

"We owned our section, but I suppose we have to call the county supervisors about the rest and to find out how we go about cleaning up." Callie let out a deep sigh as she slumped against the seat. "Nothing else to see here. Let's go to the house."

Crews from the power company were working along the road. They had cleared the roads and made burn piles in the open areas. With all the downed trees, there seemed to be a lot more open area. Callie chuckled as Luke pulled over to talk to one of the crew members. *Just like Dad seventeen years ago. Makes sense, though they've been out here working,* she thought.

"Have you gotten to Kiawah Trail yet?" Luke asked, climbing out of the SUV.

Even though she leaned toward the open window, Callie couldn't hear their conversation. Looking to her right, she spotted a car stuck in a tree. *Lord, I hope I still have a roof if that wind and water picked up a car. Ah, someone must be down by Max and Louise's. There's smoke from what looks like a burn pile.* "What's the verdict?" Callie asked as Luke folded himself back into the SUV.

"The road's clear and there's power to our neighborhood. It's about like what we've seen so far, washed out in some places, okay in others. We'll just have to go slow." Luke started the engine and eased onto the road.

Callie rode with her eyes closed the last mile to the house as she worked to control her rapid breathing. *You're in a much better place to come back from this than before. You've got Luke, your family, and friends. Get that chin up,* Callie told herself.

Luke slowed down as he turned into the driveway and Callie opened her eyes. "Oh, my," was all Callie could say as she looked at the property while Luke parked. She climbed out of the car and stood rooted, leaning on the car's open door. The high winds had mangled the old magnolia horribly, splitting huge leads from the trunk. Of course, the shed was gone again. Luke's studio seemed to be intact. The house was missing quite a few shingles and the brick skirt that circled the bottom of the house was broken in several places. It seemed to have done its job as the house still looked square on its pylons, not titling like so many others they had seen.

Luke walked up beside her, putting an arm around her waist. "It's a mess, isn't it? Ready for a closer look?"

Callie leaned against his tall frame for a moment, gathering her strength. "Sure, honey. Let's see what we've got here. Hopefully, it will smell better in there. All the rotting vegetation and dead marine life is still pretty strong."

Sand spilled off the porch as Luke took down the plywood from the porch's entrance. "We've got a small beach in here. "Okay, here goes nothing," Luke said as he removed the plywood covering the front door.

Water stains marked the walls in most rooms. Sand was everywhere. The new extension of the kitchen seemed sound. "Guess it's just as well we didn't get the new cabinets in." Callie laughed as she regained some of her cheerful outlook.

"Everything seems sound. I didn't feel any loose floorboards or shifting. Did you?" Luke asked as they completed a quick circuit through all the rooms.

"No. There's just more of everything this time. Water damage. Sand. Shingles gone. Siding gone. Thank God, nothing died in here so we're just musty and that will air out." Callie linked her fingers with his. "Okay, let's take a quick look at the studio, Alma's and then run by Max and Louise's place. I thought I saw some smoke from over that way."

The studio was in good shape and after inspecting Alma's home, both Callie and Luke felt her house was still salvageable. Crossing through the yard, they went back to the car and drove to Max and Louise's.

"Hey, Steve." Callie yelled to be heard over the chainsaw he was running.

Steve put down the chainsaw and walked across the yard to meet them. "Man, it's good to see you guys. How's things?" Steve swept Callie up in a bear hug.

"Well, it looks like both houses are repairable," Luke said. "Of course, it's up Callie and Alma to decide what they want to do once an inspector sees the place."

"How are your mom and dad? And how did you convince your dad to turn you loose with a chainsaw without his help?" Callie said as she smiled at her old friend.

"Well, you know we don't tell our parents everything," Steve said, laughing. "They think I'm down here checking things out. I thought I'd do what I could to clear some of the heavy stuff out before they get here. Nobody's getting any younger, you know. When are you guys coming back?"

"Not sure when we'll be back down, but it needs to be soon so Kim can get back to school. It's her senior year, you know," Callie said. "We've got to check Luke's parents' place in Charleston, so we'd better head out now."

"Wow, little Kim's graduating. You guys take care. Let me know if you need anything," Steve said as he began crossing the yard.

"You do the same," Luke said.

When Luke started the car, Callie said. "Honey, let's go down to the beach. I need to see it for a few minutes.

"I wondered when you would ask." Luke squeezed her hand.

Luke found a place to park alongside the road. There was still too much wreckage to park close to the beach. "Want company, or would you rather be alone for a bit?"

"No, come with me. But I'll probably be quiet. Just need to think and see the island." Callie took off her shoes, leaving them in the car.

They had walked about a mile when Callie stopped, turned, and looked back at the island. She could see the county's clean-up crews hard at work. Her eyes filled with tears. Some of the newer homes built closer to the ocean looked as if they were sliding onto the sandy beach. Piles of rubble left by the hurricane surrounded their foundations. The store, along with the diner and other shops, looked like a pile of scrap materials, more rubble.

Luke looked at her and pulled her into his arms. "Okay, my love?"

After a moment, Callie stepped out of his comfortable embrace and looked back toward the island. "I'll be fine. I feel unbelievably sad about what's not here anymore. But I want to come back. It can be even better."

Having lived through the 1970s, I can attest to banking and medical practices which were prejudicial to women during this period. A quick dip into the internet, verified the existence of a truck farm owned by a Black family near what is modern-day Mt. Pleasant as described in the early part of the book.

With regard to Max's and Alma's stories, two books were instrumental in providing historical information for this novel: Isabel Wilkerson's *The Warmth of Other Suns* (2010) and *The Color of Law*, Richard Rothstein (2017). Wilkerson follows several Black individuals as they decide to migrate to other parts of the United States and recounts their experiences along the way. Rothstein charts how the United States legislated residential segregation and how prejudicial banking and real estate practices continued to promote the status quo. Both are excellent books.

After retiring from nursing, Sherry launched a second career, writing. She enjoys writing about family relationships, mental health issues, social injustices and gardening. Sherry published he memoir *A Crazy Quilt Life,* in 2022. Sherry also writes a monthly blog for her website Writing, Sherry Comstock, Author. You can follow her there and as Sherry Comstock, Author on Facebook and 1writerslife on Instagram.

When she's not writing Sherry enjoys gardening, backyard bird-watching and visiting her children and grandchildren. Committed to encouraging a love for writing in her local community, Sherry is active in the outreach efforts of her local writers group. She lives with her husband in Burlington, North Carolina.

www.ingramcontent.com/pod-product-compliance
Lightning Source LLC
Chambersburg PA
CBHW072100300726
48975CB00003B/643